MURDER IN THE LIBRARY

A MISS MERRILL AND AUNT VIOLET MYSTERY

ANITA DAVISON

Boldwood

First published in Great Britain in 2024 by Boldwood Books Ltd.

Copyright © Anita Davison, 2024

Cover Design by Head Design

Cover Illustration: Shutterstock

A CIP catalogue record for this book is available from the British Library.

Paperback ISBN 978-1-78513-321-3

Large Print ISBN 978-1-78513-322-0

Hardback ISBN 978-1-78513-320-6

Ebook ISBN 978-1-78513-323-7

Kindle ISBN 978-1-78513-324-4

Audio CD ISBN 978-1-78513-315-2

MP3 CD ISBN 978-1-78513-316-9

Digital audio download ISBN 978-1-78513-317-6

Boldwood Books Ltd
23 Bowerdean Street
London SW6 3TN
www.boldwoodbooks.com

1

ENDELL STREET HOSPITAL, LONDON, APRIL 1916

Hannah's short walk from Charing Cross Station had brought her to the narrow entrance of the former St Giles workhouse, partially hidden by Christ's Church and marked by a pair of massive iron-studded gates with the words 'Endell Street Military Hospital' in stark white paint.

After a cold, wet winter, spring had finally come to London. Buds of colour sprang up between cobblestones and peeked over walls. Hannah consigned her heavier coats to her wardrobe and dressed in a light wool jacket and matching skirt. Giving the bell rope by the gate a sharp tug, she was rewarded by the creak of the huge door swinging open.

'Good morning, Miss Merrill.' The porter swung open the gate, bowing her into a cobbled courtyard. 'Your day at the library, is it?'

While her aunt's bookshop was being rebuilt after an air raid six months before, she suggested Hannah volunteer at the library in the nearby military hospital, not only to fill her empty days, but as her contribution to the war effort.

'It is, Mr Engle. And a good morning to you.' Hannah's

returning smile wavered as the gate closed behind her with an ominous metallic clang.

Dodging ambulances and tradesmen's vans, Hannah crossed the cobbled courtyard to the short flight of steps to the main door, held open by a slight, but bright-eyed young woman wearing the standard indoor uniform of the VAD's; a loose-fitting white overall belted at the waist which swamped her diminutive frame. 'Were you waiting for me, Dinah?' Hannah addressed her over one shoulder without breaking stride.

'Sort of, Miss.' Dinah fell into step beside her. 'I need to return these.' She nodded to the three books tucked beneath her arm. 'The patients were discharged yesterday so won't be needin' 'em.' Dinah's flat vowels betrayed her East End origins. Lowering her voice, she cast a brief glance behind her. 'Truth is, I'm avoidin' Sister 'ibbert for a bit. She's run me ragged all night.'

Hannah grasped the knob of the recreation room door, but it held fast. Leaning a shoulder against the wood, she tried again, but the door would not budge.

'It's locked.' Frowning, she examined the door as if it could explain itself. 'Was anyone using the room last night?'

'Not that I know of.' Dinah shrugged. 'Shall I fetch the key for yer?'

'If you would. It's kept on a board behind the porter's desk.'

'Won't be a mo.' Dinah laid the books on the floor and scampered back the way they had come.

Hannah shifted her feet, irritated that her day had started with a delay, though Dinah's sunny disposition helped lighten her mood. Dinah was an older sister of Hannah's bookshop assistant, Archie; a vast family, although Hannah had never quite worked out how many of them there were.

Dinah came running back in less than a minute. 'Porter says he doesn't know why the recreation room was locked.' Slightly breathless, she handed Hannah a brass key. 'Says it's usually left open.'

'That's what I thought.' The lock clicked under Hannah's hand, and she pushed open the door of the vast recreation room that contained the hospital library. The smells of old paper and cigarette smoke-laden leather assailed her, muffling the antiseptic tang that permeated the hallways.

Muted April sunshine flooded through a panoramic window that ran down one side, drawing rectangles of light onto a polished boarded floor. A full-sized billiard table took pride of place in the room, whilst at one end a small mahogany table borrowed from a titled lady held a brand-new phonograph. Glass-fronted cabinets lined one wall containing rows of neatly arranged books, the doors left unlocked so patients and staff alike could handle and choose books for themselves. The rule of the library was to provide books on any subject patients requested, so it was equipped with valuable volumes on seventeenth century furniture, old silver, zoology, and metaphysics all lent by generous patrons. Those patients with specific skills or hobbies honed their craft by making use of the donated handbooks on motors, aeroplanes and engines, while gardeners pored over books on rose-growing and argued about their preferred methods.

Hannah was also responsible for finding reference books for patients studying for the London Matriculation examination, helping them gain knowledge during their enforced leisure hours they might not have had in their previous lives.

'Weren't you meant to be on nights this week, Dinah?' Hannah's gaze went to a clock on the wall as she stowed her bag beneath the central table. 'Your shift finished over an hour ago.'

'Yeah. By rights I should be tucked up in bed in the barracks by now.' She referred to the attic dormitories allotted to the nurses.

'But we're at sixes and sevens today 'cos a patient went missing last night.'

'Missing?' Hannah turned from where she was hanging her coat on a hook in the wall. 'How did that happen?' A roll call was taken every evening before the main gate was secured until morning.

'Dunno. He left the ward after lights out and he's not been seen since.' Dinah placed the books she had brought with her on an ancient, scarred desk and wandered the room. 'Talkin' of locked doors, I couldn't get into the Johnnie Walker ward last night, either.'

Hannah's straw hat joined the coat on the hook by the door. 'Perhaps it was full?' she suggested, smiling at the name given to the basement room where inebriated soldiers taken off the streets were placed so they could sleep off their night's revelries. Cases of drunkenness had become a menace since the war began.

'More likely someone was sick in there.' Dinah leaned a hip against the billiard table. 'So it was closed off until a charwoman could be sent to clean up.'

'Well, I need to get on and I doubt this soldier you mentioned could have gone far.'

'That's the funny thing.' Dinah heaved herself effortlessly up onto the edge of the billiard table, her hands on either side of her knees, feet swinging. 'He was about to be discharged in a few days, so we don't know what 'e's playing at.'

The missing man was likely a disabused soldier reluctant to return to his unit, so had absconded. Not that Hannah could blame him for that. It was a common theme in the hospital that any soldier who claimed they wanted to return to the trenches was a liar.

'How long has he been missing?' Hannah approached the

table where the ledger recording books lent out was kept and she listed the ones Dinah had brought.

'Not sure.' Dinah rolled a red billiard ball idly between her hands. 'He wasn't in his bed when Nurse Dalglish woke the ward at six. She assumed he must be in the bathroom, but he hadn't come back by the time breakfast was served, so she reported it to Sister Hibbert.'

Hannah hefted a ledger from a drawer and placed it on the central desk ready to enter the day's borrowings and returns. Knowing the sister's reputation, sympathy surged for Nurse Dalglish at having lost a patient.

Dinah flicked the red ball with a finger, sending it across to the far cushion, and yawned noisily. 'She tore a strip off the poor girl in front of the entire ward. As if his going off was 'er fault.'

'Busy night, was it?' Hannah toured the room, collecting books discarded on chairs and one from the windowsill.

'Chaos, it were. A convoy of ambulances arrived last night that kept us busy. Most of the poor lads had lain in wet mud for hours at the casualty stations before the hospital trains picked them up, only to be bumped and thrown about all the way across the country. Many were sick on the boats after that, so were in a poor state by the time they arrived. Three of 'em died before they even got here.'

'How sad.' Hannah closed her eyes in brief sympathy, having heard similar stories in the last week alone. She approached the stage at the far end of the room where a set of full-height royal blue curtains hung from the proscenium; the Women's Social and Political Union motto, *Deeds Not Words,* embroidered in gold across the centre, together with the WHC monogram.

'Dinah?' she asked, frowning. 'Was there a performance or meeting held in here last night, do you know?' After the mystery of the locked door, she had suddenly noticed the curtains, usually left open, were drawn shut.

'Not that I know of.' Dinah dropped to the floor, her soft shoes making no sound as she joined Hannah. 'Do you want an 'and openin' them?'

'That would be helpful. They're so heavy.' Spotting a book lying on the edge of the stage, Hannah stepped up onto the platform to retrieve it. A slip of paper fell from between the pages and floated to her feet. As she bent to retrieve it, her foot struck something hard. Shoving the scrap of paper into her pocket, she lifted the bottom of the curtain, revealing a brown leather shoe – the sole clean, but well worn.

Intrigued that someone had left a shoe behind, she lifted the curtain higher. What she saw then made no sense. The shoe was attached to a leg in navy blue striped pyjamas worn by a man lying on his back on the stage. One leg lay bent at an angle at the knee, the other thrust straight out. He wore a flannel dressing gown tied at the waist with a silken cord, his arms crossed loosely over his chest.

Hannah's first thought was that he had collapsed, maybe because he was drunk or from some sort of attack. Then she saw the blood – a wide bloom of deep red seeped into the material of his pyjama jacket beneath his hands which were clasped, as if to stem the flow. More blood had pooled beneath him, the surface puckered into tiny waves that spread on the wooden floor.

Her vision tunnelled, taking Hannah back to the day she had found the body of her best friend, Lily-Anne Soames, stabbed and left in a wing-back chair in her bookshop. The same disbelief mixed with an urge to run flooded through her.

'My gawd!' Dinah's shout broke the heavy silence. 'That's Sergeant Tillman. Is 'e dead?'

'I think he must be,' Hannah said, horrified but unable to look away. Then she noticed a wheel-back chair lay on its side a few feet away, as if he had kicked it aside as he fell.

Dinah hitched her skirt with one hand, the other braced on the edge of the foot-high stage and hauled herself up beside the body. 'Where did all that blood come from?' she asked, more curious than distressed. Squatting, she reached out a hand to take the man's wrist.

'Don't touch him!' Hannah sprang forward, her hand closing on Dinah's upper arm. 'You'd better fetch someone, quickly.'

'All right, but it's not as if we can do anything for 'im now, poor bloke.' Shrugging, she retracted her hand and backed away, then the only sound above the roaring in Hannah's ears was Dinah's footsteps retreating along the hall.

Left alone with the dead man, Hannah summoned the courage to study him. His eyes were closed, his mouth contorted into a grimace, revealing a top row of uneven, slightly yellowing teeth. The skin on his face and neck was flaccid and greyish beneath a fine layer of dark stubble from his nose downwards into his neck.

She examined the book that was still in her hand; a copy of *Something Fresh* by P.G. Wodehouse. There was nothing remarkable about it; no hasty words scrawled in the margin or pages with the corners folded back. Had he been reading it when he fell? Or was it just one left by a patient the previous day?

Rapid footsteps approached, halting her speculations. Dinah appeared in the company of a pale-haired young VAD followed by two women in full nurse's uniform, their wimple-style headdresses lifting out behind them.

'Nurse Root, what has happened here?' one woman demanded.

'I don't know, Sister 'ibbert,' Dinah replied. 'We found him like this a few minutes ago.'

Tutting, Sister Hibbert bustled to the stage, grunting as she mounted the step and bent over the body.

'Is he dead?' the second woman asked, but she did not approach the stage. Hannah recognised her as Sister Kerr, a popular member of staff.

'I would say so.' Sister Hibbert peered closer. 'I cannot see what caused it, but if all this blood is anything to go by, he's been attacked.' She gestured to the two girls, but only Dinah stepped forward. 'What was this patient doing in the library at night?' She addressed the room, then turned a hard glare on the scared-looking nurse who hovered beside Sister Kerr. 'Nurse Dalglish, when did you last check on the ward?'

'I-I'm not sure, Sister.' The young nurse hunched her shoulders. 'He-he was dozing when I collected the empty cocoa cups at around ten o'clock. When I checked again at around midnight, his bed was empty. I assumed he had gone to the bathroom, but—'

'Assumed? Didn't you find out for sure?' The Sister left the stage and came to stand a few feet away from the girl. 'Patients shouldn't be out of bed after lights out.'

'I-I know, Sister, but we were very busy last night. I was helping make up beds for the new arrivals.'

'Don't shout at her, Sister,' Sister Kerr stepped between them. 'She's new here, and cannot be expected to keep track of everyone. Perhaps Nurse Root knows more?'

'No, Sister. I didn't speak to him at all last night,' Dinah stammered.

'This is unacceptable.' Sister Hibbert planted both hands on her hips, giving all appearances of taking charge. 'Nurse Root, go and fetch a couple of porters to take the body to the mortuary. Perhaps you, Sister Kerr, could fetch Dr Murray; she'll be in her office about now. When Nurse Root returns, she and Nurse

Dalglish are to wait in the nurses' common room. Dr Murray will want to talk to both of you as you were on duty last night.'

'Of course, Sister.' Giving Nurse Dalglish's shoulder a reassuring pat, Sister Kerr left the room.

'Excuse me, Sister.' Hannah stepped out from where the curtain had half concealed her. 'I'm not medical staff here, but shouldn't the body be left where it is until the police get here?'

'Who are you?' The woman's suspicious gaze moved rapidly up from Hannah's toes up to her hair.

'Er, Hannah Merrill,' she replied, unsure of her role in the drama unfolding in front of her. 'I'm the volunteer librarian.'

The woman blinked, momentarily confused, before her face cleared. 'Yes, yes, of course you are. Well, we cannot leave a dead body lying here in the library. Anyone could wander in.' Dismissing Hannah, she jabbed a finger at Dinah. 'What did I just tell you, Nurse Root?'

A neat, spare woman in her forties entered the room, followed closely by Sister Kerr. 'Ah can hear ye all the way down the corridor, Sister. I expect more decorum from ma nursing staff.'

'I can only apologise, Dr Murray.' Sister Hibbert's brusque demeanour softened into subservience. 'The missing soldier has been found, but I'm afraid he's dead.'

'What was he doing in the library?' Dr Murray approached the stage to view the body but did not climb onto the stage.

'That's a mystery to us, doctor.' Sister Hibbert held up one side of her skirt and climbed down onto the main floor. 'I was just questioning these girls, but no one appears to know anything.' She encompassed Hannah in her 'girls' remark, which made her smile.

'And you, Sister Kerr?' The doctor in charge turned her attention to the woman who hovered uncertainly behind her.

'I cannot say, Doctor. I only came on shift half an hour ago. I've asked the porter to summon the police.'

'Oh, but I don't think that's—' The blonde girl took a step forward.

'Don't interrupt your superiors, Nurse Dalglish,' Sister Hibbert snapped.

Shrivelling beneath Sister Hibbert's uncompromising tone, the girl clamped her lips shut and took a step back.

'That's enough, Sister.' Dr Murray moved to stand between them. 'Let's leave the questioning tae the police, shall we?'

'Of course, Dr Murray,' Sister Hibbert said, determined not to relinquish what little authority she had. 'I've instructed Nurse Root to have the sergeant's body taken to the mortuary.'

'Stay where ye are, Nurse Root.' Dr Murray halted Dinah, who had moved towards the door. 'The body must nae be touched. And no one must come into the library until the police arrive.'

'My apologies if I have offended, Dr Murray.' Sister Hibbert bowed her head resembling a nun accepting penance. No one crossed the doctor in charge without consequences.

'Dinna worry, Sister. You did what ye thought best.' Dr Murray turned her attention to the two VADs. 'Nurse Root and Nurse Dalglish, go with Miss Merrill and wait in the nurses' common room until ye're summoned. Sister Hibbert, you come with me and Sister Kerr, make sure you lock this door behind us.'

'Of course, Dr Murray.' Sister Kerr took up her place at the door and waylaid Nurse Dalglish, who apart from Hannah was the last person to leave.

'Are you all right, dear. You've gone very pale.'

'I do feel a little queasy.' The young nurse cast a fearful glance over one shoulder at the stage. 'But I shall be fine in a moment, Sister.'

Hannah entered the hallway, aiming a sympathetic smile at the younger nurse, who waited as Sister Kerr locked the library door behind them.

'You look a bit shaky to me, girl.' Sister Kerr slid they key into her pocket and grasped her by the arm. 'Come with me and I'll get you some smelling salts.'

'No, really, I'm all right, I don't—'

Hannah looked back, but curious staff had begun drifting out of the rooms on either side of the corridor, blocking Hannah's view of the pair. Her last sight was of the sister's face held an inch from the young nurse as she said something to her. Nurse Dalglish merely nodded, and stared at the floor.

'Are ye coming with us, or no, Miss Merrill?' Dr Murray called, her raised voice making Hannah jump. Beside her, Dinah wore a pleased smirk that Hannah was being treated like one of the nursing staff.

'Yes, yes, of course, Dr Murray.' Hannah turned and ran to catch up with her.

2

Hannah eased her back on the hard chair she had occupied for the last half hour in the nurses' common room. Furnished with second-hand and donated items, the room carried a medley of odours that ranged from old leather to wet dog and decayed flowers. Tempted to ask what was taking so long, she felt a rush of remorse. That poor man had fought for his country, survived an injury, and now lay dead on the library stage. Why was he even there? And why place a chair on the stage when the room held more comfortable options? Was he hiding from whoever might venture into the library?

'Dinah? Why do you suppose Sergeant Tillman was in the library at night?'

'Don't ask me.' Dinah perched on the corner of the wide sill where the window met the wall. 'Maybe he couldn't sleep, so went there to have a quiet read.'

'That seems an odd thing to do.' Especially when a perfectly good lamp occupied space on his bedside table. 'Might he have gone to meet someone? A woman maybe?'

'Now you're having a laugh, ain't cha?' Dinah scoffed. 'No one would be interested in 'im. He couldn't say a kind word if his life depended on it, let alone being agreeable to a woman.'

Hannah did not dismiss the idea lightly. The sergeant had been a well-built man in his early thirties. Although his features displayed the cast of death when she saw him for the first time, smoothed out in life, he would have been more than presentable.

'How well do you know Nurse Dalglish, Dinah?'

'Alice? She's all right, I suppose.' Dinah pursed her lips in thought. 'Come to think, no one knows anything about her. She don't talk much.'

'Is she a good nurse?'

'She's not been here long, but she's a hard worker. We ain't real nurses you see, not being qualified, so us VADs do all the scut work around here, but I don't mind it. I've already got my First Aid Certificate. I've passed my first aid examination and hope to train for the Queen Alexandra's one day,' she said proudly. 'I doubt Alice will though.'

'Why do you say that?'

'Have you 'eard her talk?' Dinah scoffed. 'She's posh, she is. Not a charwoman's daughter from Whitechapel, like me.' This was said without a trace of bitterness. 'She makes mistakes sometimes, like we all did when we first arrived so I can't hold that against 'er. She turned her nose up at the nurses' dormitories too, said the attics were gloomy and not private enough. Not that I blame 'er. What do you want ter know for?'

'Just curious.' Hannah noticed the nurse had not joined them. 'Where is she, by the way? Didn't Dr Murray say we had to wait in here?'

'Yes, she did.' Dinah frowned at the door. 'She must still be with Sister Kerr. I expect she'll be along when she's ready.'

Deciding to use the girl's absence to probe further, Hannah asked, 'Alice looked shocked when she saw the body, but no more than anyone else. Sister Kerr reacted as if she was having a fit of the vapours.'

'I saw that, too, but then Sister Kerr is protective of the younger nurses.' Dinah thought for a moment. 'Night shift is tough on us all, and if you ain't used to the sight of blood it's worse. And there was plenty around the sergeant.'

'I noticed.' Hannah hoped not to see anything as gruesome again. Pushing the image of the dead sergeant away she changed tack. 'Alice is very attractive, isn't she?'

'And only homely girls like me go into nursing, eh?' Dinah's tone held no resentment, only mild sarcasm.

'I didn't mean it that way,' Hannah rushed to reassure her. Dinah was far from plain, but she lacked the symmetry of features that made Nurse Dalglish striking. She tried to summon a compliment to neutralise her lack of tact, but Dinah grinned at her, unoffended.

'Just teasing yer, Miss. I learned a long time ago I weren't much to look at.' She switched her attention to the courtyard. 'Ah. I see the flatfoots have arrived.'

Hannah joined Dinah at the window in time to see a long black motor car halt on the cobbles. The rear door opened and a tall man in a dark suit and black hat emerged. He vaulted up the front steps, then paused as a lady exited the building, removed his hat and stood to one side to allow her to descend.

Hannah took a rapid step back from the window.

'Know him do yer?' Dinah smiled. 'Is he the one who caught the murderer of that lady in your bookshop?'

Hannah nodded. 'Detective Inspector Aidan Farrell.'

'Thought that must be 'im. Archie couldn't stop talking about how he was helping the police from Scotland Yard.'

Hannah's first meeting with Inspector Farrell had been over the body of her best friend in the bookshop several months before.

He struck her then as unsympathetic, with a brusque manner. The discovery of a German spy ring working out of the bookshop had changed his attitude, partly because he required her co-operation, not to mention a burgeoning interest in Aunt Violet; one her aunt remained frustratingly closed-mouthed about even now.

'It was an exciting time.' And a nerve-wracking one. By this time the inspector had disappeared inside the building, followed by a second man she did not recognise.

A short while later footsteps were heard approaching in the hall, one set lighter than the other, sending Dinah from the windowsill as the door opened to admit the doctor in charge.

'Ah, Miss Merrill!' Dr Murray said, as if she had forgotten her existence. 'This is Detective Inspector Farrell from Scotland Yard and his associate, er...'

'Detective Constable Pendleton,' Inspector Farrell answered for her, his blue eyes widening in recognition when he saw Hannah.

'I hope you'll both spare him a few moments to detail what occurred earlier?' Dr Murray asked both girls. 'Nurse Root, wait out in the hall, would you? You'll be called when required, but there's nothing for either of you to worry about.' She stared past them into the empty room. 'Where is Nurse Dalglish?'

'We aren't sure,' Hannah answered. 'She didn't follow us in here. Maybe she was called away?'

'How inconsiderate of her.' She tutted. 'Nurse Root, would you be so kind as to find her for us?'

'Yes, Dr Murray.' Dinah followed Detective Pendleton from the room, muttering as she went. 'At this rate, my shift'll start before I get any sleep at all.'

'Thank you for your co-operation, Dr Murray.' The inspector inclined his head politely. 'I'll try not to keep your staff away from their duties for long. Just a few routine questions, Miss, er, Merrill, is it?' His right eyebrow rose in a parody of innocent enquiry along with a slight, but unmistakable shake of his head.

'I'm always happy to assist the police in any way I can.' Hannah returned his gaze without flinching.

'I'll leave you to it then, Inspector.' Dr Murray reverted to her customary no-nonsense tone. 'I have a great deal of work to do, and this matter has put me behind.' The door closed behind her with a soft click.

'Sorry about the play-acting.' Inspector Farrell tossed his hat onto the side table and gestured her into the chair she had just vacated. 'Thanks for going along with it.'

'You're welcome. But why the subterfuge?' She smiled, becoming more intrigued by the second. 'What do you think of Dr Murray? Impressive, isn't she?'

'She is indeed. It was a thought-provoking first meeting.' He tugged at an earlobe with a thumb and forefinger. 'She reminds me of your Aunt Violet in some respects.'

'Goodness!' Hannah fluttered her eyelashes. 'Two strong women who know what they want. How *will* you cope?'

'I sometimes wonder about that myself.' He chuckled. 'I'd appreciate it if you didn't mention we know one another.'

'Which shouldn't be too difficult. You aren't likely to run into her in the hallways. Aunt Violet spends most of her time at the bookshop these days, and her Red Cross work keeps her busy.'

'Is it true you were the one to find the body?' He focused on the real reason he was there.

'Me and Nurse Root.' Hannah shivered slightly in the chilled room as she took up Dinah's perch in the window corner where the sun had warmed the spot. She crossed her ankles.

'This is the second time in six months you've stumbled upon a murder victim. I hope this isn't going to become a habit,' he said with a wry smile. 'With anyone else, that would be terrible luck, if not suspicious. Or should I blame incompetent doctors for allowing a patient to be murdered?'

'It's not like I go looking for them.' Hannah glared at him. 'And there *are* no incompetents here, despite the War Office's cynicism.' She had become fiercely protective of the women of Endell Street.

'No, you're right. That was uncalled for.' He dragged a chair closer and sat. 'I apologise for my clumsy sense of humour.'

'You're forgiven. Incidentally, how did the sergeant die? I saw all the blood, but it was difficult to tell exactly what caused it.'

'He was shot. I've instigated a search for the murder weapon, which could be a fruitless task in a building this size.'

'The killer could have taken it with them?' Hannah frowned. 'Could a patient have brought a weapon into the hospital with them?'

'I shall have to check, but I would imagine any weapons that found their way here would be confiscated.'

'That's what I thought. Only a staff nurse told me a Turco once brought a German Pickelhaube helmet onto the ward in a canvas bag and refused to part with it.'

'Turcos are those Algerian soldiers serving in the French army, aren't they?' He nodded sagely as if answering his own question. 'It's a tradition for soldiers to collect souvenirs from the battlefield. Been doing it since Marlborough.'

'Maybe, but this one had a severed head still inside.' Hannah fought a smile as she waited for his reaction.

'What?' His jaw went satisfyingly slack. 'You're joking?'

She shook her head. 'The Turco was most put out and insisted he needed it to prove his warrior status in his home village. Dr Murray informed him it was unhygienic and un-Christian, though as a Muslim that meant nothing to him. He gave in eventually, but he wasn't happy.'

'What happened to it?' he asked, his curiosity evidently stronger than his distaste.

Hannah shrugged. 'Buried in a local grave, I would imagine.' She had felt nauseous when she heard the same story during her first week at the library, but she delivered it with relish.

'Is there anything you can tell me about Sergeant Tillman?' he asked, taking a moment to compose himself.

'Is this an official interview?' she asked archly, testing their relationship, while re-directing him from the image of severed heads.

'It could be.' His eyes glinted with mischief as he withdrew a notebook from an inside pocket and flipped through it, a pencil poised above a page. 'State your full name.'

Hannah stared at him.

'Hmm,' he murmured. 'Witness unhelpful.' He scribbled something on the page.

'Inspector Farrell!' She rolled her eyes. 'All right, I'll apologise for the severed head story. Now, do you know what sort of gun was used?'

'Why, have you seen one lying about?' He clamped his lips shut and lowered the notebook. 'You know I cannot discuss specific details with you, Hannah. It's bad enough I have no manpower to assign to this case. This new conscription law means young men aren't entering the police force, so we're struggling.' He tapped his pencil against the page. 'But we know one thing. It was a single shot with a large calibre bullet, most probably fired from a Webley revolver, Mark five or six most probably.'

'Webleys are army issue, aren't they?'

He nodded. 'And they're not called "Man stoppers" for nothing. The entry wound was relatively small, but the exit...' He rolled his neck inside his collar. 'Big as my fist, it was. Made a right mess, I can tell you.'

Hannah pushed away the image this conjured in her head. 'Then the killer is most probably a soldier?'

'I cannot assume that at this stage. Finding the weapon is our first task, although with over five hundred soldiers in this building, unless the killer left fingerprints, it could belong to anyone.' He sounded defeated already, which did not bode well. Hannah wondered how many of the patients were fit enough to make their way to the library and use a gun. A quick assessment told her probably about half of them, maybe more.

'Hannah?' His tone was sharp, telling her it was not the first time he had asked.

She blinked, startled. 'Sorry, what did you say?'

'Dr Murray said another nurse was present when you found the body at around eight fifteen? Is that your usual start time to begin work?'

'Dinah Root, yes. She's Archie's sister.'

'Your assistant at the bookshop?' He raised an eyebrow and scribbled in his notebook.

'She was on the night shift last night so normally I don't see her, but I was earlier than usual today.'

'Was there a particular reason for that?'

A sharp retort sprang onto her tongue but she suppressed it, reminding herself there was nothing personal about his questions. Or was there?

'No reason at all,' she answered carefully. 'Call it a whim.'

'Did you have much contact with the dead man?'

'As a librarian?' She pulled a face. 'Apart from the exchange of polite greetings, like "How are you feeling?", "Isn't it a nice day?" or "Would you like to borrow a book?", I'd say no.'

His wry smile told her she was being flippant, but he made no comment. 'No one seems to know much about Tillman, but I hope to get an impression of him from his regimental commander, who knowing my luck, will be in Artois or somewhere.' She looked away quickly, and he sighed. 'Oh Lord, Hannah. I'm sorry. I forgot for a moment. That was where your fiancé was killed, wasn't it? I didn't mean to raise painful memories.'

'You didn't.' She smoothed down her skirt, conscious of his sympathetic scrutiny. 'It's been months, and you never met Gerald. No apology is necessary.'

Mention of her late fiancé always made her uncomfortable, in that most people expected her to be heartbroken, her life shattered by another young life laid waste on a muddy battlefield. When in truth her heart remained whole.

'If it helps, I could keep an ear open for you.' She found the idea of another murder case strangely appealing. 'You said you were short-handed, so I could be of use.'

'Are you implying my men aren't up to the job?' He raised a sardonic eyebrow.

'Of course not. However, the staff here are fiercely loyal. They'd be wary of saying anything incriminating to a policeman, but perhaps less so to a librarian.' She leaned forward. 'A murder on the premises is bound to create rumours and speculation.'

'This is a police matter, Hannah. You're a potential witness. I'm not comfortable asking you to help.'

'You aren't. I volunteered. And you accepted my help the last time.' Before he could respond, she rushed on, 'The fitter patients gather in the library to play billiards, cards, or listen to the phonograph. If you think women gossip, you ought to hear these men talk. My mother's bridge afternoons are less shocking. I'm very discreet. They would never know I was listening in.' Her enthusiasm grew as she talked.

'I cannot base an investigation on gossip, although...' He stared off for a moment, then shook his head. 'No, it's not professional. It might be dangerous. Remember what happened when I set you up as bait to catch a spy? You were attacked.'

'A man battered me with a door in his eagerness to get away, which hardly constitutes an attack,' Hannah scoffed. 'And you caught him. Eventually.'

She suppressed a slight shudder as she recalled the incident when a German spy had confronted her in the empty bookshop.

The click of the door catch brought their combined attention to where Detective Pendleton stuck his head round the jamb, though he did not enter the room.

'Sorry to interrupt, sir, but Miss Dalglish appears to have left the building.'

'What? I need to interview her.' Inspector Farrell glared at him as if he was solely responsible.

'I know, sir. A porter saw her getting into a handsome in the street. He wasn't aware of the situation, or he would have stopped her.'

'Let's hope she's simply gone home and not done a bunk.' The inspector sighed. 'Could you let Dr Murray know I expect her to make herself available when she returns. Oh, and I'll need her address.'

'Yes, sir.' The detective withdrew rapidly.

'Oh dear,' Hannah began, slightly sheepish. 'I apologise for not saying anything when she didn't come to the common room. It didn't occur to me she had left.'

'Hmm, that's rather odd behaviour. She was told I need to interview all the staff who were on duty last night?'

'I suppose so, but not everyone is familiar with police procedures,' Hannah pointed out.

'Even so, I don't like the idea she's avoiding me. Although something tells me her statement will be a repetition of everyone else's. No one seems to have seen or heard anything.'

'Unless she's the killer,' Hannah said.

'Well, there is that.' He exhaled a frustrated breath. 'To be honest, I'm at a loss with this one. Dr Murray informed me she has over a hundred staff and five hundred patients in this building. I have no idea where to begin.' He stroked his chin thoughtfully. 'Look, if you *do* hear something relevant on your travels, will you bring it to me? No questioning of witnesses, though. Is that understood?'

'You see? Asking wasn't that hard, was it?' It was hardly a formal request, but close enough if she was called upon to defend herself later. 'Actually, there is something which might interest you.'

'Which is?'

'When I arrived this morning, the library was locked, which is unusual. Nurse Dinah Root said the key was where it should be at the front desk. How did Sergeant Tillman know which one to take when it wasn't labelled?'

'Interesting point.' He stroked his chin thoughtfully. 'Unless someone unlocked the library for him.'

'But he couldn't have locked it again, could he? Dead men cannot lock doors. And how did the killer leave the hospital? The gates are locked at night I could try to find out if—'

'Hannah!' His sharp tone silenced her. 'This murder was not a casual act of violence. Whoever wanted Tillman dead planned it. He could still be in the building, so it could be dangerous. Please be careful.'

'I'm always careful.' She shrugged. 'Well, nearly always.'

3

Hannah arranged books on the portable trolley in preparation for her book round, while recalling her first visit to the hospital. The sight of the old St Giles workhouse with its austere, grey buildings set around a central square inside a high brick wall confirmed all her worst imaginings of a Victorian workhouse. Built on a former leper colony, it was reputed to have been used by Dickens as a model for *Oliver Twist*.

She had to steel herself during those first weeks as she wheeled the book trolley among seriously injured men, some bandaged from head to foot and others in painful looking leg or arm braces that prevented them moving. Within a few days, her time spent among the hard-working, dedicated staff and the stoic soldiers had altered her perspective – as did the light-hearted banter of the recovering soldiers eager to exchange small talk and hear news of the outside world.

Bracing her arms against the handle of the loaded book trolley, she headed for the lift to take her to St Anne's ward on the floor above. After a brief wait, the lift arrived and with a nod to the porter who sprang forward and held open the lift cage, she manoeuvred the wieldy contraption inside.

All wards at Endell Street bore the name of female saints, St Anne's being where the less seriously injured were treated before returning to their regiments. Hannah enjoyed their cheerful banter and self-deprecating jokes, but often wondered how long it would be before the laughter stopped and reality set in for those men with life-changing injuries who faced survival in an unsympathetic world.

The whirring of the heavy lift ceased, and it bumped to a halt. Sliding open the cage door, she wheeled the heavy trolley into the corridor, grateful she did not have to venture onto the three wards on the top floor in the south block, referred to as The Zoo, where the grievously injured and dying were cared for. The men there had no need for books; their groans of agony combined with the pungent smells of necrotic flesh and strong antiseptic pervaded the entire building.

In St Anne's ward, the long rows of beds were arranged against the walls with a central table that held a vase filled to overflowing with forget-me-nots, frothy-headed hyacinths, lilacs and fritillaria brought in daily from patron's gardens, their fragrance vying with the acrid, sickly smells of carbolic and disinfectant.

No utilitarian blinds, grey blankets or bare-painted walls proliferated at Endell Street. Here the men enjoyed a homely, colourful environment where the metal beds sported crimson coverlets, side tables and reading lamps. Handmade curtains adorned the row of windows that ran along one side, while landscapes donated by generous patrons hung on the walls.

Moving slowly from bed to bed, Hannah exchanged greetings with the patients about the weather, letters from home, and which books the men had enjoyed. Hannah halted the book trolley at the far end near a bed occupied by a handsome Irish corporal who was interested in the works of James Joyce. She had ordered several titles from Mudie's Circulating Library for him.

'Good morning, Corporal Doyle.' Hannah's gaze went to the copy of *The Dubliners* on his nightstand. 'I see you've finished the book. Did you enjoy it? The story of Evaline is my favourite.'

'I found it depressing, meself.' He pitched the last word as if he asked a question. 'A life wasted, if you ask me.' He lounged fully dressed on top of his made-up bed, shirtsleeves rolled to the elbows and shoeless feet crossed.

'Perhaps, but the story also has a poignancy. Though Joyce doesn't like the English much and blames us for his country's backwardness.' Realising what she had said, she stiffened, 'I'm sorry, I almost forgot you're Irish.'

'Don't ye fret.' His mouth quirked into a wry smile. 'I'm fra Belfast. A very different Ireland.' He pronounced it 'O-yer-land.'

'I see you aren't wearing your sling today?'

'First day without it.' He grasped his right upper arm with his hand and rolled his shoulder to show how well it had healed from a sniper's bullet.

'You'll be leaving us soon, then?'

'Aye, and at least I'll be walking out. Not like 'im.' His full lips turned up at the corner in a sneer, his eyes hard. 'S'pose you heard what happened in the night?'

Hannah aimed a brief nod at the stripped and empty bed opposite. 'It was odd him being found in the library, wasn't it?' she said, aiming for nonchalance.

'Someone said he'd been shot. Is that true?'

'I'm not privy to the details,' Hannah said quickly. It seemed the hospital gossip machine was in good order.

'Can't imagine what was he doing there in the middle of the night,' Corporal Doyle said. 'Probably couldn't sleep, so he went for a walk.'

'You spoke to him when he left?' Hannah asked, her interest piqued.

'Nah, but I dropped off soon after evening cocoa and slept through until the nurse woke me. Best night's sleep I've had since I got here.'

'You didn't hear the shot?'

'No. Had I done, I would have recognised it for what it was and told someone.' He turned to the soldier in the next bed. 'Did you hear anything last night, Binns?'

'Not a dicky bird,' a creaky, gasping voice said from behind a broadsheet; the legacy of a gas attack that had left him with a weak chest. 'Tillman won't be missed round 'ere though. Snide bastard!' Binns' aghast face appeared above the top of the newspaper. 'Sorry, Miss. Forgot who I was talking to.'

'I've heard worse, Private Binns.' Hannah circled the adjacent bed, handing him a thin, oversized, hard-backed book. 'I brought the manual you asked for.' That the sergeant was unpopular might be something Aidan would find interesting.

'Aw, thanks a lot, Miss. I've been waiting for this.' His eager smile stressed the puckered scar that ran from his left eye into his hairline. Crumpling the newspaper into his lap, he reached for the book and started poring over it. Barely twenty-one, he had expressed a desire to be a motor mechanic when invalided out of the army. Her Aunt Violet scoured the homes of all her friends in search of manuals on mechanical engineering, from ships' engines to motor cars, and persuaded or cajoled the owners to donate them to the library.

'He's right about Tillman, though,' Corporal Doyle said. 'Surly brute took advantage of anyone weaker than him. I don't envy the lads in his platoon. He must have ridden them hard.'

'Did he take a dislike to anyone in particular during his time here?' Hannah asked, hoping her keen interest was not too obvious.

'Hah! He hated everyone. Most of us avoided him. Not that I'm glad he's dead, but as Binns said, he won't be missed.'

'Did he have many visitors? A mother or a wife perhaps?' Even if the sergeant made no friends at the hospital, he might have had family.

'Can't say I ever saw anyone visit him, and he never mentioned family. He'd sneak out to The Cross Keys o'er the road every chance he got. The sisters usually got a porter to fetch 'im back.' Doyle hooked a thumb at the window behind him, which gave the same view of the courtyard as the library, but one floor higher. 'I saw Tillman and the porter going at it out by the gate. Those Royal Army Medical Corps blokes don't take lip from anyone.'

'Do you remember when this was?' Hannah busied herself with the book trolley, hoping he would not ask why she was asking them questions. She would have to ask Aidan how he does it without pestering.

'Hmm, when was it now?' He poked the air with a finger. 'I know, last Tuesday.'

Hannah made a mental note to find out who was on duty at the gate the previous Tuesday.

'You be askin' a lot of questions.' The corporal fixed her with a hard stare. 'Or is it because the police are 'ere?' He pronounced it po-lice.

'My apologies. Nosiness is a terrible fault of mine.' She hunched her shoulders in apology just as a nurse approached with a metal tray loaded with enamel bowls and rolls of bandages.

'Morning, Private Binns,' the newcomer said cheerfully, placing the tray on his nightstand. 'It's that time again. I've come to change your dressings.'

The young soldier's face blanched. He mumbled something

Hannah did not catch and put down his manual. The nurse unwound the bandage from his arm while the soldier closed his eyes, tension in every line of his face.

Hannah took a hurried leave of Corporal Doyle and a subdued Private Binns. Resisting an urge to run, she wheeled the book trolley towards the door while trying not to make her need to leave obvious. Among the tasks which made her stomach lurch, the daily round of dressing changes was uppermost.

She returned to the library to find the stage had been cordoned off, and the curtains pulled shut. Soldiers with slings and bandaged heads and limbs occupied all the chairs.

A game of billiards was in progress and the phonograph belted out a cheerful song by the Bing Brothers at full volume.

Despite her efforts to elicit information, Sergeant Tillman's name was hardly mentioned. The police presence, however, did not go unnoticed, repeated in nervous whispers wherever she went.

Left to her own musings, Hannah pondered who might have borne Sergeant Tillman a serious enough grudge to want him dead? Private Binns certainly seemed to despise him. Even Corporal Doyle had little to commend the man. And what was the sergeant doing in the library at night? Reading a book? Or was the book left there by someone else, its proximity to the dead man purely a coincidence?

By four o'clock that afternoon, books were returned to the shelves and billiard balls fell silent as the library emptied for tea. With nothing more to add to Corporal Doyle's unflattering portrait of Sergeant Tillman, Hannah collected her coat and hat. On her way down the short flight of steps into the courtyard, she noted there was no sign of the inspector's vehicle.

* * *

The harsh jangle of the bell over the door greeted Hannah's entry to the bookshop; it was a sound that had always grated on her nerves, but now made her smile. The previous October, when the infamous 'Theatre Raid' had wrecked the bookshop, a worker unearthed the filthy, but unharmed, bell from the rubble. Re-installed, it now stood as a symbol of resilience – her own and of a property that had stood in the same spot since Queen Victoria ascended the throne.

The refurbished bookshop boasted new light oak shelves not darkened by years of street soot and beeswax polish. Electric lighting replaced the hissing gas lamps, and the new, gleaming furniture did not smell of cigarette smoke and old biscuits. The multi-paned windows with bull-nose glass, and the slightly wonky front door at the top of a short flight of steps, had been expertly preserved. The 'Covent Garden Bookshop' sign had been replaced with a sleek, more modern style but kept its green and gold livery.

Hannah's first call on entering the bookshop, was to a velvet-lined basket in which a stocky black cat kept a baleful eye on the street. Mr Bartleby had put on weight in the last few weeks, and when she clicked her tongue in greeting, the cat ignored her, curled into a ball and nestled his chin on his paws.

Aunt Violet looked up from where she arranged books in the front bow window in an artistic display before moving to the door to greet her.

'You'll never guess what happened at the hospital this morning.' Hannah shrugged out of her coat and strode to the line of hooks on the far wall. 'Well, last night actually, but the excitement started first thing when we found—'

'We heard,' her aunt interrupted her. She leaned a hip against one of the full-height bookshelves. 'Dinah stopped in on her way home and told us all about that soldier being shot in the library.'

'Oh.' Hannah's mood dipped at the fact she wasn't the first to bring the news.

'Really, darling,' her aunt sighed. 'You must stop tripping over corpses. People will start avoiding you.'

'Not funny. And this is only my second one.' Hannah mounted the three steps up to the antique oak desk, a replacement for the original that had been turned into firewood during the raid. It stood on a platform to one side of the shop, an innovation of Hannah's design giving her an expansive view of the entire premises.

'Did Dinah mention Detective Inspector Farrell is in charge of the case?'

'Now that makes it infinitely more interesting.' Her aunt leaned her forearms on the railing surrounding the platform. 'How is he?'

'Do you need to ask?' Hannah suspected she and the handsome detective had not been strangers since he had investigated Lily-Anne's murder.

'Whatever do you mean?' Aunt Violet sniffed and continued to flick through a pile of invoices on the desk. 'I was merely being polite in asking after him.'

'I'm sure you were,' Hannah said under her breath. 'It's possible another soldier shot him, but the circumstances are odd.'

'I doubt many people get murdered in libraries.' Her aunt abandoned the paperwork and plucked a biscuit from a plate on the desk. 'What was he doing there in the middle of the night?' She spoke through a mouthful of garibaldi biscuit, just as the storeroom door opened with a bang to admit Archie.

'Miss Merrill!' His bright smile instantly cheered her up. 'We weren't expecting you this afternoon. Would you like some tea? The kettle's on.' Their recent encounter with spies and a murderer had given their assistant new confidence. He had put his wages to good use and had bought himself a moleskin waistcoat and matching trousers, though his wayward curly brown hair needed a cut.

'Tea would be very welcome. Thank you, Archie.' Hannah took her seat behind her desk in the newly extended premises provided by the acquisition of the shop next door. The air raid several months before had driven the owner into retirement, so he had sold his damaged shop to Aunt Violet and Hannah.

At the time, Aunt Violet had voted to abandon the bookshop altogether. However, reluctant to see either the shop or her independence lost, Hannah threw her energies and her money into the rebuilding. The brand-new bookshop with its electric lighting, brass fitments and gleaming polished oak bookshelves proved a more attractive environment than the old, dusty Victorian shop, and engendered a new interest in her Aunt Violet who now charmed the customers with her aristocratic demeanour. The whistle of a kettle summoned Archie back to the storeroom, where he turned back. 'Dinah told us all about that bloke shot at the hospital?'

'Hush, Archie, not so loud!' Hannah snapped, though the shop was empty of customers.

'Hannah was just about to fill us in on all the details, Archie,' Aunt Violet interrupted. 'Oh, do shut off that infernal noise. It's hurting my ears.'

'Sorry, Miss Edwards.' Archie disappeared behind the door again, and mercifully the whistle abruptly ceased.

'How much did Dinah tell you?' Hannah asked when they were alone again.

'Only the pertinent details, but the poor girl was yawning so hard, I sent her to the nurses' lodgings. She's on shift again tonight and needs her sleep.'

Archie reappeared almost immediately, carrying a tray loaded with a teapot and crockery for two, along with a plate of garibaldi biscuits.

'Have the police any idea who did it?' Archie perched on a stool and hunched over his enamel mug of tea.

'Not yet.' Hannah cradled her cup in both hands. 'Inspector Farrell is delving into his past to see if Sergeant Tillman had any enemies.'

'Could be anyone, then.'

He was right. Convoys of ambulances arriving at all hours, not to mention injured drunks who stumbled into the casualty area to be patched up, meant it wouldn't be too difficult for a stranger to slip inside unnoticed.

Hannah sipped her tea, recalling Inspector Farrell's assertion that whoever killed the sergeant had lured him to the library on purpose to do the deed in relative privacy. Did they have access to the hospital after hours? Or were they already there?

'How was he killed?' Aunt Violet asked.

'The inspector said he was shot at close range with a large calibre bullet.' She still could not bring herself to refer to him as Aidan like her aunt did. It seemed disrespectful somehow.

'If it was close range, wouldn't the killer have blood on their clothes?' Aunt Violet asked.

'I thought the same thing,' Hannah replied. 'But finding blood-stained clothing in a hospital is a fruitless task. The body had lain there for a few hours before I— it was found. There was enough time for the killer to dispose of what they were wearing.'

'Are you going to do some more sleuthing, Miss Merrill?' Archie asked, wide-eyed. 'I could help. I'm good at finding things.'

'Maybe we should leave this one to the police, Archie,' Aunt Violet said warningly.

Hannah dipped her nose to her cup, and remained silent as

she recalled the confrontation Sergeant Tillman had with the gate porter.

'Interesting,' Aunt Violet mused.

'What is?' Hannah looked up.

'That you aren't talking about it.' Her voice changed in timbre as she added, 'It's almost closing time, Archie. Lock the door, would you? Have you finished the stocktaking like I instructed?'

Archie straightened and noisily swallowed his mouthful of biscuit. 'Er, no, Miss Edwards. I'll do it right now.' Returning his empty mug to the tray, he scrambled to his feet, swept the placid cat into his arms and headed back to his cubbyhole in the storeroom.

'That was rather harsh.' Hannah frowned. 'And almost as if you were trying to get rid of him.'

'I was, but he'll get over it.' Aunt Violet returned her own cup to its saucer, then picked up a newspaper folded open to an inner page and held it towards her. 'Have you seen this?'

A bold headline announced a sentence hearing for Miss Clara Protheroe, otherwise known as Cecily Prentice, who had been found guilty of the pre-meditated murders of Mrs Lily-Anne Soames and Hannah's former bookshop manager, Montague Carstairs.

'I have, yes.' Hannah lowered her cup, pointedly looked away from the newspaper with its artist's drawing of the murderer. Losing her childhood best friend, Lily-Anne, still went deep, even though Monty Carstairs' duplicity meant his loss, if regrettable, left her cold.

'At least it's all over now, for Darius' sake.' Her aunt refolded the newspaper and placed it on the arm of her chair. 'How is Darius taking it?'

Hannah shrugged. 'It's difficult to tell, because he's reluctant to talk about it.'

The Harley Street physician engaged to assess Cecily Prentice's mental state was quoted in the newspaper as saying that her inability to discern right from wrong resulted from her father's suicide. The erudite, and expensive, medic had convinced the judge she was not responsible for her actions, and thus spared her the ultimate penalty of hanging. Instead, she would be detained in a facility for the mentally ill.

'What happens if she's cured?' her aunt asked, mildly incredulous. 'Will she be declared sane, and then they will hang her?'

'Don't!' Hannah winced. 'I'm convinced she'll be punished where she is going. You hear awful things about such places.'

Darius Clifford, and all things to do with him, were difficult subjects for Hannah. Her thoughts about her childhood playmate had recently turned to the romantic, no matter how hard she tried to keep him in a box marked 'friend'.

Darius had hinted more than once he would like their relationship to be on a different level, but whenever she got close, he would back away. At first, she attributed his reticence to his respect for her losing her fiancé, Gerald, at the front, followed by the ending of his engagement with a murderess.

He treated her these days with the gentle care of a younger sister, which she found infuriating. Should she wait for him to change his mind, or move on and consign him to the past? The latter solution sounded more practical, even less painful, but whenever she looked into his midnight-blue eyes, or he flashed her one of his devastating smiles, she lost her ability to think clearly.

'Thankfully, the whole dreadful affair is all over,' her aunt said, as if reading Hannah's thoughts. 'Now perhaps you and Darius can go on with your lives together?'

'Aunt Violet, please.' She fidgeted, uncomfortable with a subject which plagued her own solitary hours. 'He's not even hinted at us being together. Not lately, anyway. I'm content to let things remain as they are.'

'Very altruistic, darling, but I don't believe a word of it. Darius was always in love with you. He only let himself be manipulated into an engagement with Cecily, or Clara, or whatever her name is, because he lost you to Gerald.'

'Until Gerald was killed, but then it was too late.' A pang of disappointment settled beneath her breastbone. 'Then why has he been so distant? He's not even hinted at a courtship, let alone a commitment.'

'Isn't that obvious? He feels partly responsible for what happened. It was Cecily's jealousy which turned her mind. Lily-Anne and Monty were his friends too, remember?'

'That's ridiculous. None of it was his fault.'

'*We* know that, but discovering your fiancée is a double-murderer must be hard to live down with the coverage it got in the newspapers. He needs time, that's all.'

'Instead, he rushed out and joined the Secret Service,' Hannah said. 'Or was it Military Intelligence? Something like that.'

On the night the German bomb destroyed her aunt's bookshop, Darius had hinted at hopes for a different future for both of them. Since then, he had not broached the subject again, convincing Hannah the damage Cecily wreaked had soured them as a couple. Or had he since regretted his words that night? Her hopes he would come to the point had faded, but she clung to their childhood friendship and learned to accept that, for the time being at least, it was enough.

4

A firm knock on the front door brought Aunt Violet into the hall, leaving Hannah to finish clearing their supper dishes. After a moment, the sounds of soft, intimate laughter and inaudible whispers reached her. Placing the last dried plate on the rack, she entered the hall, where a gentleman's leather coat hung on the row of hooks inside the porch. A pair of driving gauntlets, cap and goggles lay on the bench below. It did not surprise her to find Inspector Farrell sharing a sofa with Aunt Violet when she returned to the sitting room.

Neither noticed her until the inspector looked up. 'Ah, good evening, Hannah.' He eased further along the sofa. 'I hope I'm not intruding, but I wondered if you had learned anything since our earlier discussion?'

'Not since this morning, Inspector,' Hannah replied, though if either of them detected her sarcasm, they ignored it. 'I didn't expect to see you twice in one day.'

'Haven't you had enough of murder and mayhem after last time, Hannah?' Aunt Violet left her seat and strolled to the sideboard. 'Sherry, anyone?' she asked, a crystal decanter held up in invitation.

'That was different,' Hannah declined. 'I had to prove my innocence somehow.'

'The evidence was circumstantial,' the inspector said. 'But I couldn't have done my job had I not considered Hannah a suspect.'

'I *knew* you thought I'd killed Lily-Anne!' Hannah said, her instincts finally vindicated. 'At least I'm in the clear this time.'

'What makes you think that?' He accepted the sherry Aunt Violet offered him with whispered thanks and a wink.

'Don't tease her.' Her aunt peered at him flirtatiously through eyelashes nature couldn't possibly have given her. 'Sherry, Hannah?' She handed her a glass, ignoring Hannah's refusal.

'What have you discovered?' Resigned, Hannah held the glass high to avoid spillage as the sofa springs yielded beneath her.

'Not much,' the inspector replied. 'But as we are collaborating on this case, I thought you might like to be kept up to date?'

Hannah frowned. Collaborating? When they last spoke, he made it clear he wanted her not to meddle in police business.

He placed his glass beside a nearby potted plant, withdrew a notebook from a pocket, and flipped to a page. 'Sergeant Alfred Tillman, aged thirty-four, was wounded in the thigh by shrapnel at Vichy in February,' he recited, as if he was in court. 'Returned to London to be treated at Charing Cross Hospital. He discharged himself early, claiming he needed to get back to his regiment. A few days later, he was admitted to Endell Street because his wound had opened and turned septic. That was three weeks ago.

'He had no visitors during his stay, and no one at Charing Cross Hospital can recall any, either. His home address is a lodging house in Ladbroke Grove, and his landlord says he was quiet and caused no trouble. I've requested a report from his commanding officer, but that will take time, as his regiment is still overseas.'

'You *have* been busy,' Hannah said, genuinely impressed. 'Did anything come of the interviews with the night shift staff?'

'Not exactly. You were right about them, incidentally. They're a frustratingly closed-mouthed group who claimed to know next to nothing about Sergeant Tillman.'

'Was there any sign of the weapon?' Aunt Violet asked before Hannah could.

'Not so far. The patients surrender their weapons before being admitted, though it wouldn't be hard for someone to smuggle one in. The place is hardly secure, despite the high walls and a guard at the front gate.'

Hannah nodded. 'We get a lot of visitors, especially high-born ladies who appear to use the hospital as entertainment.'

'Hmm. It's a puzzle. It's not as if the sergeant was there long enough for anyone to want to kill him,' he said.

'You think so?' Aunt Violet peered at him over her glass. 'I know several individuals I've been prepared to kill within fifteen minutes of meeting them.' She aimed the full force of her mischievous smile at him, making him blush.

'Go on, Inspector.' Hannah resisted the urge to roll her eyes.

'Um, yes.' He took a mouthful of sherry before continuing. 'Dr Murray said Tillman was a difficult patient, but everyone else I spoke to was non-committal, or claimed not to remember him very well.'

'That's different from what I heard,' Hannah said, bringing his attention back to her. 'Tillman was a skiver and a bully with no respect for others' belongings. I spoke to two soldiers on St Anne's ward who had nothing nice to say about him.'

'Maybe someone from his past had a long-held grudge they decided to settle.' He raised his glass in emphasis. 'A soldier he offended during his service in the army, perhaps? I've got a man going through the hospital visitors' book, but chances are a killer would have avoided signing in.'

'If the killer fired at close range—' Aunt Violet began.

'Who told you that?' Inspector Farrell straightened, his brow furrowed.

'Hannah did. Now what was I saying? Ah, yes, I know. Wouldn't the killer have blood on them?'

'My mistake, I forgot you two tell each other everything.'

'Does that surprise you?' Hannah gave him a wry look. 'But blood on a nurse's apron or doctor's coat would be commonplace. Although if the killer was in outdoor clothes, someone might have seen him.'

Aunt Violet shifted her position on the sofa to speak across from the inspector. 'From what I understand, the body wasn't found for hours, so the killer had plenty of time to dispose of what they were wearing.'

'There's also a furnace on the premises, which makes finding anything almost impossible.' Hannah sighed.

'Exactly,' Aunt Violet tutted. 'And wasn't there a shift change in the middle of it all? Anyone with a blood-stained coat will have taken themselves off home, so we'll never find it.' She rose and crossed to the sideboard. 'Refill, anyone?'

'Not for me.' Hannah shook her head. 'Maybe once all the nurses' dormitories are searched, something might turn up.'

Throughout this exchange, the inspector remained silent other than to decline a second drink.

'Just me, then.' Aunt Violet topped up her glass before returning to the sofa. 'Doesn't sound as if you have got far. Hannah appears to have gleaned more of an insight than you have.' She crossed one ankle over the other and relaxed against the upholstery.

'Perhaps I should let you ladies solve this case and I'll stay home and do some gardening.' Rising, he placed his glass on the mantel with a firm click. 'Let me know when you've made an arrest.'

'Don't be irritable, Aidan.' Her aunt pouted. 'We're simply trying to help. Between us we might come up with some theories, for which you can take sole credit.'

'I suppose it can't hurt.' He tucked both hands into his pockets and rocked on his heels.

'Now,' Aunt Violet began. 'Can the police surgeon pinpoint the actual time of death?'

'Not close enough. He estimates sometime between midnight and four this morning. When he was found, the blood was congealed.' He flushed. 'My apologies, ladies.'

'Don't worry about us,' Aunt Violet waved him off. 'I've spent almost as much time as Hannah at the hospital, and I've seen a few things. Not that I was faint-hearted before that, I might add.'

'That's entirely believable.' He scratched his ear thoughtfully. 'I still need a motive.'

'I'm not sure this qualifies,' Hannah began, 'but the gate porter had a public argument with Sergeant Tillman in the courtyard last Tuesday afternoon. The person I spoke to didn't know what it was about, but someone might.'

'That's interesting,' he murmured.

'That this Sergeant Turner had an argument with a porter?' Aunt Violet asked, confused.

'Tillman,' Hannah corrected her. Her nose tickled and, anticipating a sneeze, she slid a hand into her pocket in search of a handkerchief. Her fingers closed on a crumpled piece of paper she brought into the light and she stared at it for a moment, trying to recall where it came from. Then she remembered.

'That no one in the entire hospital mentioned it,' the inspector replied to Aunt Violet's question. 'I'll get Pendleton to check the shift schedule to find out who it was.'

He frowned at the paper in Hannah's hand. 'What's that you have there?' The inspector squinted at it.

'Probably nothing important.' Hannah shrugged. 'It fell out of the book Sergeant Tillman was reading. I thought it was a note, but it's just a series of letters and numbers.'

'Let me see.' Aidan took it from her and angled it towards the light from the window. 'There's an "O" and an "R", or it could be a "P" but a fold has blurred it. There's also an eight and some figures I cannot make out.'

Hannah retrieved the softened paper and was about to toss it into the wastebasket, when the inspector halted her.

'Let me have that. I'll give it to the boys in the back room, see if they can make any sense of it. Give them something useful to do.' He turned back at the door. 'By the way, that nurse turned up late for her shift tonight, so I didn't have time to interview her.'

'Nurse Dalglish?' Hannah frowned.

'Don't the police take precedence over emptying bed pans?' Aunt Violet said.

'Normally, yes, but somehow, I baulked at taking on Dr Murray by insisting. I'll have to try again tomorrow. Now, ladies,' he skirted a small bow, 'I'll leave you to enjoy the rest of your evening.'

'Why don't you stay for dinner?' Aunt Violet placed her empty glass on a side table and rose.

Hannah widened her eyes at her, but she did not appear to notice.

'Thank you, but no,' he replied, intercepting Hannah's surprised look. 'Another time, perhaps?'

'Well, you'd be very welcome.' Her aunt escorted him to the front door, leaving Hannah to wonder if he had refused out of disinterest in their company, or was simply being polite. She was still wondering about Nurse Dalglish's odd behaviour when the roar of Inspector Farrell's motorbike faded into the night.

* * *

The bookshop kept both Hannah and her aunt busy the following day, so there was no opportunity to talk about the murder. The hands of the wall clock crawled towards closing time, and just as she and her aunt tidied their workspace in preparation to lock up, the bell over the door announced another customer.

Summoning a welcoming, if strained, smile, Hannah looked up just as a strikingly pretty blonde girl halted inside the bookshop door. She wore the uniform of the Endell Street nurses: a grey-brown belted tunic buttoned down the front with a matching skirt to her ankles. The initials WHC of the Women's Hospital Corps were neatly embroidered in red on blue shoulder lapels. A soft cap with a flat bow at the front sat straight on her forehead with a gauze veil that hung from the back of the cap to her shoulders.

Hannah smiled in welcome as she recognised Nurse Dalglish – the orderly who had arrived with Sister Kerr in the library minutes after she and Dinah had found Sergeant Tillman's body – whose luminous porcelain skin, symmetrical features, and waif-like figure made her feel suddenly clumsy.

Archie leapt forward to intercept the newcomer, the pile of books he held hitting the floor with a thump.

Hannah gestured him away. 'Don't trouble yourself, Archie. I'll see to this lady.'

'Yes, Miss Merrill.' Archie retreated, disappointed.

'May I help you?'

The girl clutched a small leather bag at her waist, so tight, her knuckles showed white. Her wide cornflower-blue eyes darted to the front window and then back at Hannah.

'It's Nurse Dalglish, isn't it?' Hannah said, attempting to put her more at ease.

'H-how did you know?' The girl's startling blue eyes searched Hannah's face, then darted to the shop door as if prepared to run.

'I didn't mean to alarm you. I'm Hannah Merrill. I volunteer at the hospital library. I've seen you on the wards.'

'Oh, for a moment I thought—' Her eyes flickered, then cleared. 'Of course, I remember you now.' She chewed the corner of her bottom lip, darting frequent glances towards the door.

'Is there something particular you're looking for?' Hannah chose not to mention the murder right away in case it alarmed her. Something about her fragility, and a small tick beside one eye stirred Hannah's protective instinct.

'Er, I'm not sure,' she replied, in a voice as soft and attractive as the rest of her.

'While you're thinking, come and sit down.' Hannah led her towards the wing-back chair at the rear.

Shielded by floor-to-ceiling-height bookcases, the reading corner – a haven for customers to spend a quiet hour – was Hannah's pride and her nemesis. It was here she had found her friend's body in the wing-back chair that dominated the small space. The original had been replaced with a similar model in royal blue velvet, but the sight of it still gave her the odd start.

'Would you like some water, or perhaps tea?' Hannah asked when they were settled, aware of Archie making a show of rearranging books, his glance repeatedly lifting to the girl.

'Thank you, no. I'm sorry to be so jumpy, only since they found that sergeant— I mean, since you found him. I'm right, aren't I? It was you?'

'It was me, yes.' Hannah fidgeted at the unwelcome memory. 'It was most... unpleasant.'

'Everyone at the hospital is talking about it. He wasn't an amiable man, and quite rude to the staff, and even to other soldiers. He was always starting fights on the ward. But he didn't deserve to die like that.'

'No,' Hannah agreed. 'No one does. I'm surprised no one heard the shot.' Hannah scrutinised her face carefully, but her gaze remained steady. 'The library is directly below St Anne's Ward.'

'I didn't hear anything either. But then we had so many new admissions and it was very noisy with people coming and going. We didn't stop all night.'

'Is that why you went home instead of staying to talk to the police?'

'What?' She looked up, startled. 'I only did what—' She ran her tongue slowly over her bottom lip before continuing. 'I was summoned by that inspector chap that evening when I came back on shift. He was very terse with me. He told me off for leaving the hospital, which looking back I shouldn't have done. But I was exhausted after the shift.'

'He's not usually— I mean, he didn't strike me as unkind,' Hannah corrected herself, hoping she had not noticed. 'What did he say to you?'

'After he told me off, you mean?' She met Hannah's gaze briefly. 'He asked what I knew about missing sleeping powders. Not if – what.'

'Really?' He had not mentioned that during their talk.

She nodded. 'I did know something, but not what he thought. Look,' she leaned forward slightly, 'I shouldn't be saying this, but the sisters leave a few powders in the kitchen. Saves having to disturb the pharmacists at night when a patient gets restless. We aren't supposed to, but well—'

'I see. What else did he say?'

'That I was probably the last person to see Sergeant Tillman alive. But I already knew that because Sis—' She hesitated, a slow blush creeping into her cheeks.

At the corner off her vision, Hannah saw Aunt Violet, one hand held palm downwards at waist level making a brief downward motion.

Hannah responded with a tiny nod of understanding before she turned back to the nurse. 'What made you come into the library that morning?'

'I should have gone off at six, but Sister Hibbert told us a patient was missing. All the night staff joined in the search. Then said there was a commotion in the library, so I went to see if I could help. But it was too late.'

'Sister Kerr seemed concerned for you.' The nurse glanced up sharply, and Hannah added, 'I saw you with her outside in the hall, she looked as if she was holding you up.'

'Yes, I was flagging by then. Sister Kerr is so kind, and protective of all the younger nursing staff. Night shifts can be challenging, so she insists we get proper sleep between shifts. I lodge with her, so I took a cab home. I fell asleep instantly that day. Even the noises didn't disturb me like they often do.'

'What sort of noises?' Hannah frowned.

'I don't mean to be ungrateful.' The girl winced, embarrassed. 'Sister Kerr's house is clean and homely, but it's old. The beams creak and the walls are so thin I can hear the neighbours talking. I don't sleep well either, but that isn't Sister Kerr's fault, only, where I lived before was much quieter.' Her hands tightened on the bag in her lap. 'You might think I'm being fanciful, but I have this strange feeling I'm being followed.'

A dozen questions jumped into Hannah's head, but she waited for her to continue; a ploy learned from Inspector Farrell, who said most people abhorred silences and often rushed to fill them.

When the girl stayed silent, Hannah leaned forward. 'Does this feeling happen often?'

'It began about two weeks ago. I thought it was my imagination at first, but it's the same young man each time.' She frowned, lowering her voice to a whisper as if talking to herself. 'It was supposed to have been dealt with.'

'Dealt with?' Hannah frowned, confused.

'What?' She glanced up again and blinked. 'Oh, sorry, I was thinking aloud. It's nothing.'

Hannah was unconvinced. She beckoned Archie closer. Not that it was necessary, as he was at her side in seconds. 'See if there's anyone hanging about outside who shouldn't be, would you, Archie?'

Archie appeared to have lost the power of speech and could only before darting away.

'Oh, and Archie?' she called him back. 'Don't make it too obvious.'

'That's so kind, but he's probably gone by now.' The nurse brought one hand from her bag to the collar of her tunic, and murmured, 'If there really was someone.'

'It won't hurt to check. Now, what brings you to the bookshop?'

'Oh dear. I didn't intend to buy anything.' Her nervous giggle turned into a cough. 'I begin day-shift tomorrow. I need to stay awake, or I won't sleep tonight, so I did some shopping. I had just left the Strand, when I saw him. At least I guessed it must be him. I've seen him a couple of times now. So I ducked in here.'

'Could you describe this man?'

'He's more of a youth, really. He wears scruffy clothes, but he's not sinister at all. I thought he might be a... well, an admirer.' She flushed. 'Call me vain, but it's happened in the past.'

This came as no surprise, though Hannah sensed this was more than a shy girl jumping at shadows. Something had upset her badly.

'Did you mention all this to Inspector Farrell?'

'Oh no.' She shook her head, making the gauze veil flutter. 'He doesn't need to know. It has nothing to do with the murder of Sergeant Tillman.'

Hannah disagreed. Inspector Farrell had reiterated more than once that witnesses omit things they regard as trivial but could be vital to his investigation.

The bookshop had emptied by this time, the street noises beyond the windows quieting down to a low roar.

'This is a lovely bookshop.' She smiled, the tension leaving her face. 'I see it every day on my way to the hospital, but it's usually closed because I've been on night shift since I started there. Have you worked here long?'

'I own the bookshop jointly with my aunt, Miss Edwards.' She nodded to where Aunt Violet crossed the floor after seeing out a customer, her nod of acknowledgement indicating she heard every word.

'No, I'm not married,' Hannah said, in response to her surreptitious glance at her left hand. 'My fiancé was killed during the first weeks of the war.'

'I'm so sorry.' Her eyes welled instantly. 'My brother was a second lieutenant in the London Regiment. He... he was shot by a sniper at Artois. It's the main reason I became a VAD. To help those who survived, or just to do something noble, or useful.'

'Please accept my condolences for your brother.'

'Thank you, that's kind.' A shadow crossed her features showing the memory was still raw.

'My contribution to the war effort is to rearrange books in the hospital library.' Hannah aimed for some levity to lift the sudden dark atmosphere.

'Oh, but what you do is important.' Her startling blue eyes searched Hannah's face. 'There is so little to occupy the soldiers and sometimes their recovery takes a long time. The library cheers them up.'

'Do you like nursing?' Hannah appreciated the compliment.

'I do, but I'm not accustomed to so many people in one place. I mix up their names and think I've seen someone when they weren't there. There's so much to learn and I forget things.' She giggled, a light, pleasant sound. 'I put the milk on to boil for the patients' cocoa the other night and completely forgot about it. Fortunately, I went back before it boiled over.'

Hannah looked up as the doorbell jangled announcing Archie's return.

'I went as far as Drury Lane, Miss, but couldn't see anyone loitering. The streets are busy today, though.'

'There, you see,' the nurse said brightly. 'I told you it was probably my imagination.' Her high, musical laugh sounded again.

'Thank you, Archie.' Hannah held his gaze, and when he did not move, she cocked her chin in silent instruction for him to leave.

He slunk away, though did not go far.

'I apologise for being such a nuisance, Miss Merrill.' Nurse Dalglish eased from the chair and smoothed her skirt. 'I'll be going now.'

'Please don't feel you have to rush off.' Hannah waved her down again. 'And call me Hannah. We're bound to meet again at the hospital.'

'I'm Alice. Alice Dalglish.' Her hesitation was brief but telling. 'But you already know that. I'm sorry if I was abrupt before.'

Bartleby chose that moment to investigate the new arrival

wrapping his substantial body around her ankles, his tail held high.

'Oh, you have a cat. What a lovely creature.' She bent and ran a hand over his black coat, eliciting a mew of contented approval.

'His name is Bartleby,' Archie offered, easing closer.

'As in *Bartleby, the Scrivener*?' Her face lit up for a second before resuming its former sadness. 'My brother loved that story. Although I always thought it dreadfully sad.'

'Master Bartleby likes to keep an eye on us, but he's become lazy recently.' Hannah directed this remark at Archie, who had always regarded Bartleby his cat.

'Well, it was very nice meeting you again, Hannah, and you, Miss Edwards,' she said with renewed confidence. 'I really mustn't keep you any longer. Perhaps next time I'll even buy a book?' She smiled at Archie, causing his complexion to flush bright red.

'You'd be most welcome.' Hannah accompanied her to the door, followed by the cat, and held it open, mentally rolling her eyes at her assistant's gormless expression. 'You could always stop by the hospital library now you are working the day shift.'

'Thank you. I will do that.' Nurse Dalglish paused on the step, turning to stroke Bartleby between the ears before she set off towards the Strand.

Hannah watched her go, noting the admiring glances she received from passers-by, to which she seemed oblivious. It was clear the girl was upset, by the murder or her supposed follower, it wasn't clear. Her story struck a wrong note somehow. Not so much a lie, that she was holding something back. Was that deliberate, or did she know more than she realised?

'*Is* she being followed?' Aunt Violet asked, joining her at the window.

'I don't know, but *she* believes it,' Hannah replied. 'And you didn't say very much.'

'I was admiring your questioning technique.' Her aunt smiled knowingly. 'I thought you were being intrusive at one point, but you pulled back nicely. Our inspector friend would be proud.'

'Maybe I'll try again when we see each other at the hospital. Although she seemed genuinely frightened.'

'She's a right looker, I'll say that for 'er.' Archie sighed.

'Your mouth is open, Archie,' Hannah said, her attention still on the road. 'Have you done the stocktaking?'

'Er – no, Miss. I'll do it now.'

5

Two days later, Hannah waited outside the forbidding grey walls of the hospital, a hand raised to the bell rope to summon the porter. A shadow moved into her peripheral vision, causing her to glance over her shoulder. In the entrance of the narrow alley behind her, a youth aged about sixteen appeared, backlit by daylight from the street. He wore faded brown trousers and a darker jacket slightly too big for him; the shoulders overlapping the top of his arms, his face thin but pleasant beneath unruly dark hair.

Was this the young man Alice said had been following her?

Just then, he caught her staring at him. His eyes widened, and he pushed away from the wall and disappeared around the corner with the flash of a coat tail.

Suspecting he would wait for her to enter the courtyard before resuming his post, she lowered her hand from the rope pull and waited. Seconds later, he reappeared. His wary brown eyes met hers and he paled, turned and fled around the corner of the stone building.

Cursing beneath her breath, Hannah took off after him, but at the corner, he darted across the road. About to follow, she leapt back as a horse and cart rumbled past. Once the road cleared again, he was out of sight.

Defeated, she returned to the hospital gate, which now stood open as a long black motor car rolled past her into the courtyard. Detective Pendleton sat at the wheel, with Inspector Farrell's profile visible through the rear window. The vehicle eased to a halt at the bottom of the steps, where Inspector Farrell emerged from the back seat and strode up the steps. He turned at the door, gave Hannah a brief nod over his shoulder before disappearing into the building.

Hannah made to follow, when Detective Pendleton alighted the motor car and stepped onto the cobbles in front of her.

'Miss Merrill? Might I have a word?' His copper-coloured hair gleamed above pale skin that coloured after five minutes of sun, and watery blue eyes. Inspector Farrell told her he had been discharged from the army on medical grounds, but he did not go into details and Hannah had not asked.

'Of course, Detective. What can I do for you?'

'Inspector Farrell wanted me to tell you the chap who had an altercation with Sergeant Tillman is off the suspect list.' Was it her imagination, or did the detective look smug? 'The sergeant requested cigarettes from the porter, but when he declined, the sergeant made an offensive gesture and pushed him against the wall. The entire exchange was witnessed by an orderly.'

'I see. Does he have an alibi?' she asked, hoping to catch him off-guard. 'I made sure of that.' He nodded. 'He and his wife spent the night of the murder with her sister and brother-in-law in Croydon.'

'I see.' Hannah nodded, taking the steps quickly. 'I suppose it was too easy a solution, but worth considering.'

'Miss Merrill.' Following, he reached past her to open the door. 'I hope you'll pardon my presumption.'

'That depends, Detective.' Hannah turned on the top step, irritated by his patronising tone. 'How presumptuous do you intend to be?'

'Well, er... I'm aware of your previous involvement in the Soames case, but is it wise to involve yourself in an unconnected murder? You're a civilian, and a woman. Inspector Farrell has asked me to share details of the case with you, but I urge you not to put yourself at risk. For his sake and your own.'

'Really?' She held his stare for several seconds, gratified to see him flush slightly. 'I appreciate your concern, for both of us, but Lily-Anne Soames was a close friend. Her murder was hard for me and I refuse to sit back while other lives are taken if I can prevent it.'

'Our soldiers take lives every day, Miss. Many of whom are being cared for in this building.' He was apparently not willing to give up. Was it to protect her or his superior?

'I agree, but there's a difference. I can do nothing about the war, but I intend to do what I can to help tackle crimes at home.'

'Even so, Miss. I advise against making this into a personal crusade. No one can change human nature.' He hauled open the front door and stepped aside to allow her through.

'I'll bear that in mind, Detective.' She left him in the hall with her best smile, but despite her glib answer, she had let him get to her. Why did men, especially those with a modicum of authority, treat females as if they were incapable of thinking for themselves?

The library was quiet that morning. Hannah's enquiries of the staff about Sergeant Tillman met with a mixture of frustrated sighs and headshaking. She completed her book round and was on her way back to the library when a nurse in a white apron darted out of Dr Murray's office, her head down.

'Dinah, watch out!' Hannah halted the book trolley before they collided, steadying the girl's shoulder with her other hand. Something had obviously upset her. Perhaps Sister Hibbert had given her a harsh dressing down.

'Oh, I'm so sorry, Miss Merrill. I weren't lookin' where I was goin'.' Dinah raised her head, revealing red, puffy eyes.

'I thought we agreed you were to call me Hannah.' She glanced both ways along the corridor, but there was no one about. 'Come into the library for a few minutes. You can't face the patients while upset.'

'All right then. For a little while.' Dinah swiped a hand beneath her nose. 'I mustn't be late for the dressing changes, though.'

Hannah closed the library door to give them some privacy and ushered her into a chair between the billiard table and the window with a view of the courtyard. 'Now, tell me what's wrong.'

Dinah inhaled slowly before answering, her fingers plucking repeatedly at a fold in her apron. 'I've got that nice Corporal Doyle into trouble with the police.'

'Oh?' Hannah tried not to appear too eager as she took the chair beside her.

'That Inspector Funnell questioned me again about Sergeant Tillman.'

'His name is Farrell.' Hannah hid a smile. 'What did you tell him?'

'The same as I did the last time he asked if anyone showed ani-something towards the sergeant.'

'Animosity?'

'Yes. That were it. I weren't sure what 'e meant until 'e explained it was anyone with a grudge against 'im. Why didn't 'e say that the first time?'

Hannah suppressed a smile, imagining the inspector's expression in the face of Dinah's confusion. 'And did you?'

'Well.' Dinah subjected her apron to another scrunching. 'The inspector kept staring at me like 'e thought I was hidin' something, and before I knew what I was sayin', I blurted out about the cake.'

'Cake?' Hannah frowned. Whatever she had been expecting, that was not it.

Dinah's frantic nod dislodged her cap, which slipped further down her forehead. 'It happened a couple of months ago.' She shoved the cap back again with one hand. 'A young lad arrived on the hospital train from France badly cut up by shrapnel. He'd lain in a trench for a few days and by the time he reached us, his wounds were septic. He was from one of the highland regiments. Scots accent he had.'

'He could still speak?' Hannah could only imagine what he went through if he remained conscious throughout such an ordeal.

'A little, though he was in a terrible, bad way. I wasn't part of the team who cared for him, but those who did said he wouldn't last long.' Her voice hitched at remembered emotion. 'His mother couldn't afford to travel down from Scotland to visit him, but she sent him this cake. It was small, but beautifully decorated with crystalised fruit and nuts. Only he died before he could even taste it.'

'That's a very sad story, Dinah, but what does it have to do with Corporal Doyle?'

'I'm getting to that.' Dinah frowned, impatient. 'The ward sister planned to share the cake out among the patients on St Anne's ward, but it went missing. When she asked if anyone had seen it, Sergeant Tillman said he'd eaten it. Blatant, he was. Said he'd done the lad's mum a favour by not lettin' it go stale.'

'That's horrible.' Hannah shuddered. 'What happened then?'

'Corporal Doyle, that's what. I've never seen him so mad.' Dinah's eyes rounded. 'He punched Sergeant Tillman in the face so hard, he hit the floor like he was poleaxed.' Her eyes clouded. 'My dad used to say that, and I never knew what it meant, but after seeing it happen to that smug brute, I do now.'

'Was the sergeant badly hurt?' If so, it could indeed mean real trouble for Corporal Doyle.

'Not really. He had a bloody nose and threatened he'd have Corporal Doyle up on a charge for assaulting a superior officer.'

'And did he?'

'No.' Dinah shrugged. 'Sister's got a temper of her own when riled. Told him he could try, but no one would back up his story. Then the other patients got together and said if anyone asked, they'd swear on the Bible the sergeant tripped and bashed his nose on the bedpost. No one said a word about it after that.'

'Did you tell this to Inspector Farrell?'

'I didn't mean to.' Dinah's bottom lip trembled. 'It all came tumbling out. But if he reports it, Corporal Doyle could get into a lot of trouble.' She released a shuddering sob. 'And it's all my fault for not keeping my mouth shut.'

Hannah doubted anyone could be court martialled for assaulting a now-dead man. She wrapped an arm around Dinah's narrow shoulders. 'That's unlikely if the corporal wasn't formally charged.'

'You really think so?' Dinah snatched a handkerchief from her pocket and blew her nose. 'He's such a nice man. I would hate to be the one who sends him to prison.'

Hannah thought so too. Would the cake episode make Aidan look at Corporal Doyle with fresh eyes? Was killing men in battle easier the more you had to do it? Flooring a man in anger was understandable, but was Corporal Doyle capable of cold-blooded murder?

'I'll wager the fact Corporal Doyle is about to go back to the front is a priority.' Unless he killed Sergeant Tillman.

'I wish I hadn't said anything, but that inspector kept asking and asking. In the end, I only said it to make him stop.'

'You told the truth. Were other staff aware of this cake incident? Nurse Dalglish, for instance?'

'Alice?' Dinah blinked away the beginning of tears. 'The inspector asked me the same thing. What's she got to do with it?'

'Maybe nothing.' Hannah shrugged, not sure why she had asked, but despite Alice's ingénue demeanour, she was hiding something.

'I'd forgotten about it until now, but the night Sergeant Tillman died – was killed – some sleeping powders went missing from the kitchen.'

'The patients are given sleeping powders in their cocoa?'

'No, not all of them. Only those who can't settle or are in pain. Alice discovered them gone when she went back to wash up the cups.'

'Were these sleeping powders ever found?'

'Dunno.' Dinah shrugged. 'She didn't say, and later we were too busy searching for the sergeant.' She blew her nose on a handkerchief she dragged from a pocket. 'I'd better get back. Don't want the old dragon of a sister to catch me in here chattering.'

'I wouldn't worry about Corporal Doyle. No one kills someone for the sake of a fruitcake.'

But then, after what these soldiers had lived through, perhaps it took something as small as that to push a man to violence?

6

The library record showed that Sergeant Tillman had borrowed the P. G. Wodehouse novel, but there was no proof that the note belonged to him. It could have been put there by anyone.

Patients and staff came and went steadily throughout the morning, but she received no further word from Inspector Farrell. She wheeled the trolley back to the recreation room after her book round when she saw Dinah approaching, a pile of linens clutched in her skinny arms.

'Has there been any more news about Sergeant Tillman?' Hannah asked, halting the trolley as they drew level.

'Other than he's still dead, not a word. You're as bad as Archie. He questions me like a drill sergeant when I get home. Makes me wish I was back on nights again.'

'He's disappointed I haven't found out who the killer is yet.' Hannah laughed. 'He's cast me as some sort of detective since that affair at the bookshop last year.'

'More excitement than he's ever seen, that were.' Dinah's smile lit her face to almost prettiness, fading when her gaze drifted past

Hannah's shoulder. 'Oh gawd, it's the battleaxe. I'm late making up the beds.'

'Well, it's too late to bolt now. She's seen you.'

'Nurse Root!' The woman waved an imperious hand. 'Have you seen Nurse Dalglish? After all the trouble I had changing your shifts, she hasn't turned up today.'

'No, Sister. I haven't seen her.' Dinah's eyes rounded, and she bounced on her feet as preparing to bolt.

'I don't suppose you've encountered her on your round of the wards?' The woman turned a searching gaze on Hannah. 'Miss, er...'

'It's Merrill,' Hannah replied sharply. 'And no, I haven't.'

'Miss Merrill, of course.' Her eyes flickered in annoyance at being reminded. 'The police are here again this morning, disrupting the entire routine, and now this.' She tsked. 'These pampered gentlemen's daughters think being a nurse is all wiping brows and arranging flowers. It's not. It's hard, dirty work and very demanding.' Her disdainful expression showed the entire matter was, to her, an unpleasant inconvenience.

'There might be a good reason for her absence,' Hannah said, breaking the tense silence. 'Perhaps the murder upset her?' She met the older woman's steady gaze unflinchingly, conscious she had more leeway with her opinions than the VADs, who were little more than skivvies.

'That's a maybe. Most young girls who come to work here do very well, despite the demands made upon them. Others are... disappointments. The failures are allowed to leave quietly and are quickly forgotten.'

'You categorise Nurse Dalglish a failure, then?' Hannah asked. 'For missing one shift.'

'Not necessarily, but she's left her lodgings as well without a word to her benefactor. I think that speaks for itself. Now then.'

She stared along the hallway as if in search of something more interesting. 'I can't stand around here worrying about a chit of a girl too lazy to face her responsibilities. If she's not back tomorrow with an acceptable excuse, I shall have to report her to Dr Murray.' She pointed a finger at Dinah. 'And you, Nurse Root, had better get back to your duties before I put you on report as well.'

'Yes, Sister.' Dinah fled in one direction, the sister in the other, the older woman's brisk but heavy footsteps echoing down the corridor, wimple flying behind her.

Sighing, Hannah braced her arms against the heavy trolley and wheeled it over the library threshold eight feet away. A shadow loomed beside her and a figure stepped out from behind the door. Hannah jumped and brought the trolley to a juddering halt that sent several books tumbling to the floor with successive bangs.

Hannah stood an inch over five and a half feet, but Staff Nurse Bellamy was at least three inches taller. Unusually tall for a woman, but with symmetrical features and wide-set hazel eyes that made her handsome, her crisply ironed uniform and white hat fitted her without a wrinkle and looked professionally laundered.

'Oops, sorry. I didn't mean to scare you.' Nurse Bellamy bent to retrieve a book from the floor and handed it to Hannah. 'Perhaps I shouldn't jump out at people with a killer loose, but other people's conversations are so much more interesting than one's own.' Her musical voice held a mildly bored edge though she seemed in no hurry to leave. 'Though Sister livened things up a bit with her little fit about a VAD not turning up for her shift.'

'Nurse Dalglish?' Hannah's pulse raced as she manoeuvred the book trolley back into its place by the wall. 'She's run off again?'

'I assume so, unless there's been a rash of absences I don' know about.' She tilted her head and smiled. 'You're Viole

Edwards' niece, aren't you? I've seen your aunt with Dr Murray. I recognised her from the newspapers in her women's suffrage days.'

'I doubt those days are completely over.' Hannah laughed. 'She'll no doubt be waving banners outside Downing Street again as soon as peace is declared.' Her last words fell between them, creating a heavy silence neither could fill.

'Miss Edwards helped arrange that wonderful pageant of the ward saints last year, didn't she?' Nurse Bellamy broke the tension after a few awkward seconds. 'I was Joan of Arc, though I've no idea why they chose me for that role. You know, what you said just now, out in the corridor – about Nurse Dalglish being upset by that murder. Thinking about it, you could be right.'

'Why do think so? Did she say anything to you?' Hannah asked, surprised by her abrupt change of subject.

'Not exactly. But I found her in the kitchen in tears after that inspector interviewed her. She claimed the smell of carbolic made her eyes water, but she didn't fool me.'

'Did it have anything to do with her not turning up for her shift?' Hannah asked.

'Who knows.' She shrugged. 'You know she lost her brother in Artois last year?' In response to Hannah's nod, she plucked a book from a pile on the desk and flicked through it.

'You knew Nurse Dalglish before she came here?'

'Our paths crossed occasionally. We moved in the right circles and attended the same parties, Ascot, Henley Regatta and the odd wedding. She's among the many girls from well-to-do families who want to do something noble for the war – and I include myself in that – however the reality comes as a shock. My mother's an earl's daughter, but Papa's a surgeon, so I grew up discussing ailments over the dinner table.'

'Did you always want to be a nurse? Or did the war prompt you to sign up?'

'Not always. Mama wanted me to join the WVR. That's the Women's Volunteer Reserve, in case you're wondering.'

'I believe I've heard of it,' Hannah acknowledged, trying not to appear offended.

'Well, Papa said he wasn't having his wife or daughters wearing khaki and marching on parade grounds like soldiers. More likely, he was too mean to hand over the two pounds each to buy our uniforms. He said if Mama wanted to help the war, she should join the Women's Legion and do cookery and waitressing in the soldiers' canteens. It didn't occur to Papa I would be in more danger there than on a drill ground. Those soldiers can be pretty near the mark, I can tell you.'

'Did your mother join the Women's Legion?'

'She did, though Papa barely tolerates it, only because criticism would make him appear unpatriotic in front of his friends. I've promised not to tell anyone that she drives trucks full of soldiers with a female companion between Aldershot and the coast. Can you believe it? He's bound to find out one day, but for now, he's in blissful ignorance.'

'I rather like the sound of your mother.' Hannah found Nurse Bellamy's garrulous nature unsettling. They had been on little more than nodding terms around the hospital where formality was the norm, and yet she gave no sign of ending their conversation.

'Mama had me when she was seventeen,' the nurse chattered on. 'She's making up for it now, though. When the war started, nursing seemed the most obvious thing for me to do. I'll probably train as a doctor after the war, though I dread what Papa will have to say about it.' She dropped the book she held back onto the trolley and wandered over to the stage and examined the floor. 'Is this where it happened?'

'It's still obvious, isn't it?' Hannah said sadly. Two RAMC men had spent an hour scrubbing the bloodstains with bleach, but a teardrop-shaped stain clung to the varnish. Nurses and patients alike had been wandering in for no other reason than to see the scene of the crime.

'Hmm. Unless they want a constant reminder of a grisly murder, they'll have to replace the boards.' She returned to the desk where Hannah sorted books into piles. 'I saw you talking to that Root girl earlier. Did she have anything to add to your investigation?'

Hannah stiffened. 'Me? I'm not investigating anything.'

'Aren't you?' She raised a perfectly arched brow. 'From what I hear, you've been asking quite a lot of questions recently. Even been spotted listening at doors.'

'Ah, well—' Hannah floundered for a suitable response, but the nurse forestalled her.

'It was in all the newspapers.' In response to Hannah's frown, she added. 'The Soames murder case. It happened in your bookshop, didn't it?'

'Um, yes.' Hannah fidgeted, though it stood to reason everyone must know about Hannah's involvement. Scandal had long fingers, though hopefully short memories.

'Someone mentioned Sister Kerr is Alice's landlady, Nurse Bellamy.' If this girl was willing to eavesdrop, perhaps she wasn't averse to a bit of gossiping either. 'Do you know where she lives?'

'My, you have been industrious.' Her smile held mischief. 'And call me Josie. Everyone does.' She stared off for a moment. 'Now let me see... Sister Kerr lives in Camberwell – or is it Clerkenwell? No, Clerkenwell, that's it. In a circus or something, but I might have got that wrong.'

'It's charitable of Sister Kerr to open her home to other nurses.'

'Marion Kerr pleads poverty as a war widow, so I suspect she charges Alice above market rate for the accommodation.' She caught Hannah's eye and held up both hands in surrender. 'Not that she isn't an excellent nurse. And easier to work with than some.'

'Although not above taking advantage of an unworldly girl?' Hannah aimed for nonchalance, but Josie's wry smile told her she was fooling no one. 'Sergeant Tillman being shot must have been a shock for everyone?'

'It's not as if anyone at Endell Street dies of totally natural causes.' Josie's eyes lit with laughter, then hardened. 'I hope you aren't here to make trouble by being a spy for the police?'

'No, of course not,' Hannah rushed to reassure her, though she was not far off the mark. 'I'm simply curious. Were you on shift that night? Did you see anything unusual?'

'I was on shift that night, which I'm sure you already know. However, I'll oblige and play your game.' Josie smirked. 'It's difficult to say. Several ambulances arrived at once when the shift began, so we were frantically busy. I'm not surprised Alice didn't realise the sergeant had left the ward, as no one was where they were supposed to be.' Josie seemed to grow bored with the conversation, crossed her arms and strolled to the window. Her eyes narrowed at something that caught her attention. 'What's going on over there?'

'What is it?' Hannah asked, joining her.

Inspector Farrell stood by the motor car in the courtyard while Detective Pendleton firmly guided a young man into the back seat.

'Oh no.' She dropped her arms to her sides. 'Looks like they've arrested Corporal Doyle.' Josie's dismay confirmed Hannah's assessment was accurate and the corporal was a popular figure.

Hannah's stomach dropped. 'I so hoped that wouldn't happen.'

'You knew about this?' Josie glared at her over her shoulder. 'Is that what you and that policeman were talking about in Dr Murray's office? You were in there long enough.'

'I answered the inspector's questions, but never mentioned Corporal Doyle. Why would I? I'm as surprised as you are.'

'I didn't mean to accuse you.' Chastened, Josie turned back to the window. 'I suppose even charming men can kill if pushed to it. Is shooting the enemy on a battlefield any different to in a library?' A shadow flickered in her eyes. 'Sorry, forget I said that.' She changed from blithe confidence to flustered in a split second. 'I must go. My break finished five minutes ago, and I didn't even get a book!' She grabbed the nearest one from the top of the trolley without glancing at it. 'This will do.' Turning, she swept the length of the ward, the book tucked beneath one arm.

Alone again, Hannah's thoughts returned to Corporal Doyle. Not that there was much she could do other than marching into Scotland Yard and demanding Aidan release him, which wouldn't be received well.

She collected the returned books from the trolley to put away, and as she slid the last book onto a shelf, a feather fluttered to the floor at her feet.

She picked it up, about to toss it in the waste bin, but paused. She recalled an incident in the bookshop when a woman had presented Archie with a similar one as a mark of his apparent cowardice for not enlisting. The fact her assistant was only fifteen had enraged her, so she sent the woman off with a curt rebuke.

Had Sergeant Tillman given the feather to someone here in the library? Or had it been given it to him?

The question stayed in her mind until the clock struck, reminding her that if she didn't leave now, she would be late for her eagerly awaited luncheon. Shoving the feather into a desk drawer, she grabbed her coat and hurried to the Strand where she hailed a hackney.

7

'Mr Clifford is in his study with a gentleman, Miss Merrill.' Travers, Darius Clifford's butler, stepped aside to allow her into the expansive hallway of the Ilchester Place house. 'Perhaps you'd care to await him in the sitting room?'

'Thank you, Travers.' Hannah suppressed a sigh, disappointed at having to wait, and handed over her coat. Darius' mother had passed away when he was still at school and his father had retired to the country some years previously. Travers had sworn to anyone who would listen he would never leave London, so had remained as Darius' butler. Hannah had known him since childhood, and not once did his stern formality slip and let him call her Miss Hannah like most of the servants.

She crossed the triple-height entrance hall, with its wide black and white tiled floor, the space illuminated by a glass lantern two floors above. Taking a well-worn, familiar path, she entered a sapphire blue and primrose yellow sitting room. She wandered towards a double set of French doors, beyond which a stone terrace overlooked a walled garden that was Darius' pride and joy. He implied ignorance of horticulture and employed gardeners to plant things he could never remember the names of. However, Hannah had caught him on more than one occasion digging holes in flowerbeds, his hands and knees covered with earth.

The click of the door brought a rush of pleasure running through her as Darius strode into the room.

'Sorry to keep you waiting, Hannah. That chap wouldn't stop talking. I thought he would never leave. But I'm here now.'

'No need to apologise. I assume he has something to do with your intelligence work?'

Darius' fluency in German, combined with a mathematical mind that thrived on solving puzzles, made him a perfect candidate for the Secret Service Bureau. He had joined right after the air raid that had destroyed her bookshop and his fiancée had been revealed as a murderess.

'Are we still on for lunch, or are you too busy?' Hannah kept her voice light, but in her head, she prayed for the former.

'Now, would I ever pass up an opportunity to spend time with you?' The smile that accompanied this made her pulse race, hoping it was not a casual comment.

He wore his thick brown hair unfashionably long, causing it to flop over his forehead and spread on his collar. His imposing height and strong symmetrical features could unnerve at first meeting, but his smile brightened the silvery flecks in his midnight blue eyes. His rolling laugh that began deep in his chest gave him the disposition of a friendly bear and inspired trust in even the most hostile stranger.

'Was that chap who just left from Room Forty?' Hannah asked mischievously.

Her father had accidentally let slip the name of the clandestine room where intelligence officers shared their secrets and discussed strategies for foiling the Kaiser. She'd asked him how he knew about it but he became instantly cagey.

'Where did you hear that?' Darius asked, his voice guarded.

'Papa let it slip once, then was immediately mortified.' She left her place at the French doors and approached one of the twin brocade sofas placed on either side of the Adam fireplace. 'I'm sure he expected a soldier to march in and cart him away. Isn't Room Forty where you do all the secret stuff no one must talk about?'

'Please stop saying Room Forty.' Darius slid a pen into an inside pocket of his jacket. 'And you know I'm not at liberty to say anything that goes on there. That is, if it exists.'

'Which is also an answer.' His unease made her smile as she plumped up a cushion and arranged it at her back. 'When did you get back? And no, I won't ask where you've been for the last two weeks.'

'Oh, you wouldn't be interested. It was far too boring to talk about.'

Another question which answered itself. 'Papa seems convinced the Americans will enter the war sooner rather than later.'

'They're already late, but I cannot confirm or deny that conjecture. And I suggest you stop taking your father's opinions as fact. It could be misleading.'

'The newspapers say most Americans agree with President Wilson and are against joining the war?'

'American opinions changed considerably after the sinking of the Lusitania.' He switched into lecture mode when he talked of the war. 'They abhor the Germans' intention to attack any shipping they find, regardless of its country or origin, and whether or not they are military.' Darius tucked a sheaf of papers into a folder on his desk before joining her on the sofa, his arm resting on the back in touching distance of her shoulder.

'If that doesn't bring the Americans into the war, what will?' Hannah mused.

'I agree, and after a certain telegram was intercepted from the German ambassador, I'd say it was becoming more likely.'

'What telegram is this?'

'Never mind.' A telltale red flush crept up his neck, showing he spoke out of turn. 'If they do come in, Germany cannot win. Conscription has bolstered the British Expeditionary Force to a degree, although the War Office intends to expand it to married men soon.'

'Oh, Darius, that's dreadful. The thought of all those children left fatherless. Not only that, the long-term wounded won't be able to provide for their families properly. This war could handicap everyone's lives for years to come.'

'We have to win it first,' Darius muttered, then louder, 'Now, on to happier subjects. Wasn't it your day at the hospital library today?'

'It was, and you were wrong about the happier part. In fact, I have an interesting story to tell you.' His sceptical glance made her smile. 'No, really. There's been a murder at Endell Street.'

'Patient, nurse or a doctor? I imagine some are more valuable than others.'

'Don't be facetious. A patient. Someone shot him.'

'Shot? In a busy hospital? Did no one hear it?'

'Apparently not. Or no one admitted to, which is all part of the mystery. No one could have got in after the main gate was shut. The place is an old workhouse, and secure as a prison. Inspector Farrell is struggling to find a motive, but he seems convinced someone inside the hospital is guilty.'

'Not necessarily. Don't society ladies parade in and out at all hours to give their charitable time to the poor, wretched soldiers?'

'Indeed they do, but hardly any carry guns.' Hannah snorted a laugh. 'The staff don't like it when they come late and talk sanctimonious nonsense to the men who would rather relax or play billiards. Frankly, they are a nuisance. Most are well-meaning, but have an overbearing sense of entitlement as though the entire hospital exists for their convenience.' She shifted to face him. 'Yesterday, one peer's daughter came to see their chauffeur without even knowing the full name or regiment of the man she was visiting. Some poor nursing orderly had to waste time tracking him down.'

'Woah.' He held both hands up in surrender. 'I didn't mean to stir up a tirade. It was only an observation.'

'Don't pretend you aren't interested.' Hannah slapped his arm lightly. 'And you might treat it as light entertainment, but the thought that a man was killed twenty feet away from my desk is worrying.'

'As opposed to in the bookshop where you work? I cannot see the distinction. Finding bodies is not a healthy pastime, but you appear to have a knack for it.'

'Inspector Farrell said something similar, but I paid no attention to him.' She pulled a face. 'Someone with a grudge crept in during the night and shot the victim when the staff were all busy.'

'Is that the inspector's conclusion, or are you working out your next move?'

'Move?' Hannah suspected her anger showed on her face as he laughed aloud. 'It's got nothing to do with me. My brush with murder last year was more than enough, thank you. Scotland Yard can deal with this one.'

He scooted closer, his head bent to hers, enabling her to appreciate the tantalising smell of his citrus cologne. 'You are aware that part of my training is being able to detect when someone is lying?'

'I thought that was pure instinct, not something you can learn.' Hannah swallowed, taking slow, deep breaths as a blush threatened.

'Apparently it isn't. There are certain signs which rarely fail.

For instance, when you said Aidan could handle this murder, you turned away from me.'

'I was simply getting comfortable.' She fidgeted with a brooch on her lapel.

'Now you're biting the corner of your bottom lip. And if you pull that brooch any harder, you'll tear your—'

'Enough! I get the picture. And if you must know, Inspector Farrell told me to keep out of it.' Hannah avoided his gaze. 'Although he's so overworked, he agreed I could keep an ear to the ground for anything that might help the investigation.'

'I'm surprised he would involve you in police business, what with him being a consummate professional?' he said, with a certain amount of irony.

'I'm not involved exactly, only—'

'Only what?' His voice held a warning.

'The day I found the body, a VAD nurse arrived while all the fuss was going on. All the other staff were sanguine about it, apart from the fact he had a bullet in his chest, but I noticed this girl seemed anxious, almost scared. Well, today she went missing.'

'What do you mean by "missing"?'

'She didn't turn up for work, and no one has heard from her.'

'Perhaps she needed a day off if the work is as arduous as one imagines. One missed shift doesn't make her a missing person.'

'I know, and that's exactly what people are saying. But Nurse Dalglish came into the bookshop the day after the murder and she seemed... jumpy. She said she thought she was being followed.'

'What does Detective Inspector Farrell make of it?'

'I'm not sure he knows. I was going to mention it to him, but he arrested a young corporal for the flimsiest of reasons.'

'You're qualified to decide what's considered grounds for arrest now, are you?' Darius said, laughing.

'No, but if you'll stop teasing me, I'll tell you the story and you can decide for yourself.' Hannah recounted the story Dinah had told her about the fruitcake. 'Ridiculous, isn't it?' she said when she had finished.

Much to her relief Darius reacted in the way she had hoped, with a low, delightful chuckle that grew into a growling laugh. 'Farrell's superiors are on his back about this one, so he's jumping at shadows. Either that, or he's discovered something in this soldier's past convincing him the corporal was involved. That aside, is there a connection between this sergeant's murder and this nurse's absence?'

'Yes. I mean no. Let's say it's a coincidence I'm not happy with. She was working on the night the sergeant was killed, and claimed not to have seen anything.'

'Claimed? She wasn't being truthful?'

'I don't know her well enough to judge. She came into the bookshop and seemed nervous. She thought someone was following her, but Archie checked and didn't see anything.'

'I doubt Archie has much knowledge of shadowing people,' he laughed.

'Maybe not, but something doesn't sit right about the whole thing. Why would she take off like that, telling no one? What if she *was* being followed and didn't leave of her own accord? She might be in trouble.'

'You're concerned. That's understandable, but tread carefully. Hannah.' He shifted in his seat, showing he was growing uncomfortable with the conversation. 'By making a drama out of it, you could cause her and her family all kinds of anguish.'

Hannah fell silent, aware he was politely telling her to mind her own business. She couldn't shake the feeling that there was more to Alice's disappearance than mere boredom but did not know how to get her point across. The last thing she wanted was to fall out with him. But her anxiety over Alice would not go away.

'Hannah!' Darius' sharp tone snapped her thoughts back to the present. 'I said, I'm off to Folkestone tomorrow, so I won't see you for about a week.'

'Sorry, I was miles away. You're going to France?' At his surprised start, she shrugged. 'The cross-Channel ferry doesn't go from Dover any more. It's been transferred to Folkestone.'

'Er, yes, you're quite right. And that was indiscreet of me.' Darius flushed again. 'I'm going to have to watch myself closer, especially around you, or I'll be no good at this job.' He slapped his thighs with both hands and pushed himself onto his feet. 'Now, I don't know about you, but I'm hungry. Will Elena's suit, or would you prefer Simpsons?'

'Elena's is perfect. Simpsons is too stuffy, what with the guards ensuring no woman dares to venture within ten yards of the main dining room. I always feel they begrudge females even daring to enter the building.'

'It's not as bad as that. And they are waiters, not guards.' He led her down the front steps and handed her into the rear seat of the motor car parked at the kerb. 'Elena's, if you please, Harris.'

Darius settled into the leather upholstery beside her. 'Incidentally, Hannah, would you like the use of my motor car while I'm away?'

'Ooh, yes, please.' She hunched her shoulders in delight. 'Mother regards driving motor cars as unfeminine. I haven't even told her I can drive.'

'Then I shan't be the one to tell her.' Darius snorted. 'I'm more scared of Madeleine Merrill than I am the Kaiser.'

It was not until the motor car pulled up in Beauchamp Place did Hannah realise Darius had not once mentioned Cecily. She hoped now the trial was finally over it was a sign he was putting the events of the previous months behind him.

Whatever Aunt Violet said, if Darius didn't come to the point soon, she feared she might give up hope he ever would.

* * *

Hannah parked Darius' car on the Embankment outside Cannon Street Police Station next door to the New Scotland Yard Head-quarters. After a short, but slightly nerve-wracking wait in a long room lined with wooden benches filled with a variety of people, she showed Inspector Farrell's card to a desk sergeant.

'Is he expecting you?' He fingered the card with a mildly suspicious look that he then transferred to her.

'No, but—' She leaned closer, her voice lowered. 'It's concerning a murder investigation.'

'I see.' He handed the card back to her. 'Then you'd better come this way.'

Feeling mildly relieved he had not questioned her further, she returned the card to her bag before following him along a corridor that smelled of carbolic and cabbage, then up several flights of concrete stairs into a long corridor, its lower walls tiled like a butcher's shop below shiny green paint.

Finally, the policeman halted outside a door, and with a curt nod, left her there without a word.

Slightly breathless from the climb, Hannah knocked tenta-tively, expecting a curt command from the other side, only for the door to be flung open almost instantly to reveal Inspector Farrell.

'Hannah! This is a surprise.' He waved her inside a compact, featureless office that held a scarred oak desk and three chairs. 'I assume you have something important to discuss if you go to the trouble of coming here. Cannon Street Police Station isn't a place the public usually visits by choice.'

The room was small, with a shoulder-height window but held

no personal items she could see, and no pictures adorned the walls apart from a formal portrait of King George in a gilt frame which hung at shoulder height.

'They tell me you've brought Corporal Doyle in for questioning.' Hannah took the chair he offered and nervously perched on the edge. 'Have you arrested him?'

'I thought we had established the boundaries of my work and yours.' He skirted the desk and took his chair, gathered several brown files together, and shoved them into a leather satchel. 'Once inside this building, you cannot question me about my actions.'

'I know, and I apologise if I am being – inappropriate. But you can't seriously believe Corporal Doyle murdered Sergeant Tillman based on an argument over a fruitcake?'

'I assure you that cake has no bearing on this case.' He set the satchel aside, shuffled another pile of mis-matched sheets of paper and stowed them in a drawer. 'Sergeant Tillman died from a single shot to the heart, not a simple thing to accomplish, strangely. The bullet did, in fact, come from a Webley, possibly a Mark five or six, but I cannot be sure until I have the actual weapon. They are only efficient at close range; if aimed from a distance, not so much. Were you aware our Corporal Doyle is a sniper with an impressive body count in the trenches and experienced with all kinds of firearms?'

'I'm hardly in a position to know that,' Hannah replied. Not that this made her feel less for the shy Irishman. 'There are five hundred soldiers in the hospital, many with similar skills. Why pick on him?'

'His bed is situated opposite the sergeant's and there had already been a confrontation between the two. But to be honest, I did it to make the others take notice. No one was willing to discuss Sergeant Tillman, so we know almost nothing about the man. Tillman and Corporal Doyle served in different regiments.

Sergeant Tillman was wounded in Belgium at the same time Doyle was fighting in Gallipoli. Their only contact was at the hospital. It doesn't make sense.'

'No. It doesn't,' Hannah agreed, but he had apparently not finished.

'I'll admit my chief is pressuring me to solve this one, so I'm bringing in anyone remotely dubious. If it makes you feel any better, I doubt Doyle is guilty.'

'Then let him go back to the hospital.' Hannah lifted her arms in a gesture of frustration. 'He's not completely healed from his shoulder injury.'

'I might need to talk to him again. Can't risk him disappearing off to Ireland never to be seen again. Another night in the cells won't hurt him.'

'As long as it is only one night.' Disappointed but resigned to the corporal having to spend more time in custody than necessary, she decided it wasn't worth arguing about. 'Have you discovered who Sergeant Tillman went to the library to meet that night?'

'Not yet, but it was carefully planned. The oil lamp that was knocked over came from the storeroom, though why would Tillman know where that was? He also closed the curtains, which suggests he wanted no one to know he was there. He couldn't risk putting on the light, as it would have been seen from the court-yard. The stage curtains are heavy, but wouldn't have silenced a gunshot, and no one heard one.'

'Or admitted to,' Hannah muttered. 'What about the sergeant's family? Did they know anyone who might have a reason to want him dead?'

'His parents are deceased and his only sibling, an older brother, is in a nursing home in Finchley with tuberculosis. He didn't seem too concerned with his brother's death, either. Seems they didn't get on, but he was clearly in no state to plan or execute a murder. The poor chap probably won't last much longer.'

'Changing the subject, do you recall a young nurse named Dalglish from the hospital?'

'The pretty blonde VAD who arrived minutes after you found the body? I do, yes. Difficult to forget a young lady with her beauty.'

'The same. She told me you were somewhat – fierce, when you questioned her.'

'Did she indeed?' He looked up briefly from the papers on his desk. 'My questions were both thorough and appropriate for a murder enquiry. And if she had not run off the way she did, I might have been more lenient.'

'Did she explain her absence on the morning of the murder?'

'She seemed to think I had approved her leaving. She's a difficult girl to read, that one. She expressed no emotion all, even when I asked her if she knew anything about sleeping powders. Then she shut up completely and asked to be excused.'

'She's probably never been interviewed by a policeman before.'

'That's no excuse!' He slapped a pencil onto his desk with a click. 'I intend to approach that subject again to see if she changes her story.'

'What's this about powders?'

'Sleeping powders. Dr Murray said some went missing that night.'

'Do you think they are connected with Sergeant Tillman's death?'

'No, idea, but it's a line of enquiry.'

'Actually, I might be able to help with that. The nurses don't like having to go to the pharmacy during the night, so keep a few in the kitchen.'

'Ah, well thank you for that.' He underlined something on the page in front of him. 'Maybe your inside knowledge is more valuable than I thought.'

'I'll accept that as a compliment. You were equally as intimidating towards me at our first meeting, which is why I sympathise with Alice Dalglish.'

'Then I apologise to you. In my defence, most people lie to me on first meeting. It takes a few tries to get the truth out of them.'

'Accepted. But the reason I mentioned Nurse Alice Dalglish, is because she's missing.'

'Oh?' He glanced up sharply, grabbed a pad of paper on his desk and pulled it towards him, his pencil poised. 'When did this happen?'

'I don't know exactly, but she didn't turn up for her shift this morning.'

'That young lady has a penchant for not being where she's expected to be, it seems.' He sighed and placed the pencil gently on top of the paper. 'It's rather soon to assume she's actually missing.'

'True, and there could be a simple explanation, but when I spoke to her the other day, she was convinced someone was following her.'

'And you believed her?'

'I had no reason not to. She was clearly frightened.'

'Was this before or after the murder?' He picked up the pencil again, his sceptical smile fading.

'Before. After. I mean she was being followed before the murder, but she came into the bookshop after.'

'Has anyone else seen this so-called follower?'

'I did. Well, I assume it was him. A scruffily dressed youth was hanging around outside the hospital yesterday. I tried to speak to him, but he ran off.'

'He was young, you say?' The inspector's looped scrawl covered the page as she recited the physical details she could remember. 'Perhaps he was a shy admirer?'

'Which doesn't mean he isn't the reason she's gone missing.'

'Fair point. What do her superiors at the hospital say?'

'That she probably found the work too demanding and left. She's apparently from a good background but none of the hospital staff know much about her. She told no one she planned to leave, and no one has heard from her.'

'I interviewed her, so must have her details somewhere.' He shuffled through the papers on his desk. 'Ah, here it is. Number 12, Percy Circus, Clerkenwell.'

'Are you going to look into it?'

'Not yet,' he forestalled her protest. 'And I'll tell you why. You aren't a relative, or an employer, therefore I cannot base an official missing person's report on your instinct for a mystery.'

'Does it have to be official? Can't you ask around the hospital?'

'In a word, no. I cannot assign resources to locating someone, who, for all we know has merely taken a few days' holiday.'

'Have I told you recently how pompous you can be?'

'More than once, if my memory serves.' His smug smile showed he was not offended. 'And much as I hope this girl is safe and sound, I cannot do anything.'

'Darius warned me you would say that.'

'Then perhaps you should have listened to him.' He replaced the pencil at the end of the row and leaned back in his chair. 'I'll also get Pendleton to ask if anyone has reported seeing a chap fitting your description around the hospital.'

Hannah glanced up at the railway clock on the wall above his head and rose. 'I'm sorry to have bothered you about Corporal Doyle, but he's a popular character on the ward. I'm not the only one who was upset to see him carted off in a police car.'

'Don't worry about the corporal. Between you and me, he doesn't strike me as a cold-blooded killer.'

'That makes me feel better. Sort of.'

Out on the street again, she left the Swift's engine idling as she considered what to do next, though it was obvious. Despite opinion to the contrary, Hannah was convinced Alice was not the type to take off telling no one. Suppose she had not left of her own accord? Time mattered in missing person cases, and if Inspector Farrell wasn't going to act, then she would have to do it herself. Starting with a visit to Sister Kerr.

8

After two wrong turns that took her into the back streets of Farringdon, Hannah brought Darius' motor car to a halt at one of the five openings to Percy Circus. The five-storey town houses hunched together in a wide circle around a railed garden that contained several magnificent trees.

The houses were of uniform red brick from the upper floors to the roof and faced with a white stone at ground level. Although beautifully designed, many were down at heel, with scarred front doors and paintwork that was faded, peeling and in need of repair. Weeds poked through the flagstones in pathways. Rubbish receptacles indicative of multiple family occupancy were ranged along the garden walls. A home-made go-cart lay abandoned beside a lop-sided gate, while a barefoot female child bounced a rubber ball in the road.

'Excuse me.' Hannah beckoned the child closer, a threepenny piece extended as an incentive. 'Which house is number twelve?'

'Black front door, over there.' The child snatched the coin from her hand as if fearful Hannah might change her mind. She dropped it into a pocket of her grubby apron and ran off with the ball under her arm.

The houses all had railings and open wells, with steps leading to the basement area. Sister Kerr's front door was recently painted and sported a polished brass door knocker in the shape of a lion. In response to her knock, the door opened a crack, then was instantly flung wider.

'Miss Merrill!' Marion Kerr's initial scowl faded when she recognised her visitor. She looked different out of her uniform, and younger. Hannah judged her to be in her early thirties, but life had carved deep lines around her mouth and eyes, making her look older than her Aunt Violet. But then, her aunt had been cushioned through life, as a much-loved younger daughter with no hardships to worry her – financial or otherwise. Josie Bellamy had said Sister Kerr was a war widow, which explained her plain black gown and lack of jewellery, except for a thin wedding ring. Her complexion was dry and dull, with the greyish pallor of someone who spent little time outdoors.

'What brings the hospital librarian to my door?' Sister Kerr stood square in the frame, blocking the view to the inside as if protecting her domain.

'I hope you don't mind my calling on you at home, Mrs Kerr.' Hannah levelled her voice to an apology. 'I would have approached you at the hospital, but I was told you aren't on duty again until next week. Only, I've been worried about Nurse Alice Dalglish and wondered if you had heard from her?'

Sister Kerr's gaze slid past Hannah's shoulder to the motor car parked beyond her gate, giving Hannah an up and down stare of reassessment. 'Don't see many of them around here. Or lady drivers, either. Is it yours?'

'Umm, not exactly. It belongs to a friend.'

'Hmm, hope it doesn't get damaged, then.' She seemed to

consider a moment, then stepped back, the fingers of one hand hooked to beckon her inside.

'Most people I've talked to scoff and ask why I'm bothering about Alice. They assume she's a rich girl who got bored and took herself off. But I'm quite worried.' Hannah followed her into a hall that smelled faintly of lavender polish and baking, the walls decorated with olive wallpaper with tiny daisies over chocolate paintwork. 'I ought to mention I have no authority to question you.'

'Better than having to face that police inspector. Nice chap and all that, but all those questions about who was where, and doing what the night Sergeant Tillman got killed gave me a headache. But to answer your question, I've not heard from Alice Dalglish since she left.'

Sister Kerr led the way down a narrow corridor into a spacious, neatly kept rear room that doubled as a parlour and kitchen. A black leaded range took up the entire wall on one side, a scrubbed pine table on the other, beneath a window with a view of a rear yard. 'Would you care for some tea, Miss Merrill?' She gestured towards one of four chairs arranged around the table. 'I could have the kettle on in a jiffy.'

'That would be nice, thank you.' Hannah bit down a refusal; Sister Kerr might be more than willing to talk over tea. 'I was told Alice lodged with you here?'

'Who told you that?' Sister Kerr banged a kettle down onto the range with a scrape of metal.

'I can't recall.' Hannah shrugged vaguely. 'I'm sorry if I'm mistaken.'

'You aren't. Only I don't like people at the hospital gossiping bout me. I assume that's where you heard it?'

When Hannah did not answer, she nodded silently and took own cups and saucers from a wooden plate rack above her head. invited Alice to tea when she first started working at Endell

Street. A nervous little thing, she was, so I thought living here rather than that soulless dormitory at the hospital might help her settle. You know the girls all call it the barracks?'

'I do, yes.'

Marion turned from where she stood at the pantry. 'I only have sterilised milk, I'm afraid. It keeps longer, and what with my shifts, the pasteurised kind goes off before I can use it. Or I have lemon, if you prefer?'

'Was Alice settled here? And lemon would be perfect, Mrs Kerr. No sugar, thank you,' Hannah said, as a sugar bowl was placed on the table in front of her. With a curt nod, Sister Kerr removed it again.

'I always thought so. Not that she talked talk much about herself, really. And my name's Marion. No need to be so formal, is there? We aren't at the hospital now.'

Hannah smiled but decided not to reciprocate in kind. Inspector Farrell had warned her about being too friendly with witnesses.

'Alice had no real friends.' Marion leaned a hip against the range while the kettle heated, her arms folded. 'None at the hospital, that is, apart from that Dinah lass. She has some family, or what's left of them.'

'Left of them?' Hannah raised an eyebrow in enquiry, relieved she seemed more than happy to chat about her lodger with no encouragement. 'Has anyone at the hospital contacted her? Maybe she went home?'

'I don't know about that. Besides, I sensed they don't get on.' Marion's voice dropped to a whisper, despite their being alone. 'She didn't say in so many words, but I sensed there was bad blood between them. You know her brother was killed last year in France?'

The high-pitched whistle from the kettle sent her back to the range. She swilled water around in an earthenware teapot, emptying it into a square porcelain sink before spooning in tea leaves from a dented tin caddy. 'When she was out of uniform, her clothes were beautifully made. None of it looks shop-bought, that's for sure.' She grabbed the kettle from the stove, mercifully cutting off its high-pitched whistle and poured boiling water on the leaves.

'And she didn't tell you or anyone where she was going when she left?' Hannah did not expect an answer, but she might as well ask.

'If she had, her going off like she did wouldn't be much of a mystery, now, would it?' She chuckled to herself as she swirled the pot and placed it on the table. Two delicate china cups joined it, along with a matching jug.

'Do you know why Alice left the hospital that day without waiting for the police?'

Marion's chin jerked up and their eyes met.

'You hurried her away because you thought she looked faint.'

'Oh, yes. That was it.' She recovered quickly. 'What with Sergeant Tillman bleeding all over the floor, Alice turned so pale I took her outside. To have a nurse pass out is considered bad form for the other nurses. It sets a bad example. Anyway, I had no idea why she left. These pampered gentlemen's daughters are well-meaning but not equipped for hospital work. Alice got confused easily and made mistakes. Like putting saucepans on the stove then forgetting them. I put it down to being so used to having other people do things for them.'

'You seem critical of her. Perhaps it's for the best she has left?'

'It's not as if I disliked her.' She looked stricken. 'Alice is a nice, gentle girl. I'm worried about her, as it happens, and hope nothing untoward has happened to her.'

'Most people I've spoken to feel she became bored and went home to an easier life.'

'And who could blame her?' She handed Hannah a porcelain cup decorated with red rosebuds, a slice of lemon floating on the surface. 'I hate those tin mugs they give us at the hospital. Tea tastes so much better from real china.'

Hannah nodded in agreement and tasted the tea, surprised to find it was Earl Grey with a strong hint of bergamot.

'No, as I always say,' Sister Kerr balanced a cup and saucer on one palm of one hand and stirred it with the other. 'Nursing's not for everyone, is it? Nicely brought up girls don't expect to see those poor souls brought in with smashed up bones and bits of metal sticking out of them. Fair upsets us sometimes, though we mustn't show it. And the smell?' She gave an exaggerated shudder. 'Clings to the insides of your nose, it does. It's one you can never forget.'

'I cannot imagine,' Hannah said truthfully. 'Did Alice talk to the sergeant the night he died?'

Marion's eyes widened. 'You don't imagine that lovely girl had something to do with the sergeant's death?'

'No, not at all. Only, she might have seen something and become frightened.'

'Nay, I doubt that. What was there to see? And as for that Sergeant Tillman,' her upper lip curled, a common reaction when his name was mentioned, 'Alice had little to do with him, or any of the soldiers, which is as it should be.' She set her cup down firmly on the table. 'No, if you ask me, she'll come back when she's good and ready.'

Hannah sighed, aware she was getting nowhere since Marion simply repeated everything Dinah and Josie had already told her. 'When did you last see her?'

'The day Sergeant Tillman was found. But we work different

shifts so rarely see one another, even here we're like ships in the night.'

'Was Alice worried about anything?' Hannah had hoped Sister Kerr might have grown close to Alice but it certainly didn't sound like it.

'She's a private person. Contained, like; a proper lady, if you know what I mean.' She caught herself, flushing. 'What am I saying? You're a lady yourself, aren't you?'

A loud creak came from above, bringing Hannah's gaze to the ceiling.

'Don't worry about that.' Marion smiled. 'This is an old house, and when the wind is up, it rattles through the rafters. The floorboards are loose in places and creak when walked on. Noise carries.'

Hannah nodded. 'I was told you take in lodgers.'

'I do, but there's no one here at the moment. Apart from Alice. One of them billeting officers from the government came round a while ago.' She sniffed at the memory. 'He wanted me to accommodate four Canadian officers. I don't want foreigners in my house eating my food and using my bathrooms. Not when I'm at work and can't keep an eye on them.'

Hannah thought this was a lack of sympathy for a woman who cared for injured men, but chose not to comment.

Sister Kerr rose, and gathered up the tray just as a sudden, loud crash came from the rear yard, followed by a shout.

Hannah's arm jerked, spilling a few drops of her remaining tea on the table.

'The neighbours aren't exactly quiet either.' Marion shook her head as she wiped the spill away with a cloth. 'They're rowdy enough when I'm trying to sleep in the day. Goodness knows what mess and noise Canadians would create. Young trainee VADs I can cope with, but not grown men. Can't be doin' with it. Alice sometimes complained of the noise at night, but she seemed settled here.'

'Apart from the noises?' Hannah smiled.

'She must be a very light sleeper, is all I can say.'

Marion's explanation seemed plausible, but the house, if old and plainly furnished, had a homely feel – not somewhere one might feel the need to escape from.

'Would it be an imposition for me to see Alice's rooms?' Hannah asked, hardly expecting assent but if the woman refused, it might mean something. However, Sister Kerr seemed unfazed by this request other than a tiny crease appearing between her brows.

'I suppose it can't do any harm.' She placed her cup on the table in front of her and rose. 'Come on up, and I'll show you.'

* * *

Hannah followed Marion up the narrow stairs past the first floor where the chocolate-coloured doors were closed tight. The second landing was smaller, the doors closer together. Marion opened one to the right into a room that looked over the rear of the house onto a patch of garden, though the dominant view was the back of houses in the next street.

The room was filled with colourful dresses, blouses and skirts in bright colours, except for the double brass bed and a yellow slipper chair in the corner.

The surface of the plain mahogany dressing table was littered with pots of varied cosmetics, hair clips, brushes, and mirrors; a cream silk scarf was thrown carelessly over a bedpost, and a pair of patent leather shoes peeked out from under the high bed.

'Can you tell if she took much with her?' Hannah asked.

'Well, she had a soft leather bag that isn't here now.' She drifted from the open wardrobe that was over half full to the dressing table, assessing as she went. 'I can't tell what might be missing from here, but she had a silver-backed hand mirror and hairbrush she showed me once. I can't see them here.'

Things a young woman would take on a brief trip somewhere. Maybe Alice really had left of her own volition?

'There are still clothes in the wardrobe, so I can't say if she took any with her.' Marion shut the doors with a click. 'If she doesn't come back soon, or send word, I'll have to pack up her things so I can re-let the rooms. I need to—' She broke off at an insistent rap on the front door. 'Excuse me a moment while I answer that, Miss Merrill. I'll be back in a moment.' She hurried along the landing and down the stairs.

Appreciative of the timing giving her a chance to snoop, Hannah ignored the wardrobe and homed in on the bedside table. She slid open the narrow drawer and beneath a pile of embroidered handkerchiefs lay a red leather-bound volume. The title *Pride and Prejudice* was picked out in gold along the spine. Hannah tested the weight of the volume, her expert eye assessing it as an expensive, even bespoke, edition. The pages were edged with actual gold, which also featured on the embossed front cover.

She flicked open the thick binding to the flyleaf, where the name Alice Worsley-Brooke was written in copperplate handwriting. Beneath it was written *To Alice, with love from Gabriel. Christmas 1912.*

Was Worsley-Brooke Alice's real surname? And who was Gabriel?

The front door banged shut two storeys below. Marion's footsteps grew closer. Panicked, Hannah slid the book into her handbag, stepped onto the landing and pulled the door shut behind her.

'If you have a caller, I'll leave you in peace, Mrs Kerr.' She addressed the top of the woman's head as she descended the stairs.

'Ah no, dear. It was only the boy with my laundry.' Marion halted a few steps below, her face suffused with red as if she had run up the three flights. 'No luck, then?'

'Alice appears to have left in a hurry, but if she packed first, I'm probably worrying about nothing.' She glanced past Marion, but saw no one as she followed her back into the entrance hall. 'Maybe Alice just went home to her family?'

'I don't know where they hail from, but—' Her voice dropped to a whisper despite there being only the two of them in the room. 'Alice didn't say in so many words, but I sensed there was bad blood between them.'

'Did she have any callers? Or go out in the evenings?'

'Not that I know of. She sometimes went to Regent's Park of a Sunday when the weather was fine.'

Among the drab mackintoshes and Marion's uniform cape, was a kepi-style pillbox hat with a peak, and a coronet badge. Below it hung a dark blue serge tunic jacket sporting a circular badge fixed to the armband. The letters GPO in brass and some numbers were visible.

'It's my husband's,' Marion said, when she saw caught Hannah's interest. 'He was killed at Loos last year. I like to keep it there. It comforts me.'

'I understand. Well, thank you for talking to me, Mrs Kerr, er... Marion. And I'm very sorry about your husband.' She turned on the step to wave, but the door closed behind her and there came the sound of a bolt being pushed home.

She was starting the Swift's engine with the hand crank, relived to get it purring nicely when a lady strode down the path of a neighbouring house and paused beside her.

'Did you go anywhere nice?'

'I'm sorry?' Hannah unbent from her task and turned to star

at her. She wore a black coat despite the warmth of the day, and a soft cap perched on a mass of messy brown curls.

'Ah, excuse me, dear, my eyesight ain't what it was. I thought you was the friend of that young nurse who lodges with Mrs Kerr. I can see now you're quite a bit younger.'

'You saw Mrs Kerr's lodger with an older lady?' Hannah's pulse ranked up a notch.

'That's right, dear. They got into a motor car too.' She eyed the idling Swift admiringly. 'A black one with a chauffeur. Nice smart uniform he had.'

'When was this, exactly?' At the woman's start she added, 'I arranged to meet Nurse Dalglish today, but I appear to have got my days muddled.'

'Oh, I see. Well now, let me think. It was four days ago. Or was it three? No, it was four. Anyway, she had a bag with her, the nurse did. A nice leather one, which is why I asked if she was going somewhere nice.'

'Thank you so much.' Hannah slid into the driver's seat.

'You're welcome, dear.' The woman took a nervous step back as Hannah revved the engine and pulled away. Four days ago was the same day Alice came into the bookshop.

9

Hannah parked the Swift in a narrow street behind Piccadilly Circus and tipped a road sweeper two shillings to watch the motor car. The doorman bowed her through the doors of the Criterion where a waitress in a monochrome uniform showed her to a table in a quiet corner of the vast restaurant.

'Sorry I'm late, Aunt Violet, I lost track of time. I hope I didn't create more work for you and Archie?' She eased around a potted palm and greeted her with an air kiss.

'You know me. I much prefer to greet the customers and share gossip, happy to leave the machinations of bookselling to Archie. He's grown in confidence lately, but he needs more experience in how to deal with salesmen. One was trying to convince him to order two dozen bibles until I stepped in and threw him out.'

'Oh dear,' Hannah sighed. 'Who would have thought people would stop buying bibles?' Since the war began, people have lost faith in the Church. An ecclesiastical bookbinder goes bankrupt every week.

'This was a lovely idea of yours, Hannah. I haven't been out for afternoon tea for ages. I forgot how civilised it was, and a welcome change with all this sadness and gloom. How was your day at the hospital?'

'I was there earlier, but then I went to talk to a member of staff. It was all rather confusing, actually—'

'Let me order our tea first.' Aunt Violet pressed Hannah's hand on the table, halting her. 'Then you can tell me all about it.' She waved over a waitress in a black skirt and white apron and requested the Royal Blend tea, along with various sandwiches, cakes and eclairs.

'I'm surprised they still serve eclairs,' Hannah said when they were alone again, or as much as they could be in the vast and crowded dining room. 'I thought all the cream in England was being sent to the front.'

'This is the Criterion, darling, not Lyons Corner House.' Aunt Violet slowly removed her gloves with the aplomb of a vaudeville act. 'Now, what have you been up to?'

'Do you remember Nurse Dalglish?'

'That nurse who came into the bookshop the other day? What about her?'

'She's disappeared.'

'Disappeared? She's not a genie, Hannah. I assume she didn't vanish and leave a trail of bandages behind? Perhaps she took a few days off.'

'You don't have to be flippant. I'm genuinely worried about her. She failed to arrive for her shift and hasn't been seen since. Most people assume she decided nursing didn't suit her and simply left. She was probably one of the last people to see Sergeant Tillman alive. In fact, maybe *the* last person.'

'She seemed very nervous at the bookshop. I hope you noticed I didn't insinuate myself into your conversation. I thought she would reveal more to you.'

'I did, and I appreciate it, Aunt Violet.'

'Have you mentioned her disappearance to Aidan?'

'Ye-es, but he cannot do anything until she is officially reported missing. By the way, when did you start calling the inspector "Aidan"?'

'From the moment he asked me to.' Her aunt's dismissive shrug put an end to further questions. 'If he could do something, I'm sure he would.'

'He was quite pompous about it, actually. He said where she goes and with whom is entirely her own business. I cannot prove it – yet – but I'm convinced there's a connection to Sergeant Tillman's murder.'

'He appears to have ruffled your feathers. But don't underestimate him. I'm sure he'll investigate all lines of enquiry before discarding them.' Aunt Violet's last words were smothered by a loud, 'Yoo-Hoo' from a well-endowed matron in an enormous hat on which a colourful bird appeared to have expired.

'Who is that lady trying to get your attention?' Hannah nodded in the woman's direction.

'Probably someone well-connected, but her name escapes me for the moment.' She returned the wave without enthusiasm. 'Never mind her. You were saying?'

'I spoke to the nursing sister who was the first to arrive after Dinah and I found the sergeant's body.'

'Sister Kerr?' Aunt Violet smirked. 'You see, I do listen.'

'That's her. Alice lodged in Sister Kerr's house, who mentored her when she first arrived at the hospital.'

'You interrogated a witness?' Her aunt raised a sardonic eyebrow.

'No, I—' She huffed a frustrated breath. 'I suppose I did. She was happy to talk to me, but to be honest, she didn't help much. She knows very little about Alice.'

Hannah broke off, straightening, as two waitresses with wide, loaded trays set their burdens on the table and spent several minutes unloading and arranging the plates and cake stands on their table.

'Goodness, Aunt Violet – is there anything on the menu you didn't order?' Hannah smiled her thanks at the two serving girls, both of whom dropped curtsies before leaving.

'I had no time for lunch and I'm starving.' Her aunt reached for a millefeuille nestling in a delicate paper wrapper.

'Nanny always said sandwiches first.' Hannah reached across and removed the plate of cakes from beneath her hand.

'Which is exactly why I eat whatever I want, when I want.' Her aunt winked at her before she grappled the plate back and applied her fork to the layer of pink and white icing. 'Now. What do you intend to do about this missing girl?'

'Does the name Worsley-Brooke mean anything to you?'

'It's sort of familiar, but I'm not sure.' Aunt Violet lifted the lid of the teapot and peered inside, then stirred the leaves with a silver spoon before replacing it. She poured tea into two cups and handed one to Hannah.

Hannah withdrew the copy of *Pride and Prejudice* from her bag and slid it across the table towards her aunt. 'I saw this in Alice's room at Mrs Kerr's.'

'And you *stole* it?' Her aunt snatched up the book, giving the crowded dining room a surreptitious glance before examining it.

'Not stole. Borrowed. And you didn't make this fuss when I found that postcard in Lily-Anne's room. Without my snooping where I shouldn't have, we might never have discovered Cavan's estranged sister.'

'Well, she has good taste, I'll say that. And deep pockets. This is a special edition, produced to order.'

'Look at the flyleaf,' Hannah said.

Aunt Violet did so, her eyebrows lifting in surprise. 'She was using a false name?' She flicked through the pages, but finding nothing of interest handed it back.

'You're sure that it belongs to the same Alice?'

'It would be too much of a coincidence otherwise. I also ran into a neighbour outside her lodgings who said Alice and an older lady left in a chauffeured motor car a few days ago.'

'Really? Now things are getting more interesting – ah, here we are.' She smiled at the waitress who returned with a pot of hot water.

'Of course!' Hannah's teacup hit the saucer with a loud click that made the waitress jump. 'Sorry. I didn't mean you.' She waved the girl away. 'Why didn't I see that before?'

'See what before?' Her aunt frowned.

'Josie Bellamy,' she said, loud enough to draw eyes from nearby tables. 'One of the nurses at the hospital told me she knew Alice when she was younger. "Moved in the right circles" was how she described it.'

'You've lost me.' Aunt Violet topped up the teapot. 'What has that got to do with anything?'

'Don't you see? Josie must know her name isn't Dalglish, but she didn't say a thing. If she lied about that, what else is she keeping to herself?'

'There is another explanation.' Aunt Violet helped herself to a salmon sandwich, despite her cake being only half-eaten. 'Perhaps Alice has secrets she would rather not reveal, and as a friend, this Josie person was being discreet. Which suggests you ought to mind your own business.'

'Whatever's happened to you?' Hannah was mildly offended. 'You were keen to help find out who killed Lily-Anne.'

'That was different. Lily-Anne was a friend and was murdered on my property. Besides, I've learned rather a lot about police procedure since then. It's not an area in which untrained civilians should dabble.'

'Now you sound just like Inspector Farrell.' Hannah straightened, disappointed. This was not the reaction she expected from her adventurous relative.

'I do not!' Her aunt's slow smile transformed her expression but as Hannah expected, she did not elaborate. 'This Nurse Dalglish might have a perfectly good reason for not using her real name.'

'Only someone who has considered it would say that,' Hannah replied, smiling. 'Not that Inspector Farrell seems interested. In his words, "the war hasn't stopped criminals from operating, and they cannot be allowed to continue unabated."'

'He used that word? Unabated?' Her aunt slanted her a sideways look.

'No, but it's what he meant. Anyway, finding Alice is my contribution to the war effort. All I do with my free time is shuffle books around for injured soldiers. I feel I ought to be doing more.'

'You sacrificed a fiancé. I'd say that was more than sufficient.'

'He sacrificed himself. I stayed home and wrote letters. If Mother had her way, I'd be sitting in Farnham darning socks and putting care packages together.'

'Queen Mary's Needlework Guild always needs competent knitters.' Her aunt's wry smile mocked her.

'Very funny, Aunt Violet.' Hannah's hatred of sewing and needles was legendary. 'How are we going to find out more about these Worsley-Brookes?'

'I could probably ask a few discreet questions at my Red Cross Meeting this evening. All we need is a full name and we can take it from there.' Aunt Violet licked a glob of cream from the corner of her mouth.

'Two minutes ago, you disapproved of my involvement in police work?'

'Socialising is hardly police work. So, do you want my help or not?'

'I do. Thank you.' Hannah bit into a chocolate eclair, the mixture of sweet cream and chocolate almost making her moan aloud.

'What about making your new friend, Miss Bellamy, your first port of call? If she claims friendship with this Alice, you might be right about her keeping secrets.'

'She's already suspicious of me.' Hannah recalled her first conversation with Josie, who questioned her on how her investigation was going. 'She might refuse to tell me anything, especially about Alice's family.'

'Then we'll have to approach it from a different direction. I might just have an idea. But you must promise not to tell Aidan I'm helping you,' Aunt Violet said. 'It could be a dead end, and I could do without one of his lectures.'

'Don't panic. If we find out that Alice left voluntarily, there'll be no need to tell *Inspector Farrell* anything.' She emphasised his name.

'And if we don't?'

'Then he'll investigate Alice's fate himself. Girls don't just disappear without a word to anyone.'

'That's not strictly true, darling.' Aunt Violet held a smoked salmon sandwich between a thumb and forefinger at eye level. 'When I was at finishing school, Amy Carruthers eloped with a schoolteacher. She left her room intact down to her hairbrushes. Her parents thought she had drowned and had Lake Lucerne searched.' She caught Hannah's sceptical look and shrugged. 'Well, part of it. Anyway, she turned up in London a month later safe and sound. And, thankfully, married.'

'Are you saying Alice might have eloped?'

'Not necessarily, but you've caught my imagination.' Her aunt set down her cup and dabbed her mouth delicately with a napkin. 'Missing heiresses are more fun – and less dangerous – than rooting out murderers.' She slapped a dusting of icing sugar from her fingers. 'I'm staying in Richmond with the Donahues tonight, so what say we begin tomorrow? Archie can manage for a few hours without us, although he'd better not buy any bibles from persuasive salesmen.'

'How do you know Alice is an heiress?'

'A chauffeur driven motor car and a name like Worsley-Brooke?' Her aunt 'harrumphed' lightly and scanned the room. 'Where's our waitress? This teapot is empty.'

* * *

Ivy's distinctive tread on the stairs was heavier than usual, as Hannah prepared to leave for the bookshop the following morning.

'You might 'av mentioned 'er ladyship din't come 'ome last night.' Ivy slammed a tray she had clearly carried all the way up to Aunt Violet's room and back onto the hall table, spilling tea into the saucer. 'Her bed ain't been slept in.'

'Ah no, sorry, Ivy.' Hannah winced, but did not take her eyes from the hall mirror where she adjusted her hat. 'I meant to tell you, but forgot.'

'She'd better not miss supper!' Before Ivy could launch into a barrage of mutterings about Aunt Violet's irregular habits, Hannah grabbed her bag and pulled the front door closed, her maid's voice coming clearly through the wood: 'That boiled 'am I got yesterday wasn't easy to come by!'

At Charing Cross Station, Hannah joined a pressing crowd of

pedestrians, nurses in uniform and men in khaki who milled around the entrance. Buses, hansoms and tradesmen's carts negotiated the wall of sandbags that hid the statue of King Charles I on his horse. The mournful strains of a hymn from St Martin-in-the-Fields, announcing a service for a dead soldier, competed with traffic noise.

A high-pitched whistle drew her attention to where Aunt Violet gestured from the open door of a hackney at the roadside, jolting the driver on the box awake.

'When did you learn to whistle like a navvy?' Hannah asked. 'You know whistling for taxis is illegal these days. People might take it for a Zeppelin warning and panic.' Avoiding a stain on the squab, she settled into the corner seat beside a grime-streaked window, her nose wrinkling involuntarily at the smell of old tobacco and sweat.

'It's not very salubrious, I'm afraid,' Aunt Violet lowered her voice so their driver wouldn't hear her. 'All the decent horses have been requisitioned by the War Office. Only old nags and even older drivers are left.'

'Why are we in a cab?' Hannah asked. 'Had I known, I would have brought the Swift.'

'I was about to tell you, but you're being very snippy. Did you have a bad night?' Aunt Violet picked a piece of fluff from Hannah's lapel before adjusting it.

'Sort of. I keep going over my meeting with Alice. Her talk about being followed no longer seems trivial. If it ever did.'

'We're going to call in at Millie Patterson's house first to pick up my motor car. I left it there last night.'

'Er, why?' Hannah frowned, certain her aunt said she was with the Donahues the previous evening. 'I didn't know Millie drove. I thought they had a full-time chauffeur?'

'She doesn't. And they do. Goodness knows how they kept him

out of being called up. The evening became livelier when Roddy Patterson decided to keep his best champagne for ourselves instead of letting the Germans filch it. After that it seemed advisable for me to stay the night.'

'I wondered why I didn't hear you stumbling into the house at some ungodly hour.'

'Don't be ridiculous. I never stumble. Besides, the Pattersons always serve a magnificent breakfast.'

'You actually managed breakfast?'

'Naturally. Champagne never gives me a hangover.'

'You win. This conversation is over.'

'That's a shame, because you might like to know I've located the address of a relative of Alice Worsley-Brooke. Her aunt, in fact.' Aunt Violet knocked on the roof with her knuckles as a signal to the driver to leave. 'Madeleine proved more than informative. She seems to know everyone, and—'

'You went to my mother?' Hannah gaped. 'Aunt Violet! How could you? This was supposed to be between the two of us. Mother is bound to gossip, and if Inspector Farrell finds out we've been doing his job, it might constitute an offence.'

'Do stop panicking.' Aunt Violet waved an airy hand. 'I've been weaving stories for my sister for years. I'm hardly going to slip up now. Are you going to continue telling me off, or listen to what I've found out?'

'Go on then.' Chastened, Hannah slumped into her seat and pouted. Their hackney carriage was going nowhere for the immediate future; it was stuck behind a convoy of ambulances that heaved back from the Charing Cross Hospital. Every foot of the road was packed with pedestrians, but eerily silent as no one protested at the delay out of respect for the poor souls being transported.

'Your mother remembers a Daphne Dalglish, whose coming

out party she attended in the eighteen-nineties. They've been distant friends ever since. She was even at your christening.'

'Was she indeed?'

'Daphne had a younger sister, who married a Worsley-Brooke, and they had two children... one named Alice.'

'Alice is using her mother's maiden name?' Hannah smiled in triumph and wiped her gloved hand over a film of condensation inside the grime-streaked window. 'That makes perfect sense. It's what I would do if I was trying to hide.'

'Daphne herself is an Allardyce now, has been for years. The Worsley-Brookes, meanwhile, have an extensive estate in Herefordshire. They made their money through engineering in the eighteen-sixties. The previous generation had three sons and bought their way into society by marrying them off to heiresses.' Her aunt counted them off on her fingers. 'One was an earl's daughter, another inherited a title as well. I cannot recall which one. Didn't help the family dynasty, though.'

'Why didn't it?' Hannah grabbed for the hand strap as the cab pulled sharply into traffic which had started moving again.

'Most of them met a premature death before they could become parents. Quite tragic, in fact. One wife died of a weak heart, and a few months later her husband was shot in a duel over some doxy. Another wife died in childbirth, and a son fell off his horse during a Boxing Day hunt. Broke his neck. Why are you glaring at me like that?'

'I'm not glaring, Aunt Violet. I'm trying to keep up. Where does Alice come in?' The cab swerved suddenly to avoid a tradesman cart that pulled ahead of them on the Tottenham Court Road. Hannah gasped as the vehicle swayed, but immediately righted itself.

'That was close.' Aunt Violet adjusted her hat that had slipped over one eye. 'Now, where was I? Oh yes, Berkeley Worsley-Brooke the third son, married a beautiful Scots girl who claimed to have descended from the Buccleuchs. Scads of money, but no title. Her name was Dalglish.'

'Alice's parents?' Hannah nodded, working all the connections out in her head.

'Precisely. They had a son and a daughter.'

'The marriage wasn't a total failure, then?' Hannah raised her voice over the clopping of hooves that passed on both sides. 'Unless they gambled away their money?'

'The money is still there, as far as I know. As I understand it, they—'

'You mean, as my mother understands? I assume this is her story?'

'Don't be ungrateful, I had to memorise it all, didn't I?' She sniffed, mildly offended. 'Anyway, they were killed in a carriage accident on their own land. An axel broke and the entire contraption toppled into a ravine.'

'Are there ravines in Hertfordshire?' Hannah winced as the unbidden image of a carriage hurtling towards the ground jumped into her head.

'An escarpment, then.' Aunt Violet clicked her tongue in annoyance. 'They were killed outright, but by some miracle the coachman saved the horses. He jumped onto the traces and cut them, so the animals simply galloped away from—'

'I'm glad the horses were saved.' Hannah held up a hand. 'What happened to the son and daughter?'

'They went to live with their maternal aunt, Daphne Allardyce. Apparently, they grew up into exceptionally striking young people. Mind you, if they had snouts like Gloucester old spot pigs, they would still be feted with that fortune.'

'That's very harsh, Aunt Violet,' Hannah said, while silently acknowledging this was true.

'A fact of life, dear. The son, Rafe, went into the army in '14, but was killed last May at the Battle of Festubert.'

'Alice mentioned her brother,' Hannah said. 'She was close to tears even then.'

'Alice is the last surviving heir, but appears to have shut herself away as no one has seen her among her social round since then.'

'Can't say I blame her if she's besieged by fortune hunters every time she steps outside the door. And I assume her aunt is still alive if you know where she lives?'

'Very much so. Allardyce was a much older man and they had no offspring of their own. She had two step-children from that marriage though, and was raising her nephew and niece too, which was probably more than enough. Madeleine doesn't know much more than that.'

'If Daphne Allardyce is Alice's only remaining blood relative, she might have gone home if she was unsettled by the murder,' Hannah mused. 'If not, we don't want to alarm the lady by implying Alice is missing.'

'I doubt she's a frail old lady prone to the vapours. She's your mother's age.'

In Hannah's eyes that did not exclude her, but she chose not to make the point. 'How do we contrive an introduction? She might not even let us through the door.'

'Which brings me to my next piece of news, I met with some WSPU ladies last evening and—'

'Haven't the Women's Political and Social Union been disbanded until after the war?' Hannah interrupted.

'Officially, yes. But Molly Baines is hosting a fundraiser for the Princess Mary Boxes for soldiers. You remember her? Tall woman with a slight stoop and fuzzy hair.'

'I do, but how does that get us closer to Daphne Allardyce?' Hannah inhaled sharply as a cyclist veered close to the hackney

Their driver shouted a warning and after a precarious wobble, the cyclist righted himself and sped away.

'I'm getting to that.' Aunt Violet sighed, exasperated. 'When I arrived, the ladies were addressing envelopes for cards requesting donations from society ladies.'

'Rattling collection boxes on street corners is not good enough?' Hannah interjected.

Aunt Violet became interested in something in the road outside, so either didn't get – or ignored – Hannah's sarcasm.

'Aunt Violet?' Hannah narrowed her eyes. 'Don't tell me you took one of those cards when no one was looking?'

Her aunt revealed a white parchment envelope in her bag, the name *Mrs D Allardyce* written in the elegant copperplate learned at all the best ladies' academies. 'We're going to deliver it personally.'

'What a coincidence then, that Molly Baines knows Mrs Allardyce?'

'Ah, not exactly.' Aunt Violet grimaced. 'Madeleine gave me her address, so I filled out the invitation card when I got home.'

'I admire your initiative, Aunt Violet, but one day it's going to get us into trouble.'

'It already has. Sort of.' She rolled her eyes. 'I've been tasked with addressing three hundred more of the wretched things within the next week. All to send little tin boxes to the front with a bar of chocolate and a picture of Princess Mary.' She tutted. 'Filling them with bullets would be of more use.'

'Possibly, but even so, Princess Mary's pledge to issue a gift box to "every sailor afloat and every soldier at the front" is a lovely gesture for Christmas.'

'And a greater task than the princess imagined – one that will actually take several Christmases to fulfil.'

Hannah chose not to comment. 'So where are we going?'

'To St John's Wood.' Her aunt stared vaguely at her. 'Didn't I say?'

'Mrs Allardyce might not know Alice is missing. Or that she's working as a VAD at Endell Street under an assumed name.' Hannah began to lose her nerve. 'What if she thinks we're trouble-makers and throws us out?'

'My darling girl, have a little faith.' Her aunt tutted. 'I've talked my way into the House of Commons before now with less ammunition.'

10

After a detour to West Kensington to fetch the Sunbeam, kindly washed and polished by the Patterson's chauffeur, Aunt Violet drove at a reckless speed to St John's Wood.

The house in Glenfair Road was not the multi-chimneyed mansion in expansive grounds Hannah had expected, but a semi-detached Queen Anne-style red brick house built less than thirty years before. A pair of square bay windows flanked an oversized portico which offered an impressive entrance for such a modest-sized property. The house possessed no drive, only a mosaic tiled pathway to the front door behind a wrought-iron gate.

'Is this a good idea?' Hannah hesitated with her hand on the knocker. 'What if Mrs Allardyce refuses to discuss her family? Or Aidan questions her at some stage and she mentions us?'

'If he doesn't regard Alice's disappearance as worthy of investigation, I doubt he'll get this far. And if he does, I'll drop Molly's name into the conversation and lead him down a rabbit hole of coincidences.'

'Deceiving a police officer? Isn't that a crime?'

'Deceit is an ugly concept. Look at it as more like misdirection. Now knock, before a neighbour reports us for loitering.'

The butler, with his military moustache, politely asked them to wait before he went to tell his mistress of their arrival.

Hannah used the time to examine the modern square entrance hall with electric lighting, the crisp white and cream paint complemented by a plush ruby red carpet.

A fanlight over the front door, of stained-glass in a picture of a ship in full sail, cast shapes of yellow, white and blue light onto the walls and ceiling.

Several cumbersome pieces of furniture spoiled the overall feel of the room; they were older than the house and most likely brought from a much larger establishment.

'Will he come back?' Hannah asked, her nose irritated by the musty smell of mildew and dust emanating from the ancient wood furniture.

'Someone is.' Aunt Violet alerted her to the clip of hasty light footsteps approaching, which were definitely not the butler's.

A chirpy maid with a round face and ruddy cheeks made an awkward curtsey. 'Mrs Allardyce will see you now. Please follow me.'

They were shown into a well-appointed morning room off the one side of the hall. More dark, heavy furniture occupied every inch of floor space on a faded Turkey carpet. The view from square bay window showed that a high, thick hedge enclosed large, well-kept garden.

'It's more like a furniture warehouse than a home.' Hanna tucked her elbows into her sides to avoid knocking anything over

'Hush.' Aunt Violet nudged her with the toe of her boot, just a rail-thin woman in her late forties approached. She wore a floor length burgundy silk gown more suited for a cocktail party than an afternoon at home. The deep colour stripped her already pa complexion, her pallor mitigated by a pair of sparkling brown eyes.

'We appreciate your agreeing to seeing us, Mrs Allardyce.' Aunt Violet offered her hand. 'Especially as we have not been formally introduced.'

'You're Violet Edwards.' Their hostess pinned Aunt Violet with a straightforward gaze.

'Um – I am, yes,' Aunt Violet stammered. 'Though I'm not sure if I'm flattered, or should apologise.'

'A lady who gets her photograph in the newspapers as often as you have cannot expect to go about anonymously. I've always admired your independent spirit, Violet. I may call you Violet?' she asked without waiting for a response. 'We've never met, but your sister, of course, mentioned you. Not that I've seen her for some years now.' She sighed. 'You're still a spinster, I take it, or did I miss the announcement in *The Times*?'

'I'm confident you miss very little, Mrs Allardyce,' Aunt Violet replied, equally archly. 'Especially an announcement of that sort.'

'I like your spirit.' Her upper lip curled as she gave Aunt Violet's couture powder blue summer coat and matching hat a slow appraising glance. 'A woman with your beauty could have her pick. Take my advice, my dear, and apply yourself before all the decent ones take the King's shilling.'

Aunt Violet opened her mouth to speak, but their hostess was still in full flow. 'Though after my marriages, if I had my time again, I might not have bothered with them at all if. Such obvious creatures, men; of simple needs and no imagination.' Her gaze shifted to Hannah.

'And who is this?' Her gimlet eyes took in Hannah before sliding back to her aunt. 'Oh, never mind. Please, sit.' She commanded them as if addressing a cocker spaniel.

Not daring to catch her aunt's eye, Hannah obeyed, taking one of the twin matching chairs set a foot apart.

'I doubt you're here for my sparkling company, so to what do I owe this unexpected visit?' She perched on the edge of a dark green velvet sofa opposite; a piece of furniture so heavily upholstered Hannah feared it might swallow her up.

'We're inviting donations to the Princess Mary Boxes for Soldiers Scheme.' Aunt Violet retrieved the invitation from her bag, handing it to her with a flourish.

'There's still a fund for that?' She took the envelope between two fingers, giving it a cursory glance before discarding it on a nearby table. 'Wasn't there an appeal in late '14 for it?'

'Indeed, there was. As a Christmas gift.' Aunt Violet launched into her rehearsed speech. 'One which, although successful, has proved problematical. Especially when forty-five tons of brass earmarked to make the boxes were lost on the Lusitania. Then they have to be distributed to all overseas regiments in the far reaches of the globe, which will take a while, so—'

'Yes, yes, I get the picture,' Daphne interrupted, evidently bored with the subject. 'I always thought Her Highness' idea was rather ambitious myself.'

'Do you live here alone, Mrs Allardyce?' Hannah changed the subject while searching the room for signs of a younger occupant, but nothing struck her.

'My niece lives with me, though she's rarely here. Sometimes I feel she sees me as a convenience.'

'I'm actually acquainted with Alice,' Hannah ventured, sensing their host was becoming bored and might bring the visit to a premature end. 'I'm sorry to have missed her.'

'Really? She's never mentioned you.' Mrs Allardyce folded her arms, her hard stare a challenge. 'Have you known each other long?'

'Er, not long,' Hannah replied vaguely. 'We met at the Covent Garden Bookshop and discovered we had shared literary interests.'

'A bookshop?' She raised an eyebrow. 'Why am I not surprised? Such an environment would be heaven for Alice. She was always a quiet, studious girl. We were never close. She's too much like her mother – introverted and difficult to get to know.'

'Oh, I'm sure she's very fond of you, and must appreciate what you've done for her since she was orphaned,' Aunt Violet interjected.

'No need for compliments, Violet. I'm not offended. I don't blame her. I wasn't very good at hiding the fact I preferred Rafe. Everyone did.' She blinked rapidly as if near to tears.

Hannah exchanged a look with her aunt, who gave a slight nod of encouragement. 'She's a delightful young woman. So she has not been at home today?'

'Huh, Alice barely regards this house as her home any more.' She arranged her dress around herself, one arm draped across the back of the sofa. 'She's away at the moment. Staying with friends.'

'That's a shame,' Aunt Violet said, though Hannah could feel her tense beside her, like a fox smelling blood.

'Did she say which friends she planned to visit?' Hannah asked carefully. 'I ask because they might be mutual acquaintances.'

'Oh, I doubt that, my dear.' She wrinkled her nose in distaste. 'No, she did not. But she's been very restless after Rafe was killed. You know about him, I assume?'

Hannah nodded. 'Alice told me he was killed in Artois last year.'

'Such a terrible loss. Alice and Rafe came to me on the death of my sister-and brother-in-law in a tragic accident. A most stressful time. I was already a stepmother to my late husband's children, though they were almost grown by the time of Algernon's death. Mentoring four young people through life was quite exhausting.

When darling Rafe was killed, Alice was devastated. If only she had accepted Gabriel, I'm sure she would be happier.'

'Gabriel?' Aunt Violet convincingly feigned ignorance.

'My stepson.' She swiped a silver frame from the table at her elbow and handed it to Aunt Violet, who examined it before passing it to Hannah. It contained a sepia photograph of a dark-haired young man with chiselled features and penetrating eyes. It was impossible to tell their colour, but they were lighter than his hair.

'He's very handsome,' Hannah said truthfully. The eyes in the photograph stared out at her with an intense, determined stare which seemed to probe her soul, making her almost relieved to hand it back.

'He proposed to her?' Aunt Violet asked.

'Twice.' Daphne Allardyce cradled the ornate silver frame lovingly. 'Once when she turned sixteen and again last year when Rafe died. The first time, she shut herself in her room for a week; then it was because of the age difference. Gabriel was more than a decade older, but she simply couldn't see that he would have protected her.'

'Protected her from what?' Hannah asked, knowing the answer.

'Have you not been paying attention to what's happening around us?' Mrs Allardyce tutted, impatient. 'No one will be safe if the Germans invade. They will take everything we own and then we'll be—' She inhaled a slow breath. 'Alice needs to be practical. For all our sakes.' She ran a slow finger over the face in the photograph. 'She will come into everything on her next birthday. I suggested she write a will in favour of me and Gabriel, but she refused.'

'She's young still, and has plenty of time,' Aunt Violet said.

'How much time do any of us have in this war? What if some

ng happens to her?' Mrs Allardyce fidgeted, her agitation grow-
. 'She needs to secure everything for the future.'

Hannah wondered what she had in mind. Unless Gabriel
anged his nationality, whatever the Huns planned would apply
him too. Or was he a closet sympathiser?

'Do you expect Alice home soon, Mrs Allardyce?' Hannah
ed hopefully.

'Uh, no. She's gone away for a while. As I said.'

'A while?' Hannah asked.

'I'm not sure how long she's been away. I've been staying at my
use in Hertfordshire since Christmas. London is so dull these
ys, I couldn't be bothered to return after the festive season. I've
t long been back, and she was gone by then. Left me an enig-
tic note saying she needed to get away from London.'

'You don't keep in touch?' Aunt Violet asked.

'We don't check up on each other, if that's what you mean.
en I next see her, I'll let her know you asked after her.'

'That's kind. In fact, the last time I spoke to Alice, she
ntioned something about doing war work. Perhaps that has
t her away?'

'Really?' The lady's lips puckered into oblivion. 'Alice never
ntioned it to me. This boxes for soldiers scheme is more like
nething she would be involved in.'

'Actually, she was going to apply to become a nurse in a mili-
y hospital. As a tribute to her brother.'

'You cannot possibly be talking about the same person.' Mrs
ardyce huffed an incredulous breath. 'Alice would never do
h a thing. She's too refined for menial work. No, if she's
ywhere, it will be at a house party on a country estate in the
me Counties, or on a yacht in the Mediterranean. Well, perhaps
t a yacht under current circumstances, but you know what I
an.'

'And your stepson?' Aunt Violet asked causally. 'He lives town?'

'Gabriel has an apartment in Fulham, but spends most of time in Suffolk. His sister has a house on the coast there,' replied, apparently unwilling to supply details. 'Georgina, my st daughter, was widowed a year ago. She prefers the country.'

'Your stepdaughter's husband was in the services?' Hann asked, assuming he was a war casualty.

She shook her head. 'Dicky heart. That's why they moved Lowestoft. Not that it did him much good. He was dead withi year.' She replaced the picture frame on a side table, rose abrup and strode to the give the bell pull an impatient tug. The vag look she had maintained throughout changed to wariness. ' sorry I couldn't help you, but thank you for calling.' She sta straight at Aunt Violet, ignoring Hannah completely.

'Mrs Allardyce?' Hannah asked from the door. 'Do you ow black chauffeured motor car by any chance?'

'Ugh! I wouldn't travel in one of those things, they're v uncomfortable and noisy. I keep a carriage in the mews and butler acts as my driver. Why do you ask?'

'Oh, no reason. And thank you again.'

The butler arrived in response to her summons and with curt, 'Good day,' Mrs Allardyce instructed him to escort them ou

'I messed that up, didn't I?' Hannah said when they emerg onto a street lined on both sides with established chestnut trees didn't expect her to shut down like that when she was happy talk about her stepchildren.'

'We might have overplayed our hand, rather. But that does excuse her rudeness. Did you notice she promised to tell Alice y called, but she doesn't know your name?'

'She probably won't even remember me if our paths cr again. Which might be to my advantage.' Hannah turned her he and stared up at the house, but the windows remained blank, with no curious eyes watching them.

'What's on your mind, Aunt Violet?' Hannah asked, conscious they were no closer to finding Alice than the day she went missing.

'Probably the same as you. That maybe her precious Gabriel grew impatient with gentle persuasion and spirited Alice away to coerce her to marry him so he could have access to her money. I'll wager he owns a chauffeured motor car.'

'Talking of money, did you get the impression Mrs Allardyce was decamping to the country for financial reasons?'

'I did, actually. I suspect some of her artwork has been sold and lesser substitutes hung in the spaces. The gaps are still obvious. Her jewels weren't real either. No one wears marcasite if they have genuine diamonds. Not since mourning for Queen Victoria ended, anyway.'

'Trust you to spot that, Aunt Violet. Is it my imagination, or was she entirely unconcerned about the whereabouts of her niece?'

'She said they weren't close, but then she didn't exactly relish her role as stepmother to four young people.'

'Could Gabriel be behind whoever was following Alice?' Hannah slid into the passenger seat and arranged a blanket over her knees. A smart green two-seater parked on the opposite side of the road caught her attention. The vehicle faced them head on, the driver's face clearly visible through the windscreen. His expression was exactly the one in the photograph, a mixture of studied confidence and open challenge.

'Don't judge the poor man without even having met him, Hannah.' Her aunt started the motor car, allowing the engine to idle. 'What are you staring at?'

'Not what – who.' She cocked her chin at the vehicle in question. 'I'm sure that's Gabriel Allardyce.'

'And you deduce that from seeing a single photograph?' Aunt Violet followed her gaze. 'Hmm. He's certainly handsome enough.'

'A photograph Daphne Allardyce cradled like the firstborn she never had. And if it isn't him, then why is he staring at us leaving this house?' Aunt Violet began to move the car away.

'He's certainly handsome enough to be him.' Aunt Violet eased off the accelerator, bringing the motor to almost a stop. 'Perhaps you could give him a wave and remove any doubt?'

'No, don't slow down, keep going!' Hannah ordered.

'If you insist.' Grinning, Aunt Violet gunned the engine and pulled into traffic, causing a baker's van to swerve, the driver sounding his horn.

'Oh, very subtle, Aunt Violet.' Hannah rolled her eyes and pulled her hat down as far as it would go.

* * *

On her way to the hospital library the next day, Hannah debated how to approach Josie Bellamy about omitting to tell her Alice's real name. Should she tackle her head on, or tamp down her annoyance and give her a chance to explain? Not that Josie owed Hannah anything, but being lied to irked her.

She had yet to decide by the time she passed the open door to the nurses' kitchen where Dinah was stacking piles of dirty crockery.

'Busy morning, Dinah?' Hannah slung her summer weight coat over one arm, her shoulder braced against the door frame.

'Been 'ere since seven.' The young nurse kept her attention on an enormous pile of crockery. 'I'll be glad when those coppers 'ave gone an' all. They stomp about the place like they own it and interrupt our work with their questions.'

'That must be annoying.' Hannah smiled weakly, wondering i

Aidan was aware of how the staff viewed him. 'Dinah, how long has Nurse Bellamy worked here?'

'Don't rightly know, but she was probably here when the hospital opened last year. No one's been here longer than that. Apart from those who worked with Dr Murray in France, of course.'

'What do you think of her?'

'Nurse Bellamy or Dr Murray?' Dinah's cheeky grin showed she knew what Hannah meant. 'Don't give 'er much thought. She don't throw 'er weight about, if that's what you mean. Not like some.' A plate slipped out of her hands and hit the water, sending Hannah backwards to avoid the plume of suds sent over the side of the sink.

'Still askin' questions?' Dinah swiped a hand across her now damp apron.

'You know me, I'm always curious. Have you seen her today?'

'That's gonna get you in trouble one day.' Dinah grabbed a folded dish cloth from a rack above her head and snapped it open. 'And no, I ain't, but 'er name's on the roster in the office.' Dinah turned from the sink and wiped her hands. 'What do you want with 'er?'

'Any idea where she is at this moment?' Hannah asked, ignoring the question.

'Are you looking for me?' A voice at Hannah's shoulder made her jump. She whirled around to where Josie stood, pristine and efficient in her crisp white apron and wimple.

'There ya go. I found 'er for yer.' Dinah chuckled. She finished drying her hands and slapped the cloth over one shoulder, her grin wider than Josie's. 'Now that lot's done, I'll get on and count the linens.' With a brief nod to both women, she scurried off along the corridor.

The pause gave Hannah time to study Josie more closely. She

had a face with unremarkable features hard to define as either plain or handsome, though she had both charm and attraction when she smiled.

'Do you have a moment?' Hannah did not wait for a response and carried on along the hall to the library, pushed open the door and stood to one side to allow Josie to precede her.

'If you wish, and provided there are no corpses in here today.' Josie sniggered, evidently in a good mood. 'I don't have long, or Sister Hibbert will be after me.'

'I wanted to ask you why you didn't mention Alice was using her mother's maiden name while she was working here?'

'Ah!' Josie swallowed, her eyes losing the mischievous gleam they held two seconds before. 'So you are working with the police. I suspected as much when you asked questions about Alice.'

'Not really. Inspector Farrell would prefer I kept out of it. Did Alice ask you not to tell anyone who she was, or was that your idea?'

'This amateur sleuth stuff is making you imagine things.' Josie bridled. 'I admit to knowing Alice changed her name, but she did so to avoid her aunt finding out about her working here. Daphne Allardyce would have thrown a fit. And why are you so interested in Alice, anyway? You don't even know her.'

'Maybe not, but no one has heard from her in days, and I'm worried she might be in trouble. Did she mention she was being followed?'

'What? No. What a strange question. She isn't in trouble.' Josie's wariness softened to sympathy. 'I'm sorry I wasn't more open with you before, but you're carrying this too far. Alice and I lost touch, but about two months ago, I ran into her in the hallway dressed in her VAD overalls. She asked, no, begged me, to keep quiet about her nursing, convinced her aunt would drag her back home again if she found out.'

Hannah frowned at the contradiction. Daphne Allardyce didn't seem to care about Alice, but was frustrated she rejected her stepson. 'Alice is afraid of her aunt?'

'Not afraid, exactly,' Josie thought for a moment. 'Alice had little freedom growing up. Heiresses get coddled as much as royalty, and with Rafe gone, she was lost. Becoming a VAD was her first independent decision, and she was determined to make the most of it. The Allardyces have plans for Alice she doesn't agree with.'

'What sort of plans?'

'Oh, the usual thing. Marry her off to some impoverished titled bachelor who needs her money to prop up his crumbling estate.'

'By the Allardyces, you mean the aunt and her stepson? I hear he asked her to marry him.'

'Gabriel?' Josie seemed genuinely surprised. 'He's not at all interested in Alice. Wherever did you hear that?'

'Never mind.' Though, according to Daphne, it was Alice who had no interest in the match.

'Look, Hannah.' Josie's brash confidence changed to ingratiating. 'And I hope I can call you that. There's no need for you to worry. Alice is not as delicate as everyone makes out. Nor would she appreciate you asking questions about her. She'll be hiding away in an expensive hotel somewhere until the fuss dies down, no doubt.'

'Is that why she left? Because of the murder?'

Josie shrugged. 'No one wants to be involved in anything like that, do they? Only we don't all have the resources to disappear at whim.' She displayed a momentary annoyance, but it was gone in an instant. 'Alice was badly shaken by it, even though the sergeant was an unpleasant man.'

'I've heard that too. Which hotel would Alice hide in?' Hannah was losing patience. Did Josie know something or not? All her deflection was not helping.

'There isn't one.' Josie sighed. 'I was guessing. It's what I would do with a family like that.'

'You mentioned resources. Is Alice able to support herself?' Staying in London hotels was hardly cheap.

'Yes, of course. Her aunt might want to control every penny, but she doesn't have the powers to cut her off completely. The estate trustees grant her an allowance until she inherits. Alice will waltz back in when she's ready, you'll see.'

Josie bounced on her toes, eager to get away. 'Alice is fine, really. Now I must get back to the ward. Sister Hibbert is tetchy enough today. I don't want to make things worse.'

'Of course.' Hannah watched her go, though still unsettled After Josie's initial deception, how much of what she told her could Hannah rely on? Or was she worrying about nothing and interfering in matters which did not concern her?

11

A soft drizzle that threatened to turn into a downpour greeted Hannah as she stepped into the hospital courtyard on her way out that afternoon. Her head down, she picked her way across the slick cobbles of the courtyard, darting to one side out of the way of an approaching ambulance.

Her shoes squelched as she stepped through the gate and almost collided with Archie, his arms wrapped around a basket covered with a sheet of oilcloth.

'Miss Edwards asked me to bring these donated books to the hospital library.' He peered from under the peak of his cap at the steadily falling rain, his curly dark hair glistening with water drops. 'It wasn't raining when I left the shop.'

Hannah gauged the distance to the motor car was shorter than returning to the gate and waiting for a porter to let her in. 'Put them in the passenger seat, Archie. I'll take them in later.'

Ignoring the puddles, she made her way to Darius' parked car with wet feet, grateful that she had remembered to fasten the tonneau earlier.

A youth leaned against the building on the corner of Shorts

Gardens. His angular face peered out from beneath hair darkened to dirty blond curls that clung wetly to his forehead. He
wore faded brown trousers, and a faded jacket slightly too big
for him, both sporting damp patches at the shoulders and
thighs.

Hannah studied him for a moment, sure she had seen him
before, then she remembered.

'Archie!' She tugged his arm, pulling him from where he was
bent over placing the basket of books on the seat, his expression of
puzzled enquiry. She nodded towards the youth and was about to
speak when his eyes met hers. His eyes widened in recognition
before he turned and fled.

'Get after him!' Hannah yelled.

To his credit, Archie did not argue and took off at a run, his
legs pumping as he covered the distance between them.

Hannah slammed the car door and pelted after them, her long
skirt wrapped around her legs slowing her down. Her bag banged
against her hip, but determination spurred her on. She dodged
between pedestrians, shoving aside others with a barely mumbled,
'excuse me'. Some glared at her while others uttered sharp
protests, but all were ignored.

Archie stood at the corner of Shaftesbury Avenue, his foot on
the back of the youth who lay sprawled on the wet pavement.

'What do I do with 'im, Miss?' he asked, as his captive struggled uselessly.

'Have you done this before?' Hannah halted beside them, her
chest heaving as she recovered her breath.

'Don't ask.' Archie grabbed the loose collar of the youth's oversized coat and hauled him to his feet. 'Only this one wasn't too 'ard
to catch. He's a scrawny specimen. What's he done?'

'Leggo!' the boy demanded, but with his shoulders hunched
and chin on his chest, the plea had little volume. Now on his feet

he barely reached Archie's shoulder. Seeming to realise he was outnumbered, he held still.

'I mean you no harm,' Hannah said, feeling guilty at having accosted what was almost a child. 'I only want to talk to you.'

She spoke gently, mainly for the benefit of several passers-by who stopped to stare at the scruffy youth being manhandled by a larger one. Judging nothing startling was about to happen, and becoming progressively wetter, they hurried away.

'I ain't done nothin',' the youth muttered, shuffling his feet. His eyes darted in every direction, as if in search of an escape.

'I have some questions about the girl you have been following,' Hannah said.

'Who says I've been followin' anyone?' His chin jutted belligerently.

'If you prefer not to talk to me, I could always summon a policeman.' Not that there were any within calling reach in that street.

'What for?' The youth's lips twisted in defiance.

'Now that ain't no way to speak to a lady.' Archie administered a slap to the back of his neck.

'What do yer wanna know?' He looked resigned rather than afraid.

'Why don't we get out of this shower and have a drink at The Cross Keys?' If threatening him wasn't going to work she could try persuasion.

'Long as you're payin'.' He swiped a grubby hand beneath his nose that dripped with raindrops as Hannah led the way, with Archie bringing up the rear in case he tried to run.

The public bar was almost empty, its low ceilings and mass of thick, smoke-stained beams making the room gloomy and full of shadows. Hannah was conscious a handful of male patrons stared at her as she approached the counter.

'What would you like?' Hannah asked.

'Ginger beer. I don't like ale. Makes me stomach cramp.'

'I'll get these, Miss,' Archie offered, waving them to a table in the corner that gave some privacy.

Hannah caught sight of her reflection in the mirror above the bar and groaned at her dishevelled appearance, which explained the surreptitious glances other patrons were giving her. The shoulders of her jacket were dark with water, her hat sat askew over her loose bun – now sprinkled with glistening drops. Hunting in her pockets for a handkerchief, she used the first one she found to dab at her wet face. There was nothing she could do about her hair, where strands had loosened and hung down her back.

Archie joined them in less than a minute, three full glasses held expertly in his hands. He slid two tall thick glasses of cloudy amber liquid in front of Hannah and the boy, claiming a third filled with darker liquid that gave off a yeasty odour.

He slid into the bench seat, trapping the boy in the corner, while Hannah took a stool opposite, giving her a clear view of the youth's face.

'What's your name?' Hannah asked.

'Why d'you want to know?' He cradled his glass in both hands, his eyes darting around the room.

'I have to call you something.' Hannah waited, and took a tentative sip from her glass, pleasantly surprised at its spicy taste.

'It's Duffy.' He gulped half the drink in one go, smacked his lips and set the glass down on the sticky tabletop. 'Just Duffy.'

'Funny sort o' name,' Archie muttered, his glass held to his lips.

Hannah frowned at him. Shrugging, he focused on his drink.

'Have you been following a nurse from the hospital over the road?' Hannah began.

'Nah, not me. You must be talkin' 'bout someone else.'

'What if I said the lady herself told me? Pretty young woman with blonde hair? I could ask her to come in and point you out?'

'Nah, don't do that. What of it?' His initial defiance turned to wariness.

'You're useless at it, that's what of it.' Archie snorted. 'She saw you.'

'And now she's missing,' Hannah said.

'She is?' Surprise and worry flicked across his face. 'That's why I've not seen 'er for a few days. I was told to follow 'er and report where she goes.'

'Report to who?' Archie demanded.

'The man who paid me, o' course.' He threw Archie a dour look before burying his nose in his glass.

'Did this man say why he wanted her followed?' Hannah asked.

'That ain't likely, is it? And I weren't about to ask. None of me business anyway.'

'When was this?' Archie swiped a small amount of froth from his upper lip.

'A couple of weeks back. Paid me ten bob to do it.'

Archie widened his eyes at Hannah over the youth's head, in a 'your turn' gesture.

'I didn't do anything to 'er, if that's what yer askin'.' Duffy picked up his glass again and took another mouthful.

'If you didn't, then who did?' Archie's voice was low and guttural, displaying a side to him Hannah had not seen before.

'How should I know?' The glass halted halfway to Duffy's mouth. 'Come ta think of it, I read about those white slavers who kidnap girls? Some of them Belgian refugees at Olympia disappeared.'

'I sincerely hope that isn't what we're dealing with,' Hannah muttered almost to herself. She had heard rumours about human trafficking, but hoped they weren't true. 'When you were following this lady, where did she go?'

'A few places.' Duffy's neck disappeared between his shoulders in an exaggerated shrug. 'The 'ospital, of course. Then to that 'ouse in Clerkenwell. I fink it was her lodgings. She went shopping in the West End sometime, but she didn't speak to no one.'

'Would you be prepared to tell police what you've told me?' Hannah asked.

'Tell 'em what?' He snorted. 'That I took money to follow a young girl about. Nah. They'd lock me up fer sure. What's it to you? She your sister or somefing?'

'I'm just a friend, but I need to find her. She might be in trouble. What's he like, this man?'

Duffy shrugged again, cradled his glass and sipped it slowly as if he was savouring the best champagne. 'Ordinary bloke. Taller than me and thin. He wore a tan trench coat down to his ankle and a trilby pulled down over his forehead. No different from any other on the street.'

'What colour were his eyes? What about his voice or the colour of his hair?'

'Din't notice his eyes, and he had a hat on. He spoke quiet like so I had to lean in close to hear.'

'Did he smell of anything?'

'Oi!' Duffy glared at her. 'I don't go round sniffin' bloke Whaddya fink I am?'

Archie choked on a mouthful of ale, wiped his nose on h sleeve and threw Hannah an apologetic look.

'I wasn't trying to imply anything.' She inhaled a slow brea before trying again. 'This man might know where she is.'

'Not likely. And I ain't telling 'im. If the girl's gone, he mig demand 'is money back, and I don't have it no more.'

'Could you get in touch with this bloke?' Archie asked the question Hannah started.

'He said he'd be at The Coal 'ole in the Strand the day after tomorrer and be there till seven, but I shan't bovver goin' now.'

'What if I paid you to keep that appointment?' Hannah withdrew a coin purse from a slightly damp pocket and pressed a folded ten-shilling note into his hand.

'Then what?' He fingered the note with something like awe.

'Then nothing. Your relationship with him will be over.'

Duffy frowned as possibilities ran through his head, all the while keeping a firm grip on the brown banknote. 'S'pose he thinks I did something to 'er?'

'I doubt that.' If this man was responsible for Alice's disappearance, he was unlikely to turn up at all, but it was worth a try. 'Just explain you were following her, but she hasn't been around for a few days. I want to know how he reacts.'

'Well, I'll try, but—'

'No buts. Either way, the money is yours. Is that clear?' Archie leered at him, confirming Hannah's impression he was used to dealing with the likes of Dufy. She would have to ask him about it sometime.

''Ow will I find yer?' Duffy tucked the money into his pocket and cocked his chin towards the bar. 'Shall we meet back 'ere?'

'Er... no.' She contemplated giving him a short script to follow, but it would be too suspicious and she doubted this lad could carry it off without causing suspicion. 'Come to the bookshop on Catherine Street the morning after.'

'That place where the rich lady got murdered last year?' His bushy eyebrows lifted in interest.

'Um, yes. That's the one.' She avoided Archie's cheeky grin. He had warned her the bookshop would become famous for all the wrong reasons. It seemed he was right. 'If you're there by ten o'clock, I'll give you another one of those.' She nodded to the jacket pocket where he had stowed the ten-shilling note.

'Hey, steady on, Miss.' Archie looked up sharply from his glass, but Hannah shook her head. It was worth a pound to find out who wanted Alice followed.

'Aw'right. But I meck no promises, mind.' Duffy pushed his empty glass across the table towards her. 'Don't suppose there's another one o' those on offer?'

'There might be.' Hannah smiled. 'I'll order one for you on our way out.'

*　*　*

Ten minutes later, Hannah strolled back to the hospital beside Archie.

'How did he strike you?' Hannah asked, as she looked back through the pub window where Duffy's head was still visible. The torrential rain had stopped, but left rivulets of rain flowing noisily into nearby drains.

'He were a right cheeky git,' Archie muttered as they reached the motor car at the kerb. 'I'd keep clear of him if I were you, Miss Merrill.'

'Why? He's younger than you, and little more than a bag of bones. He didn't strike me as someone to be nervous about.'

'Don't let him fool you, Miss.' Archie swung open the door and retrieved the basket of books from the seat. 'I'm pretty sure he was carrying.'

'What does that mean?' Hannah frowned.

'Never mind, just make sure you're not alone if you see him again.' He placed the basket of books in her arms. 'Will I see you back at the bookshop later, then?'

'I'm not sure. I have something to do first.' She watched him saunter back along Short Street, convinced he looked taller than she remembered and walked with a certain swagger she had not noticed before.

* * *

'Back again so soon, Miss?' the porter asked, as he relieved her of the basket of books. 'Thought you was finished for the day.'

'I was, but I forgot something.' Her gaze went to the long black Arrol-Johnston motor car parked to the side of the courtyard.

Relieved the inspector was still there, she left the basket with the porter and went straight to Dr Murray's office.

'Goodness, Hannah, you're all wet!' Inspector Farrell's eyebrows lifted as she entered after a perfunctory knock. 'Is it raining? I didn't notice.'

'And good afternoon to you too.' Suppressing a sharp remark about swimming, Hannah approached the small but welcome fire laid in the grate, her hands extended to the warmth. 'You seem very comfortable, considering this is not your office.'

'Dr Murray made it available while the investigation is going on.' He leaned back in his chair, the back touching the wall. 'To what do I owe the pleasure?'

'I've come to talk about Nurse Dalglish.' She studied a photograph above the mantle, of four rows of uniformed nurses assembled in the courtyard, Drs Murray and Anderson in the centre.

'Pity.' He sniffed. 'I hoped you might know something new about our deceased soldier.'

'You're not getting anywhere?' Sympathy rose at his forlorn expression.

'Not a straightforward case, this. The man was an enigma. Most people are willing to complain about what an unpleasant man he was, but no one appears to have a particular grudge against him.'

'People kill for many reasons. Not necessarily serious ones.' Hannah's damp skirt gave off a warm wet wool smell as the heat from the fire dried the fabric. 'He might have been killed for something you or I see as trivial, but which is important to someone else.'

'Forgive me, Hannah, but that doesn't help me.' The inspector massaged the bridge of his nose. 'I've had to release Corporal Doyle because of lack of proof he was involved. I'm still baffled why no one heard the shot, when St Anne's ward is directly above the library.'

'I've heard nothing different.' Hannah shrugged.

The inspector pushed away from the desk and leaned back in his chair. 'Incidentally, I made some enquiries about Nurse Dalglish, or should I say, Miss Alice Worsley-Brooke.'

'Not Dalglish, then?' Hannah feigned innocence, but his rueful smile told her she had not fooled him.

'Don't try to tell me you've never heard that name before. Be thankful I'm not asking how you found out.'

'You wouldn't want to know. Especially as it would mean revealing my Aunt Violet's part in it.'

'Why am I not surprised?' He shook his head slowly. 'Miss Worsley-Brooke is a considerable heiress. Her aunt, Daphne Allardyce, and her stepson are her wards. His name is...' He shuffled through the papers on his desk again. 'Umm... Gabriel Allardyce.' He looked up briefly. 'Who calls their son Gabriel?' He shrugged and went back to his notebook, not expecting an answer. 'After questioning some of the staff, including Lady Nurse Bellamy, I'm inclined to believe this young woman left of her own accord.'

'She's either Lady Josephine, or Nurse Bellamy. You can't mix them.' Hannah bit her bottom lip to hide a smile. 'Her mother is a countess but her father is a gentleman, so I'm not sure that even qualifies her as a lady. Perhaps she's an honourable?'

He shot her a withering glare before continuing. 'No one seems concerned about Miss Worsley-Brooke's sudden absence. Nor did any of the staff see anyone following her.'

'That doesn't mean she isn't in trouble,' Hannah insisted.

'Even Mrs Allardyce is convinced her niece was off on some jaunt. These society women assume trouble won't ever knock at their door.'

'What if I tell you something about the youth who was following Alice?' Hannah left the fire and wandered back to the desk, but declined his invitation to sit.

'*Allegedly* following her,' he corrected. 'Do you know who he is?'

'He gave me a name,' she replied, aware it might be false.

'You spoke to him?' Inspector Farrell's glare deepened.

'Briefly.' She winced. 'It was in a public place. And Archie was with me,' she added, suddenly defensive. 'Someone paid him to see where Alice went, but he wasn't told why.'

'Don't tell me...' His eyes hardened. 'He met some chap in a pub who offered him the job for a few shillings? As if I'm not told that at least twice a week.' He folded his hands on the desk. 'What exactly did this young man tell you?'

'He calls himself Duffy, and he took the job without asking questions so he doesn't know the name of his employer or why they wanted Alice followed. I can give you a vague description of him.'

'The young chap or the man who paid him?' He sniffed, sceptically, and pulled the notebook towards him. 'Go on then, what have you got?'

Hannah described the young man, whom she remembered as

undernourished in appearance and wary in character, and how he'd been easily coerced by the temptation of money.

'That's not much to go on,' he said when he had written down all she had told him about both Duffy and his associate. 'But I'll see what I can do.' He put down his pencil with a sigh and leaned back in his chair.

'Is that it? You'll see what you can do?' she mimicked.

'I'm sorry, Hannah, but I don't have enough men to put on the ground for such a flimsy reason.' His right eyebrow lifted. 'You cannot even be sure he wasn't following the girl for his own reasons and there is no other man.'

'I didn't think of that.' Hannah sighed; the thought had no occurred to her. But Archie had seemed to believe him.

'You were discreet, I hope?' the policeman added. 'You didn' tell him anything? Like your name?'

'Of course not. But Duffy mentioned where the man wh employed him will be in the evening, the day after tomorrow.' Sh tried not to sound too smug.

'Why didn't you say so?' He snatched his pencil up agai 'Well, go on then.'

'He's meeting him at The Coal Hole pub on the Strand. Duf didn't specify a time, but I'm confident Duffy will be there becau I gave him ten shillings.'

Inspector Farrell huffed a frustrated breath. 'You don't gi scallywags in the street money, Hannah!'

'I had to, or risked him disappearing, too. Then we'd never fi out who was following Alice.'

He tapped his pencil rhythmically on the notebook during t following silence.

'I'll tell you what I'll do,' he said finally. 'I'll get Pendleton drop into the pub on his way home and see if he can spot t Duffy chap and who he talks to. It's tenuous, but he's a g copper and I'll tell him it won't hurt his chances of promotion. I may even give him the cost of a pint.'

'That's something, I suppose,' Hannah muttered under her breath.

'What was that?' He narrowed his eyes.

'I said that's nice of you to bother.'

'Hmm.' He tossed the pencil onto the desk. 'And you did well,' he added, if reluctantly. 'Considering you aren't a copper.'

'I'm glad you're finally taking me seriously.'

'I always take you seriously,' he responded with a wry smile.

She gathered her things, conscious of the wet wool smell from her skirt. 'I asked Duffy to come to the bookshop the day after to tell me what happened.'

'I wish you hadn't done that, Hannah.' He sighed again and pushed a hand through his hair. 'Now both of them will know where to find you.'

'Oh, I didn't think of that.' Hannah's mood dipped, then brightened again. 'I'm flattered you're so concerned about my welfare.'

'Pure self-preservation,' he muttered. 'Violet would never forgive me if something happened to you. You realise I might have to charge this chap Duffy? He shouldn't be taking money to follow people.'

'Must you?' Her heart sank. 'Don't private detectives do that all the time?'

'Licensed ones do.'

'He's probably an innocent in all this, and dragging him to a police station will scare him off.' She recalled Archie suspected he wasn't as innocent as all that, but decided not to mention it. 'I can't help that.' He pointed an accusing finger at her. 'And they never tell you everything they know. Remember that.'

Hannah couldn't argue with that, but hoped he would not be so harsh with Duffy.

Suddenly a thought struck her. 'By the way, have you still got that note I gave you? The one I found near Sergeant Tillman's body?'

'That piece of scribble with random letters and numbers?' He sniffed, scraped his chair back up to the desk and rooted through the papers. 'I don't have the original. I gave that to Mr Clifford before he went off on one of his secret jaunts. I copied it out, so it's here somewhere. Ah, here it is.' He handed her a crumpled scrap of paper torn from a notebook.

'Really? When did Mr Clifford start working for the police?' She glanced at the scrawled writing, but it meant no more to her than the first time she saw it.

'He doesn't. Not officially. I was scrambling around for ideas, and this was a long shot. I remembered Mr Clifford likes puzzles, so I didn't see the harm and asked him to see what he could make of it. Why do you want it?'

'I don't think I do now. If it meant anything, Darius would have discovered it by now.'

'Might I offer you a lift anywhere? The motor is outside.' He rose, tucked the pile of papers beneath one arm and grabbed his jacket off the back of his chair.

'Offering the use of a police vehicle to the public?' Hannah feigned shock. 'Isn't that against the rules?'

'If anyone asks, I'll say you're under arrest.'

'That's not funny.' She pulled a face at him. 'And don't imagine I don't know you're seeing a lot of my Aunt Violet lately. And wasn't being ambiguous.'

'I don't know what you mean.' Chuckling, he guided her gently into the hallway.

'Thank you for the offer, but I drove myself here. Mr Clifford lent me his Swift while he's away. I'll be sorry to give it back. It so... *freeing* being able to be where I want, when I want. I've driven miles since he lent it to me.'

'Do you know how to fill the petrol tank?' he asked with a smirk.

Hannah froze. 'Um...'

Grinning, he slung an arm across her shoulders. 'Come on, I'll show you how.'

12

'You seem distracted this morning, Hannah.' Aunt Violet emerged from the reading corner, a contented Mr Bartleby in her arms. 'Are you worried about that young man?'

A steady flow of customers had meandered into the bookshop since nine, attended to by Archie and Aunt Violet, while Hannah dealt with the invoices, orders and bills.

'A little.' Hannah closed the ledger she was trying to reconcile, but the figures blurred in front of her eyes, making no sense.

During the reconstruction of the bookshop, the builders had dug a staircase into the unused cellar, turning it into a storage area for stock. The shop floor storeroom was now a kitchen and a private area that had become Archie's personal domain.

A second desk positioned beside the staircase for Hannah's use gave a clear view of the entire shop while offering privacy.

'There's been no sign of Duffy, then?' Archie mounted the steps and slid a cup, from which a spiral of steam arose, onto the desk.

'Not yet, but there's still time,' Hannah replied. 'I doubt he owns a watch.'

'Five bob says he won't turn up,' Archie said, retreating.

The hands of the clock on the far wall crawled towards eleven and with no sign of Duffy, Hannah wondered if Archie was right. Then the sound of the doorbell brought her to her feet. Her heartbeat racked up a notch as Inspector Farrell and Detective Pendleton strode past Archie at his desk near the door. With only a whispered word to Aunt Violet, they approached Hannah at her desk.

'Might we have a word, Miss Merrill?' Inspector Farrell said unnecessarily, his hat held in both hands.

'Um, yes, of course.' His formality alerted her that something was horribly wrong.

He waited until she was seated then tugged up his trousers at the thighs and sat on one of the leather tub chairs opposite.

Aunt Violet discreetly escorted the last customer to the door, turning the 'Open' sign to 'Closed'.

Archie pretended to rearrange books on a bookshelf within hearing range.

'What's happened?' Hannah asked, her gaze fixed on the ridge the young detective's hat had made in his wiry ginger hair.

Inspector Farrell inhaled a slow breath, his eyes troubled as if unsure how to begin. After a few loaded seconds, he said, 'Show her the sketch, Pendleton.'

'Sir.' The young detective froze as he bent to take a seat. Straightening, he removed a folded sheet of paper from a pocket and handed it to her.

Hannah's stomach churned as she stared at a pencil sketch of Duffy's youthful face, complete with wild, curly hair and lively, expressive eyes.

'Is this an accurate representation of the chap calling himself Duffy?' Detective Pendleton asked.

Hannah nodded, unable to speak, the lengthening silence

broken by the inspector's terse command. 'Get to it, Pendleton. This is hard enough as it is.'

'Yes, sir. Sorry, sir.' The policeman cleared his throat. 'Last evening at around six o'clock, I took up a position at The Coal Hole public house in the Strand. As instructed by my superior, Detective Inspector Farrell, I observed the actions of the subject calling himself—'

'You're not in court now, lad.' The inspector rubbed the back of his neck with one hand. 'No need to drag it out.'

'No, sir. Sorry, sir.' Pendleton coughed again before continuing 'The subject, I mean, the youth known as Duffy—'

'Why do you say, "known as"?' Hannah interrupted.

'Because we haven't officially identified him,' the inspector interrupted. 'He had nothing on him with his name on. Only a few coppers, ten Woodbines and a knife.'

'What sort of knife?' Hannah asked.

'Bakelite handle, six-inch blade. Cheaply made. It's no unusual where he comes from. Young lads carry them for protection, and to show how tough they are.'

'I see. Please, go on.' She gestured with a hand, wishing the would get on with whatever it was, while suspecting the worst.

The inspector made a noise in his throat and eased his jacket out from beneath him, evidently uncomfortable.

'The – er subject ordered a drink, then sat in a corner for qui a while. He was approached by a chap in an overcoat and homburg with whom he exchanged no more than a few words, when the man left, I continued to watch Duffy.'

'And the man he spoke to?' Inspector Farrell snapped.

'I was told to watch the youth, sir. But included a description the man in my report.'

The inspector huffed a frustrated breath and signalled him finish his account.

'Duffy stayed a few moments longer, and when he left. I followed, spotting him on the Savoy Steps that run down to the river alongside the pub. He wore a mustard coat and was hatless, so was easy to spot among the crowd, but – well, I lost sight of him.' Pendleton avoided his superior's eyes as the confidence drained out of him. 'I don't know what happened, but one second he was there, and the next he had gone.'

'He gave you the slip?' Hannah asked, dismayed their link to the man who might be responsible for Alice's disappearance had got away.

'That was my first assumption.' Pendleton's face flamed, and he twisted his hat in both hands. 'I heard a woman scream, and a scuffle taking place further down the steps. A crowd was gathered round the subject who lay motionless at the bottom.' Pendleton's mouth worked, but he seemed unable to form the words. 'The... the back of his head was caved in from the edge of the step.'

'He's dead?' Hannah clenched her fists in her lap, her hands clammy as she gripped the paper drawing. 'Did you see what happened?' She didn't know why she asked when he had already denied it.

'No, Miss.' Pendleton swallowed and licked his lips. 'But when I got there, I noticed he reeked of ale, so I assume he was unsteady on his feet and tripped on the steps. They're very steep.'

Hannah turned furious eyes on the inspector. 'Do you seriously think Duffy fell?'

'It would be quite a coincidence.' The inspector shot Pendleton a hard glance. 'And you know how I feel about those.'

'It's all my fault,' Hannah whispered. The drawing of Duffy's face seemed to mock her and she shoved it back at the inspector.

'You cannot blame yourself, Hannah.' Aunt Violet appeared from nowhere and grasped both Hannah's shoulders from behind. 'If it weren't for you, the police wouldn't know about Duffy.'

'And he might still be alive!' Hannah said, her chest tight.

'It's unfortunate and tragic.' Inspector Farrell's voice was sympathetic. 'It also makes things complicated since there's no firm connection between Alice Worsley-Brooke and this Duffy. He was alone at The Coal Hole.'

'There is one. I'm sure of it,' Hannah insisted. 'I suggest you ask Mr Gabriel Allardyce where he was last night. If anyone had a reason to kill Duffy, he did.'

'There's no evidence Mr Allardyce was responsible for Duffy's actions or the girl's disappearance. At this stage even questioning him about Duffy would get me dragged in front of my superintendent and ordered to back off until I have more evidence. A situation I don't wish to create – yet.'

'Yet?' Hannah grabbed onto the word. 'Then you're not dismissing me completely?'

'Not entirely, no. But you have your wish. I'll be stepping up my investigation of the whereabouts of Alice Worsley-Brooke.'

'It's a pity a missing heiress is worth the use of police time when a nurse is not.'

'Hannah!' Aunt Violet snapped, warningly.

'I'm sorry.' Hannah muttered, contrite. Giving anyone such awful news must be a part of his job he must dread. 'I only wanted to find Alice.'

'I appreciate that, and you'll be interested to learn I paid a visit to the lady at Glenfair Road this morning.'

'Mrs Allardyce? What did she say?' Hannah straightened.

'Don't get too excited. She said two women she had never met before marched into her house a couple of days ago and asked some impertinent questions about her niece.'

'Er...'

Aunt Violet exchanged a loaded look with Hannah, who said 'admit, that was us.'

'Wait a moment.' Aunt Violet bridled. 'She recognised me immediately. Called me by name.'

'Perhaps she was being discreet for your sake, Vi?' His expression showed he was enjoying himself.

'We didn't accuse her of anything,' Aunt Violet protested.

'I don't need to hear it.' He raised a hand as if he was directing traffic. 'Mrs Allardyce was strangely ambivalent about her niece's whereabouts. She maintained Alice is being entertained by friends somewhere in the Home Counties. As for the suggestion she was being followed, she almost had the butler toss me out on my ear for voicing something so crass.' He eased back in the chair, his legs stretched out in front of him. 'Either she's a remarkable actress, or she has no genuine affection for Miss Worsley-Brooke. She intimated it was all a misunderstanding, and her niece would return when she chooses.'

'Then she probably knows where Alice is.' Hannah's voice rose slightly.

'Eminently possible.' Inspector Farrell stood, replacing his hat. 'But I could hardly accuse her. In some echelons of society, a certain aversion exists for the police.' He stared pointedly at Detective Pendleton, who stepped aside smartly to allow him down to the main shop floor.

Pendleton turned back at the bottom. 'I'm really sorry about Duffy, Miss Merrill.'

'I'm sure you did your best, Detective.' The only person Hannah blamed other than herself, was the person who pushed Duffy down those steps. And she was convinced he was pushed.

'I knew that Duffy was a wrong 'un. I saw it in his eyes,' Archie said at her elbow.

'Possibly, Archie.' Aunt Violet rested a hip on the balustrade, her arm around Hannah's shoulder. 'But clearly he didn't throw himself down those steps.'

'We'll never know now, will we?' Hannah sighed. 'What made me think I could outwit a dangerous man, Aunt Violet?' Hannah sighed. 'Now I've caused that young man's death.'

'No, of course you didn't. That boy was on a dangerous path, accepting money to follow people. Do you really think Gabriel Allardyce had anything to do with it?'

'I don't know.' Hannah thought for a moment. 'Daphne seemed very keen for them to marry when we spoke to her. It might explain why Alice became a VAD and chose to live under an assumed name in lodgings.'

'Perhaps the elegant Mrs Allardyce is in league with her step-son? People will often do anything necessary where money is involved,' Aunt Violet said.

'Dare I keep searching for her? Or will it put her in more danger?' Hannah asked. 'Or are we both being used by the Allardyces?'

'In what way, used?' Aunt Violet shifted on the rail, apparently uncomfortable, but not willing to leave just yet.

'What if they've engineered all this and have Alice secreted away somewhere? Then when she turns up, alive, well, and married to Gabriel, any accusations we make about her being pressured into the marriage will be put down to hysteria.'

'That sounds overly elaborate, but not implausible, though its purpose eludes me. Alice is an heiress in her own right, so her cousin requires her consent to have access to the Worsley-Brooke money.'

'They could make her look unbalanced and incapable of managing her own affairs. She left home and went to live in lodgings, became a VAD against their wishes. Then she started hearing strange noises in the night and imagined she was being followed. Suppose they hired Duffy just to frighten her?'

'That's not all he was—' Archie began, silenced by a curt gesture from Aunt Violet.

'Alice is an orphan,' Hannah said. 'How hard would it be for her family to have her committed to a lunatic asylum so they can take charge of her money?' Her aunt's incredulous expression faded quickly into thoughtfulness. 'You see!' Hannah pointed a finger at her. 'It's not so outrageous, is it?'

'It's certainly a chilling concept, and where money is concerned, people do terrible things. How do we prevent it?' Her gaze drifted off. 'Although marriages aren't that simple to arrange. It takes three weeks for banns to be read and she's been gone less than two.'

'What about a special licence?' Hannah said. 'They've been granted since last year for servicemen about to be sent to the front who want to marry quickly. You can marry within a few days without having to post banns.'

'How do we stop it if we don't know where Alice is?'

The room went quiet as they pondered the thought and Archie went to greet a customer who had just entered the shop.

'Aunt Violet,' Hannah ventured, watching him. 'Do you know what it means for someone to be "carrying"?'

'I do, actually. It means they are armed with a weapon if some sort. Why do you ask?'

'Oh, no reason. I heard it somewhere.' Hannah's hands shook slightly as she remembered what Archie said about Duffy being involved in something dangerous.

She also owed Archie five bob.

13

'Don't worry, Ivy, I'll answer the door.' Hannah abandoned
uninspiring breakfast and entered the hall just as Ivy shou
something unintelligible from the scullery. Hannah smiled as
threw open the door.

'That's a wonderfully welcome smile. I hope it's for r
Darius' impressive frame stood beneath the wrought iron can
his blue eyes filled with amusement.

'You're back!' Her fingers on the door catch tightened as
emotion of the last two days welled, and she fought an impuls
throw herself into his arms. Pride won out.

'Day before yesterday. I would have called earlier, but I ha
few things to sort out at the War Office.'

'Then you had better come in, or you'll have the neighbo
talking.' She gestured him inside. 'They've taken an interest in
visitors since Inspector Farrell began parking his motorb
against the garden wall.'

'I always approve of giving the neighbours something to t
about over the teacups,' he said, laughing as he followed her i
the kitchen. She gathered up her half-eaten breakfast and star

to take it to the scullery when he placed a thin brown file onto the pine table. 'I brought you this.'

'What is it?' She paused, plate in hand and stared at it. 'Messrs Rasen, Falcon Limited, Shippers and Exporters,' she read aloud. The plate joined her teacup and a teapot.

'Ignore that.' Darius flipped open the front cover. 'It's um... an address we use at... well, use your imagination. Anyway, I'm about to take it to Inspector Farrell, but as you found the note, you might like to see it first.'

'Note?' Hannah frowned at the file then up at Darius. 'Oh, the one inside the book Sergeant Tillman was reading when he was killed. Inspector Farrell told me he had asked you to look at it, what with you being so good at puzzles.'

He nodded and flipped open the front cover. 'It's a list of names of men serving in the second unit of the Eighth Battalion, London Infantry Regiment.'

'Why have you brought this to me?' Hannah asked, taking a chair.

'Humour me.' He slid the file closer, a finger pointed at a name halfway down the page. 'Look at this.'

'Captain Peter Gorman, 8784355,' she read aloud, then frowned. 'I've never heard of him.'

'No, but you've seen this before.' He spread the crumpled note beside the file and pointed to a series of numbers beside the letters, 'P', 'O' and 'R' on the note.

'The numbers are the same, but what does it mean?' Hannah frowned.

'I thought it was a location co-ordinate or a code, but I was trying to be too clever. It's so simple I ought to have seen straight away that it's a regimental number. Captain Gorman's, in fact.'

Her pulse raced as a thought struck her. 'If he's a patient at Endell Street he could be Sergeant Tillman's murderer?'

'It was the first thing I checked, but he was never a patient there. In fact, he's dead. His body was discovered at Ypres last February and originally identified by his identity tags.'

'Then what has he to do with anything?'

'I'm getting to that. See here. Tillman and Captain Gorman were in the same regiment.'

Hannah picked up the scrap of paper again, her confusion turning to excitement. 'The Post Office Rifles.'

Darius nodded.

'The London Postal Workers who enlisted together at the beginning of the war formed their own regiment.' He straightened, and her heart rate settled again.

'Like the "Pals" regiments?'

During Kitchener's recruitment drives, men from the same area were given the opportunity to serve with their friends, neighbours and work colleagues instead of being sent to random battalions.

'But what's the connection, unless—' She ran her finger down the list of names, searching for a specific one. Her gaze latched onto it and she smiled. Shuffling the pages into the file, she tucked it under her arm.

'We need to go to Scotland Yard.' Hannah pushed back her chair and rushed past him into the hallway where she grabbed her coat from the hook with her free hand.

'Exactly what I said when I arrived,' Darius said, following. 'But why the urgency?' He took her coat from her and helped her put it on.

Rapid footsteps followed, and her aunt's head appeared over the upper balustrade. 'Why didn't you tell me Darius was here? I would have come down.'

'Good morning, Miss Edwards.' Darius called up to her. 'I hope you are well.'

'Don't be silly, it's Violet to you. Now what are you two up to?'

'No time for social niceties.' Hannah looked up at the landing as she shrugged into her coat. 'I know who killed Sergeant Tillman.' Tucking the file beneath her elbow, she grabbed her bag with her other hand. 'We're going to see Inspector Farrell.'

'Wait for me, I'm coming with you.' Her aunt ran down the stairs, fastening her jacket as she went. 'So, who is it?'

'I'll tell you both on the way.' Hannah hauled open the front door, flooding the hall with spring sunlight. 'We're about to make Inspector Farrell's day. Maybe even his career.' She glanced back over her shoulder to where Darius remained on the doorstep.

'Well?' Hannah demanded. 'Are you coming?'

'I would think so, since I did most of the work.' He slammed the door behind him and strode past them to open the gate before they reached it. 'Perhaps Inspector Farrell will stop making jokes about me sitting in gentlemen's clubs making up games to play on the enemy.'

'He was just teasing you. You perform a very important job.' Aunt Violet closed the gate behind her.

'Surely you aren't jealous of Inspector Farrell?' Hannah tossed the file onto the passenger seat and walked around to the driver's side door.

'Maybe a little.' Darius said, suddenly downcast. 'I can see the cut and thrust of investigative work appears more dynamic than my job.' His wry smile conveyed something she could not define. 'Do you ever boast about my important job?'

'Definitely not. I might tell the wrong person some vital secret and put your life in danger.' She went to open the driver's door but he shooed her away.

'Move over, I'll drive.'

'Why can't I drive?' Hannah pouted. 'I've been all over London while you were off on your secret mission. I'm quite capable.'

'I'm not suggesting otherwise.' He swung open the passenger side door and gestured her into the seat. 'Only I got up at dawn and took a hackney all the way here to deliver this file. And, well, to be fair, it *is* my motor car.'

'Spoilsport.'

'Will you two stop squabbling?' Aunt Violet swept past them and slid into the passenger seat ahead of Hannah. 'You can take the jump seat. I'm far too mature to perch on the back like a piece of luggage.'

Hannah tutted in annoyance, but bundled her full skirt around her knees and squeezed into the tiny jump seat. She was barely settled when the motor car sprang forward with a roar, so she had to clamp a hand on her hat or risk it ending up in the river.

* * *

'Excuse me, Miss, but you can't go in there!' The officer outside Inspector Farrell's office attempted to block Hannah's way. 'How did you get past the desk sergeant?'

'He was busy, and we didn't want to waste his time,' Aunt Violet explained, as Hannah sidestepped him, her fist lifted to knock.

'I wouldn't bother trying to stop them if I were you,' Darius leaned in close and whispered to the bemused policeman. 'The younger one can be quite intimidating.'

The officer scratched his head and turned away, muttering 'Well, I ain't taking responsibility.'

'Intimidating?' Hannah glared at Darius, who shrugged. There was no time to pursue the matter, as the commotion had brought the inspector to the door.

'What's going on?' He looked from Hannah to Darius an

finally to Aunt Violet, his anger visibly melting. 'Miss Edwards! What can I do for you?'

'There are three of us.' Hannah shoved past her aunt, forcing the inspector a pace backwards. 'We need to speak with you, and it's important.'

'Why don't you come in?' He rolled his neck inside his collar and returned to his desk. 'Take a seat.' He directed this at Aunt Violet, who was already seated, leaving Darius to close the door behind them.

Hannah placed the brown folder on the desk while Aidan dragged two chairs from the corner of the room, settled Hannah into one, but remained standing.

'And what is that?' Inspector Farrell peered at the file, then back at Aunt Violet.

'I've no idea.' She shrugged. 'Having come late to this party nothing has been revealed yet.'

'We'll get to that.' Hannah moved the file to one side and sat. 'I now how Sergeant Tillman was killed and by whom.'

'This should be interesting.' Aunt Violet took the chair Darius eld out for her, her bag placed squarely on her lap.

Darius took up a position behind both of them, and waited.

'Suppose...' Hannah dragged out the word, 'the murderer was a staff and only pretended to leave the building when they ished work that night? But actually they were hiding in the sement?'

'In the Johnnie Walker ward?' The inspector's mouth curved o a knowing smile. 'Of course, that ward wasn't in use that ;ht. Keep going, Hannah.'

'Dinah said the door was locked when it shouldn't have been. guess is, the murderer hid in there before going to the library ere Sergeant Tillman was waiting. Having shot him, they locked the door, put the key back on its hook then returned to the Johnnie Walker Ward for the rest of the night.'

'Why conceal it?' Aunt Violet asked. 'Why not find the sergeant's body right away?'

'The gates are kept locked at night, so if the alarm was raised sooner, the police would have stopped anyone going in or out. The killer began work as normal the next morning and claimed they weren't there when Tillman was killed.'

'The question is, why was he killed?' the inspector asked. 'The only people who disliked him enough to wish him harm were still at the front.'

'I would have thought that was obvious,' Hannah said. 'He was blackmailing whoever killed him. And she used the sleeping powders that went missing to drug the patients' cocoa.'

'She?' Aunt Violet demanded. 'Hannah, do you know who the killer is?'

'Sister Marion Kerr!' Hannah and the detective said together. At Hannah's surprised start he pointed a finger at her. 'You aren't the only one who can put these things together. I'm the detective, remember.'

'But why was the sergeant blackmailing Sister Kerr?' Aunt Violet asked.

'Darius will explain. He's the one who put this together.' She nodded to where Darius had straddled an empty chair.

'That file is a list of the men in Sergeant Tillman's platoon who fought at Ypres last February,' Darius began. 'The War Office sent it over a few days ago, but I didn't see it until I arrived back in London.' He pulled the file towards him. 'Sergeant Tillman worked at Camden Post Office before joining the army.' Inspector Farrell started to speak, but Darius raised his hand, halting him. 'But you already know that. You also know his supervisor described him as a difficult man to work with, but he made particular enemies. He bullied his subordinates, apparently. Especially this man.' He pointed to a name halfway down the page.

The inspector frowned at the list, then his eyebrows rose. 'Good heavens.'

'Exactly. Private Albert Kerr,' Hannah read aloud over Darius' shoulder. 'He was reported killed in action, 26 February 1916. Sister Marion Kerr's husband. She has his postman's tunic hanging in her hall.'

'Might I ask what you were doing in Sister Kerr's house?' Inspector Farrell's eyes narrowed at Hannah for a second. 'Don't bother answering that. Well, go on then. You were saying...'

'Most London area postal staff joined a regiment they called—'

'The Post Office Rifles,' the inspector finished for her. 'Yes, yes, I'm aware of that. But Albert Kerr was killed some time before Tillman's murder, so I'm not sure where it gets us.'

'Sergeant Tillman and Albert Kerr not only worked at the same Post Office, they served in the same regiment. Let's assume Albert Kerr mentioned Tillman's name to his wife and the fact she worked at Endell Street.'

'That's a bit of a leap,' Inspector Farrell tossed his pencil onto the desk and folded his arms. 'But plausible. Go on.'

'Sergeant Tillman was injured in the same attack in which Albert Kerr was reported killed in action,' Darius said. 'He was Albert Kerr's commanding officer, so it's possible Marion might have believed he had sent him into danger unnecessarily.'

'Which we cannot prove with both men dead,' Inspector Farrell said. 'We'd have to find a survivor of the same attack and hope they saw something. If we accuse Mrs Kerr of shooting the sergeant, she'll claim it was pure coincidence that Tillman was admitted to Endell Street. And where would Sister Kerr get an army issue revolver? The RAMC men aren't armed, their weapons taken off them before they arrive at the hospital.'

'It was the gun Albert Kerr brought back from the war.' Hannah dropped her gem into the conversation and sat back, waiting for them to catch up.

'Kerr was a private,' Inspector Farrell pointed out. 'Squaddies aren't issued with revolvers, only rifles. And anyway, Kerr didn't come back from the war.'

'It wasn't his gun. He took it from this man.' She pulled the file towards her and placed a finger on a name lower down the page.

'I thought *I* was going to explain.' Darius adopted a look of feigned disappointment.

'Sorry,' Hannah murmured, clearing her throat.

'Captain Peter Gorman,' Inspector Farrell read aloud. 'He's marked as missing, assumed killed in action at the same attack as Kerr, so—' He raised his gaze to Hannah's, then nodded. 'I see. Private Albert Kerr isn't dead.'

'And the penny drops.' Darius' deep chuckle made Hannah's spine tingle. 'Who said women shouldn't be police detectives?'

'It wasn't me,' Aunt Violet said.

'So.' The inspector pulled a notepad towards him. 'Sergeant Tillman observed Private Kerr swap Captain Gorman's identity tags with his own on the battlefield?'

'That's exactly what he did.' Hannah nodded. 'He probably took his uniform jacket too. As a private roaming the countryside he would have been subject to questioning by any high-ranking officer he came across. That he had a handgun too would also be suspicious. Privates carry rifles.'

'How very astute of you, Hannah.' Aunt Violet directed a triumphant smile at the inspector.

'It wasn't all me. Darius found the list,' Hannah reminded him.

'So Kerr is a deserter.' Inspector Farrell spun a pencil between the fingers of his right hand as an aid to thought. 'And he's been holed up at his house in Percy Circus ever since he got back?'

'That's our assumption.' Hannah exchanged a look with Darius, who nodded. 'Protected by his wife, and successfully so, until Sergeant Tillman tried to profit from it.'

'Has the body in France been confirmed as Captain Gorman's?' Aunt Violet asked.

'I was about to ask that.' Inspector Farrell winked at Aunt Violet, a gesture Hannah pretended not to see.

'The War Office have agreed to look into it.' Darius consulted the file again. 'The body was interred in the Cuinchy Cemetery, so will be exhumed. According to his army record, Albert Kerr has a puckered scar on his left tibia. A result of an accident with a plough at his father's farm when he was fourteen. What's the betting the body at Cuinchy bears no such scar?'

'And then there's this.' Hannah pulled the white feather she found in the library from her bag and held it up.

'A feather?' Inspector Farrell frowned. 'Aren't those being handed to civilians as cowardice for not enlisting?'

'Not this one.' Hannah leaned back in her chair and smiled. 'I believe Marion used a pillow to muffle the gunshot. It must have taken her a while to collect these up before she left the library afterwards.' She twisted the feather in her fingers. 'Only she missed one.'

'Well done, darling.' Aunt Violet squeezed Hannah's shoulder. 'This Sister Kerr is nothing if not efficient. What a shame she couldn't have put all that ingenuity to something less... criminal?'

'I have to agree.' Inspector Farrell turned an admiring smile on Aunt Violet. 'And although I must congratulate you, Hannah, I can't give you the credit for any of this,' he reminded her. 'My superintendent won't want to hear your part in an official investigation.'

'I'm aware of that.' Hannah sighed, though the thrill of having solved the murder was delicious enough. 'If Sister Kerr had poisoned the sergeant, say with morphia, it would have pointed straight to a member of staff.'

'I always believed it was the staff, my difficulty was in locating which one.' Inspector Farrell rose abruptly, the back of his chair hitting the wall with a bang as he headed for the door. 'Constable!' His voice echoed in the corridor. 'Find Detective Pendleton and tell him to scrounge up three men and report to the main gate in five minutes.' He turned back, changed his mind, and poked his head round the jamb again. 'Oh, and I'll also need a police van to pick up two criminals as well.'

'Now all the excitement is about to happen, I expect you'll send us home?' Hannah said, despondent.

'Maybe not.' The inspector turned back from the door. 'To show my appreciation for your diligence, you can accompany me to make the arrest.' He raised a finger in front of her face. 'As observers only. No meddling, is that clear?'

'Perfectly.' Hannah suppressed a triumphant smile as she turned on Darius.

'Does he mean it?' Aunt Violet asked, as the inspector's rapid footsteps receded down the corridor.

'I'm not sure, but I'm not waiting for him to rescind it.' Hannah leapt to her feet and darted after him, both Darius and her aunt close on her heels.

he journey took longer than they expected. Without the benefit
f police bells clearing their way through traffic, horses and hack-
eys delayed them at every junction. Percy Circus was blocked by
e type of police van nicknamed a Black Maria and Inspector
rrell's police car. Leaving the Swift at the kerb fifty yards away,
ey walked the rest of the way to number twelve and paused at
e bottom of the steps.

The occupants of nearby houses lined up beside the railings,
men in aprons and men in workmen's jackets and cap; even a
ker's boy straddled his bicycle.

Marion Kerr stood on her doorstep, her arms folded as she and
pector Farrell conducted a conversation, while Detective
dleton was flanked by two forbidding looking police officers
rby.

'I can't hear a thing from out here,' Aunt Violet said, making
effort to lower her voice. 'Let's get closer.'

'Perhaps not.' Darius placed a hand on Hannah's arm, halting

'But any interference could make things difficult for the
ector.'

'Don't be stuffy.' Aunt Violet lightly slapped his shoulder. 'He said we could observe, so let's observe.' She squeezed between him and Hannah and glided up the steps.

An officer at the gate barred their way with an upheld arm as she approached but, giving him a wide smile which seemed to startle him, she swept away his arm with a confident, 'We're with Detective Inspector Farrell.' The policeman stared after her and didn't seem to notice when Hannah and Darius followed.

Marion had planted her feet apart on her front step, effectively blocking entry into the house. 'And you're certain you are unaware of the whereabouts of Miss Alice Dalglish, Mrs Kerr?' Aidan's tone was calm and non-threatening.

'How do *I* know where she went?' Marion's shrug dismissed him. 'My lodgers come and go as they please.'

'I thought we were here about her husband?' Hannah turned her face away and whispered to Darius, 'Why is he asking about Alice?'

'The inspector clearly hopes she doesn't know why he's here,' Darius replied. 'If her husband isn't in the house Farrell will have to leave and then she'll be able to warn him and then he'll disappear.'

Hannah agreed, though the way Marion guarded the door convinced her Albert Kerr must be somewhere inside the house.

Their off-stage conversation finally alerted Marion to their presence as her gaze skimmed over Aunt Violet and settled Hannah. 'What are *you* doing here?'

'We're still looking for Alice, Mrs Kerr,' Hannah said. 'Are you certain you haven't seen her?'

'I told him the same as I told you.' Marion gestured to detectives. 'Alice left days ago.'

'We're wasting time,' Inspector Farrell snapped, and waved the two uniformed officers. 'One of you come with me, and you he pointed a finger at the second man '—stay here and make sure Mrs Kerr doesn't leave.'

'Hey! You can't just march into my house like...' Marion's protest tailed off as the policemen strode past her and thumped up the stairs. She followed them inside, continuing her tirade that they had no right to treat law-abiding people in such a manner, all of which the officer ignored.

Seconds later, the sound of breaking wood, followed by triumphant shouts and a scuffle came from somewhere above them.

Marion turned and made a break for the front door. She started to descend the front steps, elbowing Hannah in the stomach as she passed. However, the officer at the gate grabbed her arm as she made to fight her way past him. At the sudden pain to Hannah's midriff, she doubled over, losing her balance and fell.

'Hannah!' Aunt Violet reached for her, but Darius got there first, caught her around the waist from behind and righted her. His reassuring smile as he asked her if she was all right sent heat into her cheeks. She adjusted her hat, nodded to show she was fine, but felt bereft when he released her.

Further scuffling from the landing announced Detective Pendleton and an officer manhandling a scrawny man in rolled-up shirtsleeves down the stairs.

'He was holed up in the attic just like you'd thought, Inspector,' Detective Pendleton announced, triumphant. 'Had a truckle and bedding up there, too. Been there a while, I'd say.'

'Not Bert. Not my Bert!' Marion's face twisted in anguish and she wrapped her hands tightly around the newel post. 'Hasn't he been through enough? Why can't you leave him alone?'

The captive kept his head down and barely glanced at his wife, whose sobs had receded. She stumbled after them, crying. 'I'm sorry, Bert. I didn't tell them. I swear I didn't.'

Once, Hannah would have been sympathetic to the woman's distress, but the knowledge she was in fact a murderer smothered any instinct to offer comfort.

Inspector Farrell gestured Hannah and her aunt into the kitchen-cum-parlour where she had been served tea on her first visit. The room looked shabbier than she remembered it, and claustrophobic with so many people crowded inside. Hannah and Aunt Violet commandeered chairs, while Darius remained on his feet.

Detective Pendleton leaned his back against the wall, his arms folded in front of him. Inspector Farrell spread both hands on the surface of the scarred pine table where Marion sat, her sobs reduced to an occasional sniff and hiccough.

'This is Private Albert Kerr, a fact of which I am sure you are aware.' Inspector Farrell inclined his head at Hannah in silent congratulation, though an answer was hardly necessary after Marion's outburst.

'Aye. Thass me.' Albert Kerr stood with his back to the fireplace, where the remnants of a fire had burned to white ash.

His voice was lower than Hannah expected, resigned but defiant. About five feet seven inches tall, he had medium brown hair, thick eyebrows and a badly cut moustache beneath a chiselled nose. His heavy-lidded, wide brown eyes were probably animated when he smiled, but were now dull. Whatever fight left in him had fled, and he stood with his shoulders slumped and stared at the floor, darting uneasy glances at each of the six-foot-tall policeman who stood on either side of him.

The inspector launched into a rapid speech about holding Private Albert Kerr in custody on charges of desertion, dereliction of duty and several others that went over her head. Albert Kerr acknowledged nothing, didn't even speak until the inspector said, 'Miss Worsley-Brooke—'

'Never heard that name,' he said, and stared at a spot over the inspector's head.

'You knew her as Alice Dalglish.' When he did not respond, the inspector turned to Marion. 'Where is she, Mrs Kerr?'

'How should I know?' Marion's upper lip curled and she snorted. 'I've already told you – she packed a bag and left.' She cocked her chin at Hannah. 'I told *her*.'

'I know what you told me,' Hannah said. 'Did you deliberately drive her away?'

'Don't know what you're talking about.' Marion lifted her chin. 'She was a flighty thing and scared easily. Even before the sergeant was killed, she thought someone was following her. Why would I do anything to frighten her away? I needed the money, what with Bert to feed.'

'And I never laid eyes on the girl,' Albert added.

'I doubt that, and you must have known she lived here,' the inspector addressed Albert. 'It's difficult to keep still for hours at a time. She probably heard you moving about. Is that what frightened her?'

Albert shrugged. His disinterested gaze drifted to the range, then the floor again, but not once did he look at his wife.

Hannah's pulse raced as another piece of the puzzle fell into place. 'That's why you sent out your laundry,' she blurted. 'The delivery boy brought it back that day I was here!' Why hadn't she realised it before?

'Laundry?' The inspector frowned. 'What's that got to do with anything?'

'You have been busy with your snooping, haven't you, Miss Busybody?' Marion sneered.

'Quiet!' the inspector snapped. 'Go on, Miss Merrill.'

'A widow with a single female lodger couldn't risk allowing

Alice or the neighbours to see a man's clothes on her washing line.'

'Good observation, Hannah.' The inspector smiled and nodded. 'Not sure I would have put that together myself.'

'I did that girl no harm,' Marion insisted.

'Yet you told Miss Worsley-Brooke you would implicate her in the murder of Sergeant Tillman by claiming she drugged the men on St Anne's ward that night.' Inspector Farrell said.

'Tillman!' Marion spat, her eyes hard a second before emptying into resignation. She clamped her lips shut and turned her head away.

'No matter.' Bored with the conversation, Inspector Farrell straightened. 'I'm sure we'll persuade you to be more co-operative down at the Yard.'

'All right!' Marion propped her elbows on the table, her face cupped in her hands. 'I had to, don't you see? That man bullied the younger soldiers and was rude to the nurses. He even tried to blackmail me!'

'Hardly justification for murder, but go on,' the detective prompted.

'He was Bert's boss at Camden Post Office and made his life a misery.' Her gaze darted to her husband, but he ignored her, much less acknowledge her. 'He turned up at Endell Street a few weeks back. Told me he knew Bert wasn't dead, and if I wanted him to stay quiet, I had to pay him.'

'How could Tillman know your husband had made it home to England?' Inspector Farrell split a look between Marion and Albert.

'I didn't ask him!' Marion snorted. 'I just told him to get lost because Bert was dead. I thought he was bluffing.'

'But he wasn't?' the inspector said, his voice softening.

Marion shook her head. 'Said he'd have a quiet word with the

War Office anyway. He could always claim he'd been wrong. I couldn't risk it.'

'How did he discover you worked at Endell Street?'

'That was my fault.' Albert stared at the floor. 'Marion wrote to me in France and told me about the job. Tillman must have heard me telling the lads how proud I was of her.'

'Tillman wouldn't give up.' Marion sighed, leaning back in the chair that creaked beneath her. 'We arranged to meet in the library so I could pay him, but I knew he wouldn't be satisfied with one pay-off, so I took the gun Bert brought home from France in case he got shirty. I pretended to leave at the end of my shift, and hid in the Johnnie Walker ward until after lights out. Tillman was sitting in a chair on the stage when I got there with this smug expression. Said it was a good start to our association. I knew he'd try to bleed me dry, so I picked up a cushion from a chair and shot him.' Marion's eyes held no remorse, only triumph.

'I told you, you didn't have to kill him, you daft bint!' Her husband's furious snarl brought all eyes in the room towards him.

'What else was I going to do?' Marion stared at him as if they were alone in the room. 'With that Dalglish girl's regular rent money we almost had enough to leave the country. I wasn't going to let him ruin that!'

'That telegram from the War Office saying I was dead meant Tillman couldn't prove anything. All you had to do was keep yer mouth shut, woman!' Albert made a lunge at his wife, but was held back at the last second by the two policemen. 'I could have hidden somewhere else until—'

'Until what, Mr Kerr?' Inspector Farrell raised an enquiring eyebrow, but Albert stayed silent. 'Not that it matters now. You'll be going to a military prison, which will make a police station cell seem positively inviting.' He cocked his chin at the officers. 'Take them both away.'

'Wait!' Hannah said. 'Marion, did you take money from Alice besides her rent?'

'We've already established this was all about money.' Darius spoke for the first time since they entered the house. 'You don't need to ask that question. Leave it to the inspector.'

'No, I want to know for myself.' Hannah turned furious eyes on Marion. 'Well, did you?'

'She told me she thought someone was following her. I... I agreed to help her, that's all.'

The inspector held up a hand at the approaching officer, halting him. 'What form did this help take?' He bent over her, his face inches from hers. 'What did you do?'

Her face crumpled. 'I... I told her I could get someone to talk to him. Get him to stop.'

'How much did she pay you to organise that?' When she did not reply, he added, 'I could always add extortion to your crimes.'

'A few pounds.' Marion shrugged. 'She had plenty to spare, so never missed it. It was Bert's idea.' She stared at her husband accusingly. 'It would have worked. That chap wouldn't have stuck around once he dealt with him—'

'Dealt with him, how?' Hannah asked, just as a thought struck her. 'Your husband killed Duffy?' Albert started to speak, but she added, 'That was the name of the boy who was following Alice.'

'I didn't kill no one!' Albert launched himself forward. His chin jutted at Hannah, but he was jerked backward by one of the officers. Instantly he relaxed, his chin lowered to avoid the inspector's eye. 'The newspapers said it was an accident.'

Marion glared at her husband, sending him a message Hannah could not interpret, as he was roughly bundled out of the room, at which Marion promptly burst into tears, which had little effect on the inspector.

'Take Mrs Kerr to the van, Pendleton,' he snarled, with barely concealed disgust.

* * *

'That wasn't nearly as satisfying as I imagined,' Aunt Violet said, as the room emptied leaving the three of them in the heavy silence. 'Though I have no idea why.'

'It was awful.' Hannah longed to get out of the plain but homely parlour with its old, but well cared for dresser filled with china teacups of varying patterns and sizes. Marion must have spent years collecting them from markets and second-hand shops. Their intricate flowers and tarnished gold rims seemed to mock her.

The atmosphere took a strange turn from the thrill of the chase, by Marion's heartbreaking sobs and Albert's open defeat.

'They were bound to be caught, Hannah,' Darius whispered, as if sensing her discomfort. 'None of this is your fault.' With a firm hand in the middle of her back, he guided her into the hall and past the Post Office jacket on its hook by the door. In the street, the Kerr's neighbours had formed a semi-circle on the pavement, their expressions varying from curious to disdainful, but with little sympathy directed at the Kerrs. The muttering grew louder as Marion and Albert were helped none too gently up the step into the police van.

One policeman followed inside, the other secured the rear door. He headed for the driver's cab, but Inspector Farrell stopped him with a shout.

'Officer! Come with me. Miss Worsley-Brooke's rooms might give a clue where she went.'

Hannah was about to tell him she had already looked there, but changed her mind.

'There's not much else we can do here,' Darius said from behind her. 'We might as well go.'

'In a moment.' Hannah held up a hand. 'I'll check if Inspector Farrell needs anything else from us, then I'll join you. I won't be long.'

She caught up with him on the second landing outside the open door to Alice's rooms. The wardrobe doors were flung wide, the contents in a rough pile on the brass-framed bed while an officer stood at the window making notes.

'What are you doing?' Hannah asked, forgetting why she was there herself.

'The Kerrs won't be coming back anytime soon. Maybe never. I'll arrange to have all these things packed up and stored as the property of Miss Worsley-Brooke.' He tapped the policeman on his shoulder, whose back was turned towards them. 'List everything, and don't forget the chest of drawers over there. That bureau, too.'

'Where will they take it all?' Hannah stared at the ensuing chaos.

'A storage facility somewhere, I expect,' the officer shrugged, his attention drifting elsewhere.

Hannah surveyed the mountain of exquisite lace, taffeta, and velvet dresses accumulating on the bed coverlet. Underclothes, gowns, shawls, cloaks and gloves, hair clips and ribbons were tossed haphazardly onto a peacock-blue negligee. Among them was a small sheaf of letters held together with a blue ribbon.

The first envelope was addressed to Miss Alice Worsley-Brooke at Glenfair Road, in strong, looped handwriting characteristic of a man's hand. From an admirer perhaps?

The date on the postmark was partly obscured by what appeared to be mud, but she could make out the date May 1915 which showed they were probably written by her brother, Rafe, sent from the front. Sadness filled her at the thought of this last correspondence from a lost soldier being stored in a damp warehouse. What if Alice returned home to find them gone, possibly lost in some anonymous depository?

The officer was busy with his notebook and Inspector Farrell's footsteps were receding on the stairs. Hannah slid the letters into her bag. Descending the steep staircase a moment later, she spotted Aunt Violet and Inspector Farrell in deep conversation on the pavement while Darius hovered at the front door.

The inspector nodded as she reached them, murmured something to her aunt she did not catch, and approached Darius.

'Thank you for your assistance with those military records.' The inspector took Darius' hand in a firm grip. 'My superintendent will be delighted, and perhaps now we can all look forward to a restful Easter break.'

'What happens to the Kerrs now?' Hannah asked, joining them.

'The fact Mrs Kerr took a revolver with her and removed the key from the porter's desk to lock the library door afterwards, indicated she had it all planned. The judge won't be sympathetic if she plays the victim. A good afternoon's work all round, I'd say.' He snapped a salute to them before striding to where Detective Pendleton waited beside the black police vehicle.

'Everything all right, Hannah?' Aunt Violet asked as she led the way back to Darius' motor car.

'Yes, everything is fine.' Hannah stared after the inspector. 'He's very self-satisfied.'

'And why shouldn't he be?' Darius settled into the driving seat beside her aunt, leaving Hannah on her perch in the jump seat. 'He's just made two significant arrests.'

'The capture of a murderer and an army deserter will certainly enhance his career,' Aunt Violet said, as the engine burst into life.

'And what were you saying to Inspector Farrell before we left?'

Hannah tapped her aunt's shoulder as the motor car negotiated the central railed garden, then headed towards Kings Cross, a hand clamped on her hat to prevent it being tossed into the road.

'Nothing that would interest you.' Aunt Violet stared straight ahead. Hannah could only see a slip of her profile from where she sat, but Violet seemed extremely pleased with herself.

As they approached Hammersmith Bridge, Hannah straightened as a thought struck her. 'Duffy's death wasn't an accident.'

'What did you say?' Darius glanced back, shouting over the buffeting wind just as a bicycle appeared from a side turning and swerved towards them.

Hannah gasped. 'Oh, watch out!'

'Don't panic, I've seen him.' Darius swung the motor car expertly to the right, missing the bicycle's rear wheel by an inch.

'Albert lied,' Hannah shouted above the wind.

'He probably did.' Aunt Violet twisted in her seat. 'Don't worry. Aidan will get the truth out of him once they are back at the Yard.'

'I forgot about the beer. Don't you remember, Aunt Violet? When Duffy was found, Pendleton said Duffy smelled of beer.'

'I don't actually, but what's odd about that? He'd been sitting in a pub for over an hour.'

'Duffy hated beer,' Hannah shouted. 'He never drank it. Why would he smell of it?'

Darius eased his foot off the accelerator and glanced at her over his shoulder. 'Do you want me to turn around?'

Hannah shook her head. 'There's no point. Inspector Farrell will have left by now. I'll call him in the morning.'

'If you're sure. I'd be happy to drive you to the Yard and meet him there.'

'No. It can wait.' Hannah relaxed back in her seat.

It was not until Darius brought the vehicle to a jarring halt at the gate of Hannah's house that any of them spoke again.

Aunt Violet unfolded her tall frame from the bucket seat and pulled down her jacket. 'I don't know about the two of you, but I could do with a drink.'

'I'm game.' Darius dropped his driving gloves into his cap and hurled them onto the driving seat. He strode to the gate and held it open for both ladies.

Hannah was about to mention it was still afternoon but kept silent. The sight of her own front door made her emotional with its solid familiarity after all the drama.

'What about you, Hannah?' Aunt Violet asked.

'I could handle a sherry.' Perhaps it might help her get Marion's expression when she saw Albert being led away out of her head.

15

The next day being Sunday and Ivy's day off, Hannah knew better than to wake her aunt before ten o'clock, so she prepared a scratch breakfast for herself, while the previous day's events played in her head. Marion's fate was a foregone conclusion, and with her husband facing the fate of an army deserter, the thought neither of them would survive the year sent a chill through her.

Her aunt's invitation to for Darius to join them for a drink had extended into the evening and an omelette supper, ending late with a promise to repeat it soon. Hannah had forgotten about Alice's letters, but was determined to tell her aunt about them as an idea germinated.

She collected the newspapers from the mat and was soon absorbed in a report of how three aircraft of the British Royal Naval Air Service bombed Constantinople and Adrianople. 'I wonder what it's like to fly in an aircraft,' she murmured to herself, just as the sound of rapid footsteps on the stairs brought her head up to where Aunt Violet passed the kitchen door on the way to the sitting room.

'Have you seen my handbag?' she called out.

Scraping back her chair, Hannah abandoned her fantasy of soaring through a blue sky and followed. Her aunt wore an emerald-green day dress that skimmed her slender curves, her swan-like neck encircled with onyx beads and pearls on a gold chain.

'I was about to make more coffee. Would you like some?' Hannah asked, while admiring her aunt's clear complexion that retained its youthful glow, and her dancer's build. She hoped whatever family trait that kept her aunt so well-preserved at forty might be passed on to her.

'No, thank you, darling. I'm on my way to luncheon with the Pattersons.'

'Luncheon?' Hannah glanced at the clock, surprised to see it was already past eleven.

'Ah, here it is.' Her aunt dragged the offending item into the open and peered inside. 'By the way, I spoke to Aidan on the telephone this morning, when you were having your bath.'

'I'm still not used to you calling him that.' Hannah leaned a shoulder against the door frame. 'Was he still gloating about yesterday?'

'You cannot blame him. It's quite a coup and will do wonders for his chances of promotion. He asked if he might call in on us this afternoon.'

'He's coming here?' Hannah scanned the room for anything out of place, but Ivy had done her usual expert job. 'Shall I make myself scarce?'

'What? Oh no, at least, not on this occasion.' She dropped the handbag on the sofa and joined it, lounging with her feet up on a footstool. 'He says he has something to tell us. Apparently, after some vigorous questioning, Albert Kerr made a full confession up to the part about Duffy. He maintains Alice had left the house days before he could put his scare job in place.'

'Of course he's going to say that. He's hardly likely to confess, is he?' Hannah chose not to ask what 'vigorous questioning' entailed, although she had a fair idea.

Seeing her pained expression, her aunt straightened and planted both feet on the floor. 'I forgot, you're still upset about Duffy, aren't you?'

'Don't say his name, Aunt Violet. Each time I hear it, my stomach knots. And if Albert Kerr didn't kill him, then who did? We still have no idea of the person who employed him to follow Alice. Did they kill Duffy because they knew he had spoken to me and didn't want him identified. Unless—'

'Unless what?'

'Suppose Alice saw or heard something that implicated Marion in Sergeant Tillman's murder? She would want to make sure Alice kept her mouth shut, wouldn't she?'

'Or Alice could have discovered Albert was in the house, and that's why she ran away?'

'You mean the noises she heard?' Hannah nodded. 'Possibly. But why didn't Marion stick to the story about Albert being killed in action at Ypres? She could have claimed ignorance of his desertion. She even had a telegram to prove his death.' She sighed. 'It's all so sad. Marion might have saved herself, but she couldn't save Albert.'

'With both the Kerrs in custody, it's all academic now.' Aunt Violet bent and swept her shoes from the floor. 'Now, I must go, or I shall be late.'

'Before you do, I...' Hannah hesitated.

'I know that tone.' Her aunt swung her shoes in one hand by the heels. 'What's wrong? And don't say nothing. I know you too well.'

'Yesterday, when I was with Darius at the Kerrs' house, Aidan was having Alice's things removed. He didn't want to leave them among the Kerrs' belongings in the event of a court case and probate.'

'Sounds like he's already got that pair hanged,' Aunt Violet said, then flushed. 'Sorry, that was inappropriate.'

'But accurate. I watched a cack-handed policeman toss all Alice's beautiful belongings into a heap as though they were nothing. As if she was already dead so her things didn't matter any more.'

'Did you see anything interesting among them?' Aunt Violet's wry sideways betrayed her.

'You know I did.' Hannah pushed away from the door frame, plucked her handbag from beside the sofa and retrieved the letters. 'I couldn't stop myself. They were just lying there on the bed.'

'Show me.' Aunt Violet placed her shoes back on the floor, took the letters from Hannah and skimmed through the envelopes.

'I'm guessing they were sent by her brother from the front before he died.'

'Well, I don't imagine he sent them through a medium.' Aunt Violet's lip twitched.

'Not funny.' Hannah rolled her eyes. 'I couldn't stand the thought of them being shoved into a storage box in a basement warehouse somewhere if Alice isn't found. Or if she—'

'Don't complete that sentence, darling. I know what you mean. And it was a nice sentiment. Daphne Allardyce might be glad of them as they were written by her precious Rafe.'

'Don't talk about Alice as if she's dead. Anyway, you're missing the point.' Hannah lowered herself onto the sofa beside her. 'They were sent to Alice at her aunt's house, but see the last one here? It's got another address scribbled on the back.'

'Number eight, Carlyle Mansions, Cheyne Walk, Chelsea,' Aunt Violet read aloud, then shrugged. 'A friend, perhaps?'

'Or where Alice went when she left Marion's house?'

'Possibly.' Aunt Violet tapped the letters against the palm of her other hand. 'You should show these to Aidan.'

'I would have, but he was so smug, stomping around the house in Clerkenwell giving orders like a circus master. He's taking full credit for the Kerrs being in custody.'

'He's a police officer, Hannah. That's what he does.'

'I know – but he doesn't know about this address. Maybe Alice is there?'

'It's possible, I suppose, but if Aidan finds out about it, he won't be pleased about you swiping evidence.'

'He was right there in the room.' A lie, but a small one for which she felt no remorse. 'If he wanted them, he could have taken them.' She took the letters back and replaced them in her bag. 'Shall we pay a visit to Cheyne Walk? It would be a feather in our cap if we find Alice before the inspector does.'

'It's very tempting.' A mischievous gleam entered her aunt's eyes. 'If we go now, we could be back in plenty of time for his visit.'

'I thought you were lunching with the Pattersons today?'

'It's a flexible arrangement. There will be scads of guests, so I doubt I'll be missed. Shall we take my Sunbeam or Darius' Swift?'

'Darius took it back last night, don't you remember? I'm going to miss it. That motor car gave me such freedom, I could go anywhere without having to deal with cabs and trains.'

'You should buy one of your own.' Aunt Violet hunted for her shoes where they had been kicked under the sofa and slid her feet into them.

'Huh! Can you imagine what my mother would say?'

'Hannah, you're an independent young woman, and way past worrying about what my sister thinks.'

'Hmm, what colour should I get?'

'Is there a choice?'

'There should be. Not everyone wants black or green. And if I purchase one, you must allow me to tell Mother myself.'

'Agreed. And that's the easiest promise I've made all week.'

* * *

Aunt Violet halted the Sunbeam on Chelsea Embankment beside a short pathway leading to a Portland stone portico. The words Carlyle Place above double-glazed doors gave entry to a block of mansion apartments.

'They must have spectacular views of the river from those bay windows.' Hannah closed the passenger side door and joined her aunt on the pavement.

'We need to be prepared.' Her aunt halted her in front of the bevelled entrance door. 'If a doorman challenges us, we're here collecting donations for Princess Mary.'

'You mean for the gift boxes, Aunt Violet.' Hannah giggled. 'Princess Mary doesn't need money.'

'You know what I mean.' Her aunt led the way into a cavernous entrance with high ceilings and glittering crystal light fittings. The floral green and gold wallpaper created a luxury hotel feel.

'There's no one here.' Hannah approached the empty porter's desk where a notice said to press the bell.

'Don't!' Aunt Violet warned Hannah, whose hand hovered over the bell. 'We'll make the most of his absence. It's the first floor, isn't it?'

'Yes. Number eight.' Hannah intercepted her on her way to the lift. 'If we're sneaking around, shouldn't we take the stairs in case there's an attendant?'

'Good thinking.' Aunt Violet changed direction and followed Hannah up the stairs and along a thickly carpeted hallway.

'Here it is.' Hannah halted at a door displaying a brass number eight set at eye level, with a matching doorbell set into the wall beside it.

'There's no name on the label,' Hannah observed, as the two-tone notes sounded somewhere inside the apartment.

'Maybe there's no one in?' Hannah said, after a good thirty seconds of silence. 'Or the flat has been vacant since Alice left?'

'Now, where are they?' Her aunt threw open her capacious bag and rummaged inside.

'What *are* you doing, Aunt Violet?' Hannah eased rapidly sideways to avoid her aunt's flying elbows.

'I was once enamoured of a man who showed me how to manipulate locks. He gave me this set of picks in a darling leather case, and I could have sworn—'

'Don't you dare!' Hannah wrestled the bag shut, and came smartly to attention a second before the door was flung open, revealing Josie Bellamy.

Hannah gasped. 'What are you doing here?'

Josie appeared quite different out of uniform, in a cream embroidered blouse and dark layered skirt, her chocolate-brown hair swept onto her head in layers of silken waves. Her lipstick and face powder, forbidden for nurses, emphasised small blemishes on her skin. She had layered it on too thick and it did not suit her.

'I could ask the same of you.' Josie glared back at her from beneath lowered brows without a trace of embarrassment. 'How did you find out about this place?' She braced a hip against the doorframe, blocking entry to the flat.

'I gather you know this young woman, Hannah?' Aunt Violet raised a sardonic eyebrow her mother would have been proud of.

'You gather correctly.' Hannah recovered herself. 'My aunt

Violet, who I believe is a person you're aware of already? Aunt Violet, this is Nurse Bellamy.'

'Indeed?' Aunt Violet stared Josie down in a way only Aunt Violet could. 'Strange our paths have never crossed. But then I don't spend as much time at the hospital as I used to.' Aunt Violet strode past her, forcing Josie to move back. 'Please don't keep us out in the hallway, it's hardly polite.'

'I suppose you had better come in.' Ignoring Hannah, Josie led the way into a small but well-appointed sitting room decorated in a modern style, in an understated taupe with accents of cream. A sofa and three chairs upholstered in a vivid peacock blue sat in a cosy arrangement on a matching rug. Lampshades in the same colour dotted around the room completed a space Hannah suspected had been professionally designed.

'I won't offer you any refreshment as it's the maid's day off.' She slumped onto one of the compact but stylish sofas without offering them seats.

'Are you going to explain what has been going on, or do I summon Detective Inspector Farrell and let him question you?' Hannah's frustration found a voice. 'He will probably want to do it at Scotland Yard, because he has a low opinion of witnesses who lie to him.'

Aunt Violet wandered to the bay window. 'Darling, you were right,' she said, as Hannah took the chair set at right angles to the sofa on which Josie sat. 'The view of the river from here is magnificent. Do you live here alone?'

'Yes. I mean, well, no. I have a maid, of course.'

'Of course,' Aunt Violet muttered archly, turning back to the view.

'What I told you before was true.' Josie heaved a deep sigh, but her left eye twitched slightly. 'Alice wanted to honour her brother, so I suggested she join the Volunteer Force. She isn't close to her aunt – she's too controlling – so swore me to secrecy. I know Daphne Allardyce. She's a cold one in that she absolutely hated having four half-grown children to raise.'

'And moving into lodgings with Sister Kerr?' Hannah asked. 'Whose idea was that?'

'I suggested she move in here with me, which she did for a short while.'

'But Alice didn't stay?' Hannah said, the question why Rafe wrote to her there explained. 'She went to lodge at Sister Kerr's house?'

'That's right.' Josie crossed one leg over the other, her foot swinging at the ankle. 'Alice felt too many people in Chelsea know us and word would have got back to her aunt. Daphne would certainly have disapproved. Nursing isn't what people like the Worsley-Brookes do.'

'You do it.' Aunt Violet ran a hand over a polished table, then peered at her finger.

'My family isn't as influential as theirs. We have a title, but they have more cash,' she replied with asperity, as if fate had allotted her less than she deserved. 'But I didn't know she was missing. When Sister Hibbert said she hadn't turned up for her shift, I thought she had simply taken off after the murder because she didn't want to be associated with it.'

'Have you heard from her?' Hannah asked.

'No, which is worrying.' Josie blinked rapidly. 'It's not like her to go off without a word. After you spoke to me about her—'

'When you told me to mind my own business?' Hannah interrupted. 'Not in those words, but the sentiment was the same.'

'Well, it seemed premature at the time. She had only been gone a day or so.'

'Is this your apartment, Miss Bellamy?' Aunt Violet asked. She strolled the room, eyeing up paintings and examining the odd ornament.

'My parents pay my rent. I could hardly afford this on my nurse's salary. They're all right, but living at their townhouse was stifling with all their rules.'

'I sympathise.' Hannah exchanged a smile with Aunt Violet. 'My parents aren't happy about my not living with them either, but I prefer it.'

'Oh, it's not forever. I expect to marry soon and have a residence of my own—' She realised she had moved into personal territory and stiffened. 'I'm sure you aren't here to talk about me. So why *are* you here?'

'It's obvious, isn't it? I'm worried about Alice,' Hannah said, surprised Josie seemed far less concerned. 'Did she tell you she was being followed?'

'Only once. A young chap had followed her from the underground and hung about outside the hospital. She never mentioned it again. I thought she must have imagined it.' Something flickered in her eyes, making Hannah wonder if she now regretted not paying more attention.

'I shouldn't be telling you this...' Josie said, following Aunt Violet with her eyes as she adjusted the position of a lurid red and black Japanese statue, something Hannah suspected she did deliberately. 'That morning you found Sergeant Tillman, Alice said some sleeping powders went missing from the kitchen.' She flicked a piece of cotton from her skirt.

'The staff keep sleeping powders in the kitchen?' Aunt Violet turned from her study of a landscape on the wall and stared at her. 'Does Dr Murray know about that?'

'Only a few. For emergencies,' Josie said, defensive. 'If a patient cannot sleep. It saves having to knock up the pharmacist after hours.'

'Go on.' Hannah waited to see if her story matched Dinah's.

'Alice was worried about being accused of something and held responsible for the man's death.'

'How, when he was shot?' Hannah asked.

'The detective who questioned her made her nervous. Not the red-headed chap, the one who glares at you and leaves long, awkward silences between questions.'

'I think I know who you mean.' Aunt Violet smirked. 'Fair hair and very blue eyes?'

'Yes, that's him.' Josie smiled knowingly. 'He asked about the sleeping draughts, but when Alice claimed not to know anything, he clearly doubted her.'

'You think she might have been worried about being implicated in drugging the men on the ward?' Hannah asked. Though Alice didn't strike her as the type who would just up and leave. 'Wouldn't that make her look guilty?'

'How could I know what she was thinking?' Josie examined her fingernails, growing bored with the subject matter. 'She didn't tell *me* anything.'

'Could Gabriel Allardyce have had something to do with her disappearance?' Hannah asked. 'Perhaps he found out she was a VAD and confronted her?' She imagined an argument with a defiant Alice challenging a young man who believed she was acting beneath her station. Without knowing more about Gabriel this remained only a vague idea.

'What?' Josie glanced up sharply. 'So he spirited her away somewhere?' She snorted with derision. 'Gabriel is the kindest man on earth and would do nothing like that. He always felt responsible for her and Rafe since they lost their parents so young.'

'Didn't Gabriel ask Alice to marry him?' Aunt Violet asked,

turning from her study of a vase. 'Some men don't take rejection well.'

'Nonsense. That was something Daphne Allardyce put about, but there was never any truth to it. Gabriel felt sorry for Alice because she was in a terrible state when Rafe was killed. He thought she was about to have a breakdown. Her aunt was worried she wouldn't be able to cope once she inherited. The family estate is a heavy responsibility.'

'I imagine it is,' Hannah said, thoughtful. Or will be when it comes under Alice's control.

'I'm sure Gabriel is fond of her, but his intentions are purely altruistic, if that's what you are suggesting.'

'Have you seen him since Alice went missing?' Hannah asked.

Josie fidgeted, apparently unwilling to discuss Gabriel. 'We had afternoon tea at Harrods recently, but he didn't mention Alice.' She chewed her bottom lip. 'If he was worried about her, I'm sure he would have said so.'

'What about you? Wouldn't he want to know Alice hasn't been heard from for days?' Aunt Violet asked.

'What for? He's not interested in Alice, and she certainly isn't interested in him.' Josie's face flamed crimson. 'I wish you'd stop implying Gabriel has done something wrong. Alice is probably somewhere in the Home Counties and when she comes back, we'll have a good laugh about her worrying everyone with her silly prank.' She launched out of her seat, her arms folded across her chest. 'Now, I've nothing more to say to either of you, so you may as well leave.' She headed for the front door, evidently expecting them to follow.

'We didn't mean to upset you. My aunt and I are only concerned Alice might be in danger,' Hannah said, once they stood in the communal hall with Josie blocking her front door.

'What sort of danger?' Josie studied her for a moment, then

gave an impatient snort. 'See? You have no idea what you're talking about.' She slammed the door in their faces, her angry footsteps receding along the hall.

'What a surly young woman.' Aunt Violet led the way down into the entrance hall. 'Did you notice the rash on her face?'

'I did.' Hannah nodded. 'It looked sore. What do you suppose caused it?'

'I cannot say, but she ought to use a more superior quality brand of face powder if her skin flares up easily.' Aunt Violet pushed open the door that led to the stairs. 'Though I doubt she would appreciate cosmetic advice from us.'

Arriving back at the car, Aunt Violet tossed her bag behind her seat, grabbed the crank handle from the floor of the Sunbeam and strode to the front.

'Somewhere in the Home Counties,' Hannah repeated what Josie had said, and remained on the pavement, shivering in the brisk wind that blew off the river.

'What was that?' Aunt Violet asked, as the engine burst into life.

'It was what Daphne Allardyce said to the inspector. Josie said exactly the same thing just now.'

'I doubt it means anything.' Aunt Violet tossed the crank handle back onto the floor before sliding into the driver's seat.

'Perhaps Josie was right and Alice feared being accused of drugging the ward?' Hannah bundled her skirt in one hand and climbed in beside her aunt.

'Making her Marion's accomplice? Is that likely? And Aidan wouldn't have accused her without evidence.'

'We know that, but Alice didn't. Then being followed made the poor girl lose her nerve and take off. Only—'

'Only what?' Aunt Violet pressed down on the accelerator and the Sunbeam lurched forward with a growl, pushing Hannah back hard in her seat. She clamped a hand on her hat to save losing it into the river. 'Josie has lied to me twice now. They were lies of omission, but still count as dishonesty.'

'We're not authorised to question Miss Bellamy, and she knows it.' Her aunt raised her voice over the rushing wind. 'In her mind she's simply protecting her friend. She owes us nothing, and lying to us has no consequences.' Aunt Violet raised her voice over the buffeting of the wind. 'When news gets out that Marion Kerr is in custody, Alice will probably come home of her own volition.'

'I hope you're right, Aunt Violet.'

16

'I'll be away this weekend, Hannah, so I was wondering if you'd like to borrow my motor car again?' Darius turned from the sideboard in the sitting room of Hannah's riverside house, a crystal whisky decanter in his hand.

'Won't you be needing it?' Her smile deflated. 'Or are you off on one of your secret missions?'

'Now you know I cannot talk about that.' He pressed her forearm as he joined her on the sofa.

'You could have telephoned instead of coming all the way to tell me.' Her cheeks heated at the memory of her childish delight at seeing him unexpectedly on her doorstep. 'But thank you, that would be very welcome. Although you realise there's a risk you won't get it back?'

'Won't get what back?' Aunt Violet entered the room and headed straight for the sideboard, where she poured herself a gin.

'Darius' motor car. I shall be a free spirit again for a while,' Hannah replied.

'Hmm.' Darius frowned. 'Perhaps I shouldn't have offered.' At her disappointed expression he grinned. 'No, you can have it.

Although my intentions aren't purely altruistic. I doubt I'll be able to use it much when the price of petrol doubles when rationing is introduced in a few weeks.'

'What?' Aunt Violet spat out a mouthful of gin. 'That's a shilling a gallon! We'll won't be able to go anywhere at that price.'

'We all have to make sacrifices, Aunt Violet.' Hannah retrieved a handkerchief from her bag and used it to dab at the damp spots on her aunt's skirt.

'All available fuel is needed for the war, so rationing has become a necessity.' Darius' rueful smile did nothing to mollify Aunt Violet, who mumbled, 'Outrageous,' under her breath.

'That's enough, Hannah, the stain has gone now.' Aunt Violet snatched the handkerchief from Hannah's hand. 'You seem distracted, darling. I thought you'd be thrilled at having the motor car back for a while.'

'Oh, I am.' Hannah's thoughts had taken an entirely different direction. 'Alice Worsley-Brooke has been gone ten days now, and no one has heard from her. For all we know, Daphne Allardyce has got her married off to Gabriel.'

'You've been reading too many Regency romance novels,' Aunt Violet scoffed. 'Young women don't get forced into marriage in this day and age.'

'Forced is too strong a word. More like coerced.' Hannah chewed her bottom lip as an idea took root.

'You've never met the man,' Darius pointed out. 'Perhaps he's as concerned about Alice as you are?'

'Or he gave up trying to convince her, and she's already dead, her body stowed away where no one will find it.' Frustration at not being taken seriously sent her off on an unlikely tangent.

'Hannah, now you're being ridiculous.' Aunt Violet laughed. 'And concealing bodies isn't as easy to accomplish as you might imagine. At dinner the other night, a police surgeon told me there are few foolproof methods of disposing of a body completely. Even pigs don't eat everything.'

'I'll take your word for it.' Hannah frowned. 'When did you meet a police surgeon?'

'Um, quite recently. We dined at Beauchamp Place with some friends of Aidan's.'

Hannah's next question was cut off by the throaty roar of a motorbike.

'Ah, that will be him now.' Aunt Violet sprang to her feet, her heels clattering down the tiled hall floor.

Hannah turned an astonished look at Darius, who grinned. 'It seems your aunt and the inspector have taken a shine to each other.'

'Well, she's being very secretive about it. Has she told you anything?' Darius knew her aunt almost as well as she did.

'Not really. Only I met Aidan at my club the other night for dinner, and he talked about her constantly.'

'You had dinner with Inspector Farrell?' Did everyone refer to him as Aidan but her? 'I didn't realise you two socialised.'

'It's not unusual for two single chaps to be mulling over life together. Actually, he requested my help in a case he's working on. The Secret Service Bureau works in collaboration with the police when their cases overlap with ours.'

'The Tillman murder or Miss Worsley-Brooke's disappearance?' Though there wasn't much left to do regarding the Kerrs.

'Neither, actually, nor will I be drawn.'

Aunt Violet's distinct laugh accompanied Inspector Farrell's low tone from the hall, seconds before the pair bounced into the room. He had removed his riding goggles and his ankle-length leather coat, leaving him in casual trousers and a light jacket, which indicated he was not on police business.

'Mr Clifford! I didn't realise you were here!' He approached Darius and shook his hand energetically. 'Good to see you again.'

'Last-minute impulse, but if you have business to discuss with the ladies, I'd gladly...' He pointed his glass at the door as a prelude to leave.

'No, no, Nothing I have to say cannot be said among friends and might even make everyone's day. Especially yours, Hannah.' He relaxed into one of the twin sofas facing each other and spread himself across the entire space.

'Well go on then, what is it?' Aunt Violet handed Darius a crystal glass that held an inch of amber liquid before perching beside him. Smiling into her eyes, he shifted sideways to make room.

Darius resumed his seat beside Hannah, his glass dwarfed in both hands held between his splayed knees.

'Now we're all comfortable,' the inspector began, 'I have news. I had a visitor yesterday. A Mr Gabriel Allardyce.'

'How interesting,' Aunt Violet said, one eyebrow raised.

Hannah's mouthful of sherry went down the wrong way and she spluttered, swallowing quickly before spitting some over her skirt. 'He turned up at Scotland Yard? Just like that?' She swiped a discreet hand across her mouth, relieved to find it dry.

'He did. Our conversation was most revealing.' The inspector took a slow sip from his glass as the anticipatory silence stretched. 'Mr Allardyce informed me his stepmother was visited by two ladies who claimed Alice had disappeared in strange circum-stances. A rumour he was eager to refute.'

'Ah!' Hannah murmured.

'Exactly.' He scowled at her. 'He said the woman was scared to death that something awful had happened to her stepdaughter.'

'That wasn't the impression we got,' Aunt Violet muttered at his elbow, adding, 'You can drop the dark looks, Aidan. You know it was us. Daphne Allardyce recognised me.'

'Yes, well.' His hard gaze swivelled towards her. 'I managed to smooth things over with the man and explain you only had Alice's interests at heart. In fact, you're both lucky you aren't in serious trouble.' He pointed a finger at each of them.

'But does he know where Alice is?' Darius asked, joining the conversation, having observed the by-play as if watching a tennis match.

'He does.' The inspector saluted him with his glass. 'He was eager to inform me that Miss Worsley-Brooke had not intended to create either concern or suspicion over her actions. She did not mention she was being followed as she felt it was unconnected with the murder.'

'But I told you she was being followed. Or thought she was,' Hannah said.

'I needed to hear it from her, but she seemed to be avoiding me.' The inspector sighed. 'You have to agree, her behaviour was odd. She lodged with a woman we now know is a killer, ran from the hospital before she could be questioned with no reasonable explanation, then quit London altogether. It occurred to me she knew Albert Kerr was hiding in the house and was culpable in harbouring him.'

'More likely she found out by accident and ran off in case she became Marion's next victim,' Hannah said.

'No more theories, please, Miss Merrill.' His hard gaze swivelled towards her. 'I've had as much trouble as I can handle unravelling who's been asking who what, and whether it's relevant to my murder case or not. In fact, you're both lucky you aren't in serious trouble.'

'We apologise.' Hannah encompassed Aunt Violet in this

admission of guilt. 'But you weren't taking her disappearance seriously. No one was.'

'Not true, I was very concerned. But might I remind you murder investigations are my purview, not yours.' He shifted on his seat as this sank in. 'Miss Worsley-Brooke is currently staying in Lowestoft with Mr Allardyce's sister, Mrs Georgina Ure-Reid. At his invitation, I plan to go down there in a few days to hear the story from Miss Worsley-Brooke's own lips.'

'Of course, Daphne Allardyce said her stepdaughter lived in Suffolk,' Hannah said. 'It makes sense she would be with her? That must have been the lady Alice left Percy Circus with in the chauffeured motor car.' An idea stirred in Hannah's head and grew rapidly, and she inched forward in her seat. 'When are you going to speak to Alice?'

'My workload is quite busy at the moment,' the inspector said after a brief pause. 'But it's Easter soon and I haven't had a break for a while. It strikes me that would be a good time to take advantage of Mr Allardyce's invitation.'

'Easter by the seaside.' Aunt Violet waggled her shoulders. 'Sounds delightful.'

'I agree. So why don't we all go?' Hannah asked, surprised at herself for being bold enough, though Darius seemed not only unfazed but amenable to the idea.

'Hannah!' Aunt Violet's mouth formed a perfect 'O'. 'What *are* you suggesting?' Though the gleam in her eye showed she wasn't as shocked as she pretended.

'I doubt the weather will be up to much,' Darius said, thoughtful. 'However, a couple of days beside the sea will make a pleasant break. Where are you staying, Inspector?'

'Mr Allardyce suggested somewhere called the Hotel Victoria.'

'I'm game. As long as I'm not being invited to act as chaperone.' Her aunt pulled a face.

'I don't need a chaperone.' Hannah glared at her. 'Unmarried young women are doing a lot of things on their own they would have been aghast at a couple of years ago. And even if I did need one, you wouldn't exactly be my first choice.'

'Whatever can you mean by that?' Aunt Violet blinked, her glass held aloft.

'Now, no squabbling.' Inspector Farrell adopted a smug smile. 'This might tie up the case nicely. My supervisor might even cover my expenses.'

'Hmm.' Darius stared into his glass. 'I doubt we'll find much to do there so early in the season.'

'We don't need entertaining.' Aunt Violet rose and approached the sideboard, where she refilled their glasses. 'These coastal hotels always have some sort of tea dance and evening musical entertainment. And there's bound to be a promenade for a bracing walk. It could be fun.'

'That settles it then.' Darius took the glass Aunt Violet handed him while aiming a wink at Hannah that made her cheeks heat. 'If the inspector books rooms for us, I'll arrange travel permits for the station checks.'

'Station checks?' Hannah repeated, confused.

'We might not need them, but with new military installations popping up all over the East Coast, there are restrictions on who enters the area. And the benefit of the four of us going, means if I'm required to leave suddenly, Hannah won't be left alone.'

'Why would you have to leave?' Hannah asked.

'One never knows when an emergency will crop up. That's why they're called emergencies.'

'Honestly.' Hannah placed her empty glass on a side table with a firm click. 'Since you joined the Secret Service Bureau, I swear you talk in riddles.'

'It's a prerequisite of my employment.' Darius' smug grin only annoyed her even more.

'Well, I'd wish you'd stop. It's incredibly annoying.'

* * *

"We're leaving late, aren't we?" Aunt Violet said, as she climbed into the first-class carriage with the help of the inspector's extended hand. 'The day will be gone before we get there.'

'It's Easter Sunday, Vi, and this is the last train this evening. We were lucky to get tickets at all.' The inspector's last words were drowned out by the shriek of a whistle that echoed along the platform. 'It wasn't intentional.'

'I doubt we'll get there in time for dinner.' Aunt Violet handed Darius her vanity case which he stored on the overhead rack, pushing aside Hannah's leather grip bag to make room for it.

'Take the window seat, Hannah. I'll take the corridor.' Inspector Farrell moved his coat to allow her to sit. 'Would you do me a kindness,' he whispered. 'Don't keep referring to me as "Inspector". People get nervous in the presence of authority.' He cocked his chin towards to where a man in a Homburg had paused outside their carriage door while giving their party a worried look before hurrying past.

'Um, well if you wish, I promise to make an effort.' She plumped down on the hard bench next to him. However he would always reside in the box in her head marked 'policeman', despite his growing attachment to Aunt Violet.

'I hope this is the right train.' Aunt Violet kicked a wicker basket beneath the seat before sitting. 'You rushed us through the station so fast, I didn't have time to check the notice board. Are you sure this isn't the Edinburgh Express?'

'Trains to Scotland go from King's Cross, Vi.' Aidan spoke from the depths of a newspaper he had opened on being seated.

Hannah peered through the grime-streaked window onto the platform partially obscured by engine smoke as the train filled with naval officers filled the other first-class carriage. Sailors in white hats prowled the corridors dragging kit bags behind them as they searched for somewhere to sit, exchanged loud greetings with those they knew or apologised for stepping on the toes of strangers.

A sequence of doors slamming preceded another whistle as the train lurched forward, then chugged out of the station and gathered speed. They emerged into late afternoon light, leaving the vaulted and glazed station roof behind.

The next half hour passed in companionable silence, listening to the clickety-clack of the wheels as they passed over the joints in the rails, the gentle sway of the carriage making Hannah's eyelids heavy.

'Perhaps the journey might pass quicker if you told us what else came to light after the Kerrs were arrested?' Aunt Violet pulled the basket from beneath the seat, unwrapped several brown paper parcels and lined them up on the basket lid.

'As you wish.' Aidan re-folded his newspaper, resigned to not being left at peace to read. 'Albert Kerr admitted desertion but stuck to his story about being nowhere near The Coal Hole when Duffy died.'

'Did you believe him?' Hannah shrugged off her lethargy to ask.

'I doubt it. Though the lad was known to us, so it's possible he had other enemies.' He accepted a crustless sandwich and devoured it in two bites. 'Good idea of yours to bring sustenance, Vi. I was relying on a buffet car, but they don't appear to have one on this service.'

'The only food on this train will be in the baggage car intended for the navy,' Darius said, smiling.

'You were saying?' Hannah prompted, eager to hear what he had discovered about Duffy's death.

'Marion Kerr thought she was on to a good thing with Alice and charged over the odds for those rooms at Percy Circus. They also intended to relieve her of as much as they could before leaving the country. We found two second-class tickets for a steamer to Halifax leaving from Liverpool, departing the ninth of September.'

'Sandwich, Hannah?' Aunt Violet offered a sheet of brown paper piled with neatly cut sandwiches.

'Can you prove Albert killed Duffy?' Hannah declined the sandwich, suspecting it was fish paste, but accepted a garibaldi biscuit. 'Albert Kerr claimed it was an accident and Pendleton actually didn't witness him pushing Duffy.'

'That's where proper police work comes in,' Aidan said smugly. 'A witness reported seeing a moustachioed figure in a dark green overcoat with a grey velvet collar shove Duffy down the steps. He hurried away, like the good, I'm-not-getting-involved Englishman he is, but conscience-stricken, he came into Cannon Street Station to give a statement. Too late then, of course.'

'Did you find a coat like that at the Kerr house?' Darius asked.

'No,' Aidan replied, disappointment carving a frown on his forehead. 'If Kerr thought he had been seen, he probably disposed of it. He's unlikely to own up to a crime we cannot prove. At least we've got him for desertion.'

'Or the army has,' Darius reminded him.

'I still feel it was partly my fault Duffy was killed.' Hannah sighed. 'I wasn't exactly discreet when I asked Marion all those questions.' *Had Duffy seen Albert Kerr at Percy Circus when he followed Alice home? Did Albert kill him in order to keep his secret?*

'Don't blame yourself, darling.' Aunt Violet leaned forward and patted her knee. 'You acted out of concern for Alice. No one could have known Albert Kerr was still alive.'

'No one except Sergeant Tillman.' Darius grasped Hannah's hand that lay on the seat between, making her pulse race. 'Did Sergeant Tillman's commanding officer get back to you, Aidan?'

'He did.' Aidan examined the contents of a sandwich before biting into it. 'Tillman and Albert Kerr were manning a gun emplacement outside the Bluff at Ypres, when a German howitzer hit their trench.' He took a bite of his cucumber sandwich before helping himself to a second, earning a sharp slap on the hand from Aunt Violet.

'Be fair, Vi. They're quite small. And by the look of that basket, you have plenty for all of us.' He shuffled back in his seat, his professional persona stripped away to show the man beneath. Hannah decided in that moment that she actually liked him. Perhaps calling him by his given name would be easier than she imagined.

'Ivy went to a good deal of trouble preparing this food, so everyone gets their fair share and no more.' Her aunt shifted the basket further out of his reach.

'As I was saying,' Aidan held up his second sandwich in emphasis, 'Tillman was hit with flying shrapnel, so too injured to move, he lay still to wait for the stretcher bearers. He watched as a relatively uninjured Albert Kerr removed Captain Peter Gorman's ID tags along with his wallet, revolver and tunic.'

'He didn't kill him, did he?' Aunt Violet asked. 'I hope the poor man wasn't simply wounded and could have been saved.'

'No, Vi. Gorman was dead,' he replied dispassionately. 'He had part of his face missing, so had to be identified by his tags.'

Suddenly nauseous, Hannah discarded the rest of her biscuit.

'Which were, in fact Kerr's tags,' Darius pointed out while

chewing a slice of chicken and ham pie. 'Gorman was a captain though, so Kerr must have had to grow a moustache to pass as him.'

Hannah stared at the generous slice of pie on his lap, wondering where her aunt had obtained such a rare delicacy, but her own appetite had gone.

'I always thought officers being mandated to grow moustaches was a peculiar rule.' Aunt Violet held up a greaseproof paper-wrapped cube. 'Ginger cake?'

Darius grinned and reached for it. 'It was instigated in the 1860s and is still in place today.'

'Kerr didn't have enough facial hair at first, so must have kept Gorman's tunic to wear when his own grew in.' Aidan unwrapped the cake carefully, the smell of ginger and cinnamon filling the carriage. 'Then he hitched rides on troop vehicles with a story about being lost on the battlefield and had to get back to his unit. Not an unreasonable claim with so many displaced soldiers out there.'

'Did you find the gun Marion used to kill Sergeant Tillman?' Despite her queasiness, the enticing smell made Hannah's mouth water.

'Ah, Mrs Kerr wasn't so clever about that.' He rapidly chewed a mouthful of food and swallowed. 'She hid it in the cellar. Probably planned to sell it.' He peered at his sandwich. 'Where did you get this ham, Vi? It's delicious.'

'Don't ask.' She waved him off. 'Perhaps Marion planned to use the gun again. In my experience, if a method works once, one is tempted to repeat it.'

'I won't ask how you know that Aunt Violet.' Hannah shuddered. 'With all the military hospitals in London, what were the chances of Sergeant Tillman being sent to the same one where Marion Kerr worked?'

'Ah, now that's the interesting part.' Aidan seemed to enjoy himself. 'Tillman was shipped home to Charing Cross Hospital. His leg wound healed well enough for him to be discharged. A month or so later, the landlord at The Cross Keys remembered a man with a limp who collapsed in the public bar. A couple of customers took him to the casualty room at the nearby Endell Street hospital, where he was admitted with a septic leg wound. Dr Murray thought nothing of it at the time, but with hindsight, she's convinced he re-infected it himself to gain access to Marion Kerr and begin his blackmail campaign.'

Hannah winced, chewed the remains of her biscuit, and slapped crumbs from her fingers. 'Albert Kerr boasted about his wife to Tillman, so that's how he knew she worked there.'

'Those two deserved one another,' Darius said from his corner seat. 'No doubt they'll both hang.'

'Mrs Kerr will. The Army will take care of Albert,' the inspector said.

'I'd rather be shot than hanged,' Aunt Violet murmured.

'Let's hope you'll never have to make that choice.' Aidan grunted as Aunt Violet's elbow contacted hard with his ribs.

A silence fell as each of them ruminated on this thought as the train rattled and swayed through the open countryside.

'I know she was awful, but I'm still sad for the Kerrs,' Hannah said after a moment. 'Marion was trying to re-start their lives and their marriage, and we cannot imagine what Albert went through at the front.'

'When questioned,' Aidan shifted slightly to face her, 'Marion admitted they had no intention of stopping Duffy from following her, even when Alice paid them. And the noises in the attic were exaggerated to rattle her.'

'I take it back. I have no sympathy for either of them.' Hannah turned her head and stared morosely out of the window.

'We've all had enough doom and gloom for one day.' Darius licked a glob of butter from his thumb and crossed one leg over the other. 'I intend to enjoy a well-earned break in spectacular scenery and forget all about murders for a few days.'

'A sensible idea,' Aunt Violet said. 'Anyone want the last sandwich?'

Darius and Aidan made a grab for it, collapsing into enthusiastic laughter when Darius won.

17

The train juddered to a halt, startling Hannah out of a light doze. Blinking awake, she eased a stiffness in her neck and attempted to focus on a wide sign announcing Lowestoft Central.

'Welcome to the Sunshine Coast.' Darius nudged her fully awake. 'Lowestoft is called that because it enjoys the earliest sunrise in Britain. You'll see daylight at about four in the morning.' He left his seat and took down the suitcases from the overhead racks and lined them up in the corridor.

'I don't intend to be up that early, but I'll take your word for it.' Aunt Violet tugged down her jacket and slung the strap of her bag over one arm.

'We'll have to fend for ourselves, I'm afraid.' Darius helped Hannah down the step before reaching back for Aunt Violet. 'Looks like the navy has commandeered all the porters.'

'Aidan appears to have things in hand.' Hannah suppressed a yawn as the policeman hauled the two largest cases onto the platform before rushing away.

'I managed to flag down the only taxi left in the station forecourt,' he said between rapid breaths on his return. 'It will be a bit of a squeeze, but I'm sure we'll manage.' Darius and the inspector carried their cases across the footbridge and out into the street, leaving Aunt Violet and Hannah to cope with the picnic basket, handbags and various outer garments.

'How far is the hotel?' Hannah asked once they had climbed inside, her voice strained. She felt decidedly claustrophobic with a suitcase on her lap blocking her vision and Aunt Violet's vanity case on the floor behind her knees.

'Once we are across the bascule bridge, it's less than a mile,' Darius replied from the front seat. 'The Hotel Victoria is on Kirkley cliff with a superb view of the sea. It has an excellent reputation, so I'm sure we'll all be comfortable.'

'That's a relief,' Aunt Violet said from her position squeezed between Hannah and Aidan. 'I wasn't looking forward to a boarding house with rough blankets and paper-thin walls.' She smiled sweetly at Aidan. 'Not that you would have booked one on purpose.'

Their brief climb up the southern cliff proved, as promised, mercifully short. The taxi pulled up on the sweeping drive of a Victorian red brick building. Two bell boys came running out of a central arched entrance manned by a military-looking doorman who beamed at Darius. 'Good evening, Mr Clifford. Welcome back, sir.'

'Er, thank you, Sanders. Nice to be back.' Darius inclined his head at the porter and flushed slightly when he saw Hannah staring at him. Though she knew better than to question him. Why had he not mentioned he had been here before?

Darius and Aidan sorted the luggage, while Hannah and Aunt Violet admired the dining room with its stunning view of the sea and the harbour.

'They have a ballroom with a maple sprung floor and announcements of weekly dances held during the season,' Aunt

Violet read from a notice mounted on an easel. 'Has anyone brought their bathing costume, because there's a bathing beach in front of the hotel with diving boards?'

'In April? I'm not that brave, Aunt Violet.' Hannah nodded to where Aidan strolled towards them from the reception desk.

'I'm afraid the dining room closed half an hour ago, so it's fortunate we had an early dinner in London and a snack on the train.' He handed both Aunt Violet and Hannah their room keys. 'If anyone's hungry, the kitchen will send up a light meal and coffee.'

'Where's Darius?' Hannah asked, accepting the key with its oversized label.

'Making a telephone call.' Aidan peered back over his shoulder. 'He's checking in with his office.'

'On Easter Sunday?' Aunt Violet tutted. 'Surely even the War Office is closed today? I'm surprised the trains are even running.'

'They aren't,' he replied. 'Didn't you notice it was a troop train? Darius managed to wangle a carriage, which wasn't easy. There's a war on, you know,' he added without a trace of irony, while gesturing for them to mount the curved staircase. 'By the time we get settled it will be too late for much. I suggest we meet in the main dining room for breakfast and make plans for the day.'

Aunt Violet halted on the staircase and glanced back to where Aidan had not moved from the bottom of the stairs. 'Our rooms are on the second floor.'

'I know, but first I'll contact the local police station and let them know I'm here.'

'Whatever for?'

'These provincial police don't welcome the Met second-guessing them, Vi.' His jovial tone failed to hide an underlying frustration. 'And this is still a police investigation, so I'll keep it formal.'

'Don't be so stuffy.' Aunt Violet sniffed. 'We're on holiday. And I know it's barely eight thirty, but the journey was rather tiring so I'm going to have an early night. What about you, Hannah?'

'Um, yes. I am rather tired, it feels like a long time since we left London.'

'I'll, um, keep Darius company for a bit. Shall I?' Aidan said from the bottom of the stairs. 'See where the land lies and all that?'

'What land does he mean?' Hannah asked, as she and her aunt reached the first landing. 'What are they up to, Aunt Violet?'

'I've no idea. But it's decidedly suspicious if you ask me. Where's your room?'

Hannah examined her key. 'I'm on the third floor.'

Aunt Violet leaned forward and planted a kiss on Hannah's cheek. 'You never know, this time away might give you and Darius a chance to spend some time together and sort yourselves out. You've been dancing around the serious question for far too long.'

'Goodnight, Aunt Violet.' Hannah smiled weakly, but lately the flame of hope she held out for Darius to declare himself was dying fast. They got on so well, but he treated her like a younger sister he liked to indulge, as though there was nothing romantic about it. Perhaps her aunt was right, and a short break away from London might help them establish some sort of understanding.

They parted with a hug, and Hannah found the door that corresponded with the key fob. It was a small but charming room set under the eaves, and one step away from being an attic. The homely room had yellow walls, a green floral bed cover, and a bay window that made her sigh in pleasure.

She waylaid a passing chambermaid and ordered tea, then drank it while watching the sunset from an upholstered chair by the window.

Ten o'clock came and went with no call or appearance from

Darius. She placed her tray outside her door, undressed, and got into bed.

She slumped onto the luxuriously soft bed and wrapped her arms around a pillow, burying her chin in the crisp white cotton. 'Sometimes, Darius Clifford, I wish you weren't so much the gentleman.'

* * *

Hannah woke the next day to a bright spring day that flooded the room with light. She threw open the window and breathed in the sea air over a glittering calm sea, the only sounds this high on the cliff were the calls of seagulls and a distant ship's horn.

She was more than ready for a hearty breakfast and dressed quickly.

'You were right, Aidan,' Hannah said, joining him and Aunt Violet at a window-side table in the dining room. 'That sea view is spectacular.'

'I'm glad it proved to be a good choice. For the first time in weeks, I slept like a baby.' He held out his cup to a hovering waitress who poured his coffee.

'Which tells us you've never had one,' Aunt Violet commented, delicately nibbling a triangle of toast. 'My niece will tell you once a baby is in the house, sleep is an impossibility.'

'Your niece?' He aimed a frown at Hannah.

'She means my sister, Iris,' Hannah explained. 'She has four. All under six. By the way, where's Darius?' She scanned the dining room, but although it was busy with guests, there was no sign of him.

'Er...' Aidan swallowed visibly. 'He's checking the status of the situation with his colleagues at the Bureau.'

'Really? Then why did you and Darius spend the evening in

the hotel bar?' Aunt Violet adjusted the shawl around her shoulders. 'And if you're wondering, that lovely man at the front desk cannot lie to save his life.'

'I assume you aren't allowed to tell us what it was about?' Hannah asked, conceding that Darius might have a valid excuse for his non-appearance the night before.

'I'll leave it to him to explain. I had a word with the porter who gave me Mr Allardyce's telephone number.'

'Do they have telephones in darkest Suffolk?' Aunt Violet said archly. 'And it's barely nine o'clock. Wasn't he annoyed at being disturbed so early?'

'They rise early in the country, remember? Now stop interrupting and let me finish. I told him I was here with friends—'

'Does he realise Aunt Violet and myself are the friends you are talking about?' Hannah interrupted him.

'Er, come to think of it. No. However Mr Allardyce invited us all to dinner tonight at his sister's house somewhere up on the cliff. He's even sending a car to fetch us.'

'Dinner?' Aunt Violet's jaw went slack. 'But I don't have any suitable clothes.'

'What did you intend to wear tonight?' Aidan asked, bemused.

'That's entirely different.' She narrowed her eyes, offended. 'Had I known we were dining with local society, I would have brought something more... sophisticated.' She scooped a spoonful of marmalade from a crystal pot which she dumped unceremoniously onto her toast.

'Are you sure it isn't a trap?' Hannah pushed her scrambled eggs around her plate. 'A few days ago we thought Alice had been kidnapped, and Gabriel Allardyce was our prime suspect.'

'*Your* prime suspect.' Aidan popped a piece of toast into his mouth. 'I gave him the benefit of the doubt.'

'Have you told Darius about this dinner invitation?' Hannah suppressed a sharp retort that sprang to her tongue.

'He's had other things on his mind, but I might have mentioned it.' Aidan nodded to where the man himself manoeuvred towards them between tables of diners.

'I apologise for being late,' Darius said, mildly breathless as he took the last empty chair and scooted it closer to the table. 'I owe you all an apology, but a situation discussed in London recently has become something of a crisis down here.' Snapping open his napkin, he laid it across his lap.

'If I didn't know better,' Hannah began, aware she sounded snippy, 'I would say that was a coincidence. However, knowing you, I very much doubt it.'

Darius paused as the waitress filled his cup, dismissing her with a smile.

'Ah, I see what's going on.' Aunt Violet wrapped her hands round her coffee cup, her elbows on the table in a stance which would have made Nanny bring out the ruler. 'I wondered why you were so keen for us to make this trip together. Was it out of generosity or subterfuge?'

'He didn't bring us here, Aunt Violet,' Hannah pointed out. 'We invited ourselves.'

'I confess to taking advantage of an opportunity that presented itself. When you suggested this trip, Hannah, I asked my superior if I might follow up on a situation which has developed here in Suffolk. He agreed and asked me to report back.' Avoiding Hannah's eyes, he eased his collar away from his throat with a finger.

'What sort of situation?' Aunt Violet asked.

'You cannot ask him that, Aunt Violet.' Hannah experienced a pang of disappointment, having hoped he had made the trip for her, but apparently not. 'And you're forgiven, but only because Alice is no longer in danger.'

'If she ever was,' Aidan muttered through a mouthful of toast.

'Can't you tell us anything?' Aunt Violet pouted.

'All right, but only because what is happening now might affect us all in the next few days.'

'Goodness! This is beginning to sound worrisome.' Aunt Violet leaned back in her chair, a triangle of toast held high. Hannah agreed while sensing a shift in the mood around the table. Even Aidan seemed overly preoccupied with his tie.

'What I am about to tell you is... sensitive.' Darius paused as a roar of guffaws erupted from a nearby table but died down again quickly. 'Our listeners in London picked up worrisome messages a while ago between the Germans and Irish nationalists.' He broke off again as the waitress delivered his breakfast.

'Irish nationalists?' Aunt Violet whispered, her gaze on the waitress' retreating back. 'Those chaps who demand Home Rule for Ireland?'

'Those *chaps*,' Darius repeated with emphasis, 'have negotiated with the German High Command to create a diversion.'

'What sort of diversion?' Hannah felt panic building, but forced herself to remain calm. They had come all this way to get away from the war and it was following them.

'They plan to attack shipping in the North Sea on the same day the Irish nationalists announce a free Ireland in Dublin,' Darius said.

'An attack?' Aunt Violet straightened, the colour draining from her face. 'What's going on, Darius?'

'Where will they make this attack?' Hannah's throat dried. She had never heard her aunt sound so worried before. 'Surely not here?' Her gaze drifted to the window where a calm sea glistened on a misty horizon. It was a beautiful, calm morning, with the sea like glass. *This cannot be happening.*

'The Imperial German Navy is at sea now, but we don't know exactly where they are heading,' Darius went on. 'Our primary concern is they might try to break into the Downs, where a hundred merchant ships are waiting to enter the Port of London.'

'Is that what the telephone calls were about last night?' Hannah's hands felt clammy as the implications sank in.

Darius nodded. 'A man named Casement was developing the Irish relationship with Germany.'

'I've heard that name,' Aunt Violet interrupted. 'Wasn't he arrested?'

'He was.' Darius cut into his fried egg and loaded his fork, halting it halfway to his mouth. 'We hoped that would stall the rebels, but apparently not. The rising is going ahead in Dublin despite our efforts to derail it.'

'Don't they call themselves freedom fighters, not rebels?' Hannah observed.

'I'd rather not debate the political rights and wrongs, Hannah.' Darius frowned a warning. 'Last night, a German cruiser struck a mine north-west of Nordeney.'

'Where's that?' Hannah interrupted.

'It's an island off the North Sea coast of Germany,' Darius replied. 'The cruiser was forced to turn back with a flooded torpedo compartment. This slowed the attack but hasn't stopped it. Now we have learned that the Irish nationalists occupied the Dublin Post Office on Easter Sunday and publicly declared a free Ireland.' He lowered his voice to little above a whisper. 'The Foresters are on their way from Watford as we speak to put an end to it.'

'The Foresters?' Hannah frowned.

'The Sherwood Foresters,' Aidan said, a triangle of toast held in mid-air dripping butter. 'Known as the Robin Hood Regiment, for obvious reasons.'

'I don't like the sound of this.' Aunt Violet set down her knife and fork and fidgeted in her chair.

'Don't worry, Vi.' Aidan covered her hand on the table with his. 'Those U-boats won't get within twenty miles of the coast.'

'Don't treat me like an ignoramus.' Aunt Violet snatched her hand from beneath his. 'You don't know any more than Darius, and he's the spy.' She gasped and clamped a hand over her mouth, giving the dining room a sweeping glance. 'Sorry. It just slipped out.'

'Is this what you meant when you said you might have to leave in a hurry, Darius?' Hannah asked.

'I didn't want you stranded here if I'm sent elsewhere.' Darius pushed his uneaten breakfast away and leaned his face close to hers. 'Things have got serious quickly, which I didn't foresee. I thought...' His hand grasped hers on the tabletop and she did not remove it. 'I'm sorry the timing is so bad. Especially as I really looked forward to a few days away from London with you.'

'Are we in any danger?' Hannah's delight at this admission was subsumed by alarm.

'I sincerely hope not. I'm going to call at the Customs House in town to liaise with the naval attaché there.' He tossed his napkin onto the table, scraped back his chair and rose to his feet. 'It means, ladies, that you'll have to amuse yourselves for a while, but we'll meet up again later.'

'What about you, Aidan?' Aunt Violet plucked a piece of bacon from his plate, though her hand shook slightly. 'Won't you join Hannah and me for a bracing walk along the promenade?'

'If there's going to be trouble at sea, the local constabulary might be glad of some help.' Aidan spread the last of the tiny pat of butter on a triangle of toast.

'I'm sure they can do without the services of a metropolitan policeman. They have enough of their own.' Aunt Violet's frustration matched Hannah's. 'Besides, what help can you be if there really is an attack?'

'I'm sure something will occur to me.' He planted a swift kiss on her cheek, to which she did not react. 'You might as well enjoy this holiday now we're here.'

'Well, that's us dumped.' Aunt Violet slumped into her chair as both men strode out towards reception.

'We did rather make it easy for them.' Hannah sighed. 'Not that we had much alternative. But I hope they're wrong and the Germans are bluffing.'

'Well, I'm not going to spend all day worrying about it.' Aunt Violet patted Hannah's hand. 'Why don't we go up and plan what we are going to wear at Mr Allardyce's dinner? What did Aidan say the house was called?'

'He didn't. Only that it's somewhere on the cliff,' Hannah replied. Was it her imagination, or did the sea suddenly look rougher and the sky darker?

* * *

After reviewing their wardrobes, Aunt Violet settled on her oyster silk gown for the dinner party. Hannah's dusky pink gown, if less stylish, was certainly beautifully cut and enhanced her slender figure.

By luncheon there was still no sign of either Darius or Aidan, so she and Aunt Violet took a light meal in the hotel dining room before setting off for a walk in the town.

'It's all so normal and quiet,' Hannah said, as they strolled the seafront arm-in-arm. 'Do you suppose anyone here suspects what we know?'

'I doubt it,' Aunt Violet said. 'The navy would avoid saying anything to prevent chances of a panic.'

Hannah's stomach tightened at the thought of the townspeople being hurt or killed if the Germans arrived. The guilt she had felt the previous October returned, when she had known about a planned Zeppelin raid on London that the War Office had insisted on keeping quiet. It made practical sense, but her heart still grieved for the people who died that night.

'Would knowing make any difference?' Aunt Violet asked. 'How do you choose which people to save and who to leave to their fate? It's a sad fact of the war.'

'It's heartbreaking, and the way you say it makes me sound naïve.'

'No, just still young enough for your emotions to overrule everything. Life is rarely fair. The good are often unrewarded and the bad don't always get what they deserve.'

'Then what was the point of eating my greens, or keeping my elbows off the table?'

'None whatsoever.' Her aunt laughed.

Once back at the hotel, they found Darius and Aidan occupying armchairs in the hotel lounge. Both men wore grave expressions that changed instantly to bright but fragile smiles when they entered.

'Did you have a nice day?' Darius asked.

'An uneventful one,' Hannah replied. 'We walked down to the Marine Parade and strolled the pier and shops. At least the weather held.'

'Are we still going to dinner with the Allardyces, or are we about to be obliterated by the Germans?' Aunt Violet asked, her voice arch.

'Don't be pessimistic, Vi.' Aidan swallowed, but avoided her eye. 'Mr Allardyce's motor car is expected for seven thirty.'

'Our cruisers are on alert to intercept any destroyers that get too close to the coast.' Darius rubbed his hands together. 'Now, how about afternoon tea before we have to dress for our dinner?'

'Good idea.' Hannah smiled brightly, a pang rising at his obvious attempt to keep their spirits up.

Aunt Violet drew Hannah towards a sofa by the wall of glass that gave a panoramic view of the sea. Her voice lowered. 'I get the impression we might be outnumbered if this attack happens.'

'Are we outnumbered?' Hannah asked, mildly panicked.

'By size maybe, but not cunning or strategy. We have the best navy in the world, darling.'

'Just as well, because it sounds as if we'll need it.'

18

The chauffeur who collected them at precisely the time prescribed by Mr Allardyce drew the motor car to a smooth halt beside a Victorian house four storeys high at the end of a drive lined with thick rhododendron bushes.

'What an unusual and beautiful house.' Aunt Violet peered through the car window as they drew to a halt beside two steps leading to double front doors. 'It looks like something one would see in a child's storybook.'

The structure appeared to have grown from the rock; each ascending floor was slightly smaller than the one below, so it resembled a gothic castle. Semi-circular balconies extended from the upper floors, designed to give a view of the sea. The cliff rose twenty feet behind the property, offering some shelter from the worst sea winds. 'All it needs are a few turrets,' Hannah agreed.

Aidan alighted onto the gravel first, turning to hand out Aunt Violet and then Hannah. Darius came last, and all four stared up at the stone edifice with awe. The double front door was thrown open by an extremely handsome man who must have been waiting for the car to arrive.

'Detective Inspector Farrell.' He strode forward and shook Aidan's hand vigorously. His rich, round tone matched his outstanding looks. 'I'm delighted you accepted my invitation.'

'If that's the butler, I cannot wait to meet the man of the house,' Aunt Violet whispered.

'Behave yourself.' Hannah hushed her. 'That's Gabriel Allardyce, the man who was outside Daphne Allardyce's house in Glenfair Road that day, remember?'

'Is it really? Then I wish I'd paid more attention,' Aunt Violet whispered.

He turned and repeated the action with Darius. 'And you must be Mr Clifford. Welcome to Swan's Nest.'

Turning, he approached Hannah with an enquiring smile, which she returned, confident he knew exactly who she was.

'Hannah Merrill,' she said, taking his outstretched hand. His smile revealed he was about to raise it to his lips, so giving it a firm shake she released it, indicating Aunt Violet. 'And this is my aunt, Miss Violet Edwards.'

'We're delighted you accepted our invitation.' He swept Aunt Violet's hand into his and planted a kiss on her knuckles, turning to Hannah with a 'look what you missed' gleam in his eye. 'Two more beautiful women to grace our home this evening.'

Their host drew them into an interior that was unexpected. Instead of dark oak and lowering beams the predominant colour was white with gold and cream accents, with Victorian coving with gold leaf detail, chandeliers, and marble fireplaces alongside matching floors, archways between rooms and pedestals where small plaster busts were arranged. The cantilevered staircase rose in a wide curve to the upper floor. An abundance of gilt and crystal reflected the light from tall windows.

'I apologise for whisking Miss Worsley-Brooke away from London during a police investigation.' His gaze flicked from Aidan to Hannah and back again. 'Alice feared for her safety, so I thought it best for her to stay here with my sister.'

'Did your stepmother know where Alice was that day we called on her?' Hannah asked, refusing to be silenced by Aidan's warning frown. 'Only I'm sure you were parked outside when we left.'

'Ah.' He swallowed. 'Pure coincidence, I assure you. I had gone there to explain Alice's predicament, but she pre-empted me with an attack of the hysterics about two ladies who claimed she was missing.'

'We didn't mean to upset her,' Hannah replied, chastened.

'She'll recover. She asked me to tell you she donated to your Princess Mary boxes scheme too.'

Hannah inwardly winced, but polite enough not to relish her discomfort he turned his benign smile on Aidan. 'I apologise for my stepmother's lack of co-operation, but having her niece connected to a murder was quite a shock.'

'I get a lot of that.' Aidan sighed, adjusting his tie, which appeared to have become too tight.

Hannah took the first empty seat she came to on a sofa at right angles to the fireplace and sneaked another look at Gabriel. He didn't seem like a ruthless seducer, but then she had been wrong before.

A well-preserved woman in her forties stepped through a curtain separating the room from what appeared to be a dining room. Her champagne-coloured gown accentuated her still slender figure. A circle of sparkling stones encircled her unlined neck, which Hannah speculated were genuine diamonds, but she would have to get closer to make sure. Her blonde hair was swept up on her head, fastened at her temples with matching clips.

Despite their not being related, Georgina might have been Alice's older sister, though her eyes were blue rather than green.

'And this is my sister, Georgina Ure-Reid.' Gabriel presented her like a duchess, showing his obvious affection for her.

'Welcome to Swan's Nest, everyone.' Her voice was soft, slow and compelling, her features a subtle version of her brother's, but no less attractive.

'Your home is stunningly beautiful.' Hannah aimed the compliment at Gabriel.

'Thank you. Although to be accurate, it's Georgina's house. I take unfair advantage of it whenever London palls. All the principal rooms face the sea with breathtaking coastal views which never fail to impress me, no matter how many times I come here.' Gabriel gestured for them to be seated. 'Please make yourself comfortable. Withers will serve aperitifs of your choice before dinner.'

'And I'm quite envious of this house, Mrs Ure-Reid,' Aunt Violet said as they shook hands.

'Georgina, please.' Their hostess' smile was enigmatic. 'I married a man who claimed to be a wealthy businessman, but who turned out to be a professional gambler. He dragged me around Europe for several years, dodging creditors and raising funds to play his next game. One summer, he had a rare spate of good luck and won this house in a game of vingt-et-un. He died soon afterwards,' she said, with no apparent regret. 'I never remarried.'

'I like her,' Aunt Violet said, when Georgina excused herself.

'Of course, you do. She could be your twin, but for the hair,' Hannah whispered. 'And possibly the diamonds,' she added mischievously, earning her a sharp dig to the ribs.

The double doors to the hall slowly opened, followed by a silent heartbeat creating a sense of anticipation. Then a figure appeared in the frame and a young woman entered. Her sapphire gown revealed her creamy white shoulders, the fabric shot through with silver that glimmered as she walked. The slow way it swept the floor as she glided towards them showed it was heavy.

Hannah took a few seconds to recognise her. She looked very different from the nervous girl in the grey-brown uniform that day in the bookshop. Her confidence took a dip at her beauty. She glanced sideways to gauge Darius' reaction, but he was talking to Aidan, enabling her to relax.

'Alice!' Hannah left her seat and swept towards her. 'I can't tell you how pleased I am to see you, um, again.'

'It's a pleasure to see you too, Miss Merrill.' She took both Hannah's hands in hers as if they were old friends. 'I cannot help feeling guilty knowing you were trying to find me. Because as you can see, I'm quite safe.'

'You met my aunt at the bookshop.' Hannah reclaimed one hand which she used to indicate her aunt. 'And this is Mr Darius Clifford, my um... good friend.'

'I also am delighted to see you safe and well, Miss Worsley-Brooke.' Darius inclined his head, smiling.

The rolling boom of a dinner gong brought conversation to a halt, and Gabriel clapped his hands. 'Ah, I hope everyone is hungry. My cook is most inventive, which is becoming more necessary with all these food shortages. However, living in the country has its advantages. We have a substantial vegetable garden.'

'You can grow produce up here on a cliff?' Aunt Violet asked, incredulous. 'We live by a river and even our potatoes are hardly impressive.'

'The garden is lower down and very sheltered.' He extended a hand towards the dining room. 'Shall we go in?'

Georgina led them through a double arched doorway into a cavernous dining room. A circular floor-to-ceiling bay window across almost the entire far wall gave a magnificent view of the sea. The room was luxurious, with high ceilings, ornate decorations, parquet flooring and a huge marble fireplace. Crystal candelabra and vases of spring flowers decorated a circular marquetry dining table in the centre.

'I've put you to a lot of trouble, haven't I?' Alice said, when they sat over bowls of clear soup on which artfully cut pieces of vegetable floated. 'It wasn't my intention, but I found myself in a difficult situation. I now realise I handled it badly.' Her vivid blue eyes sparkled now they were no longer filled with anxiety.

'You were so nervous in the bookshop that day, I was quite concerned,' Hannah replied. 'Then when you disappeared, I'm afraid I overreacted, I—'

'Don't apologise.' Alice covered Hannah's hand on the table. 'You tried to help me, but I was in no state to recognise it.'

'Despite the misunderstanding, Alice and I appreciate your efforts, Miss Merrill.' Gabriel tore a bread roll in half and spread some butter on it.

'Did Sister Kerr really kill Sergeant Tillman?' Alice's blue eyes widened but held resignation rather than shock. 'Gabriel told me he was blackmailing her.'

'She did.' Hannah nodded. 'Did you see something that night? Is that why you left without a word to anyone?'

'I left the day of the murder because Marion insisted I go home and get some rest. When Inspector Farrell asked me the same question, I explained, but according to him, Marion denied it.'

'I don't mean to be rude,' Hannah began. 'But that seems like a strange reason to leave town.'

'I agree, but the night Sergeant Tillman was killed, I saw Sister Kerr, Marion, coming out of the kitchen just before I went in to make the cocoa. It didn't make sense as she wasn't supposed be on night shift but I thought I must have got it wrong. Sometime nurses do extra shifts if we are busy and thought no more about it. Hospital corridors aren't quiet places with people and trolleys being wheeled back and forth at all hours. I went into the kitchen to make the cocoa, to find someone had put the milk on to heat, which never happens. I asked Sister Hibbert, but she muttered something about missing sleeping powders and ignored me.'

'Those sleeping powders explained how the killer carried it off with no one hearing the shot,' Aidan interjected.

'Then when the body was found,' Alice went on. 'Sister Kerr claimed she had only just come on shift. Well – no one does three shifts in a row.'

'I recall she hustled you out because you felt faint,' Hannah said.

'Which was a lie.' Alice 'tsked', visibly annoyed. 'She wanted to get me outside the library to warn me to keep quiet about seeing her the previous night. I didn't know why it was important then. That only occurred to me later.'

'If the cocoa was drugged,' Aunt Violet's sultry voice drew all eyes, 'why didn't the sergeant sleep through the night as well?'

'Sergeant Tillman only drank tea,' Alice replied. 'Marion would have been aware of that. When Dinah came running to say Sergeant Tillman was in the library, I could tell Marion didn't want me there.'

'She was protecting herself, not you,' Hannah said. 'No one could seriously imagine you had killed the sergeant.'

'Which wasn't how it felt at the time. I mean, who would take the word of a novice volunteer nurse against a respected member of staff?'

'There are many layers to crime, Miss Worsley-Brooke. I like to think I'm experienced enough to tell the difference between someone capable of murder, and someone being manipulated. Your behaviour when questioned was concerning but there was nothing I could arrest you for,' assured Aidan.

'And what made you suspect Alice in the first place?'

Georgina's long, elegant fingers stroked her necklace as she fixed him with a challenging stare.

'Forgive my policeman's logic, Mrs Ure-Reid, however Miss Worsley-Brooke didn't help herself. She lodged with a killer and might have been culpable in harbouring a deserter. I couldn't ignore that.'

'I'm relieved to hear I am no longer in your sights, Inspector.' Alice's smile lit up her face even more. 'I apologise for being less than candid.'

'That's enough depressing talk for tonight.' Gabriel clapped his hands together, prompting the hovering maids to remove the empty soup plates and sherry glasses, replacing them with the fish course.

'We're very proud of our fish here in Lowestoft,' Gabriel said as Hannah applied her fish knife to a sea bass. 'These were freshly caught this morning.'

'It's delicious.' Hannah savoured the white fish in wine sauce 'Do you always eat so well here? It's becoming difficult to find things like fresh fish in London these days.'

'We send most of it to markets and to the troops, naturally. Mrs Ure-Reid joined the conversation. 'But we keep some thing back for ourselves.' She exchanged a look with Gabriel, which may or may not have been conspiratorial.

Hannah chose not to speculate. She had been wrong abou Gabriel once already, so chose to keep her thoughts to herself. And the fish really was good.

* * *

'I can hardly believe I was lodging with a murderess,' Alice said, a she tucked into an entrée of thin and crisp vol-au-vent pastry with mutton cutlets. 'Marion didn't seem at all the type.'

'She must have unnerved you to make you leave so abruptly,' Hannah said.

'The footsteps in the night didn't bother me nearly so much as being followed.' Alice twirled the silver fork in her fingers. 'That day at your bookshop, I was so confused. I didn't want to go back to the house, so I wandered around Liberty's for a while before I remembered Georgina was in town, so went to her hotel.'

'I took her to lunch, and she told me everything.' Georgina gestured to her brother to pass the salt. 'When she mentioned being followed, that settled it. I instructed my driver to take us to this Circus place where we packed a bag. She shared my suite at Claridge's that night, and the next day we drove here. I couldn't possibly have left her there.' She wrinkled her nose in distaste. 'It's hardly the sort of place I want a relative of mine to live.'

'It wasn't that bad, Georgina. And Marion was kind to me until the night the sergeant was murdered,' Alice said, oblivious to the irony of that remark. 'She struggled to pay her bills, and with her husband dead, I was glad to help.'

'Only he wasn't.' Aunt Violet held up her fork on which clung a miniscule piece of pastry. 'Dead, I mean.'

'You left at an opportune time, under the circumstances,' Hannah said, to cover the awkward silence this provoked.

'I didn't know Marion had killed anyone, but at the time several things struck me as wrong. Georgina promised to tell no one where I was.'

'Except Gabriel,' Hannah interjected.

'Yes.' Alice's expression softened. 'Georgina rang him from the hotel. He said I should tell the police everything, only I had lied to my family already about becoming a nurse, so I was too nervous.' Her eyes narrowed at Aidan. 'You can be quite intimidating, Inspector. And you made it clear you regarded me as unreliable.'

Hannah sliced a sideways look at Darius, whose bemused wholesome dimple-revealing smile made her pulse race.

'Mr Allardyce?' Darius began. 'If you didn't know the police were actively looking for Alice, what made you visit Scotland Yard?'

'I told Gabriel about Sergeant Tillman being killed and how Marion had behaved,' Alice began. 'He said I wasn't directly involved and shouldn't worry. Only then he showed me the sketch in the London newspaper of the young man who died.'

'His name was Duffy,' Hannah murmured. 'And he was murdered.' Though no one appeared to hear her.

'It was such an excellent likeness.' Alice shuddered. 'I recognised him at once. I knew we couldn't pretend it was nothing to do with me any longer, so I asked Gabriel to come and see you. To explain.'

'Yours is a story I intend to dine out on, Alice,' Aunt Violet said. 'Though if Hannah hadn't found your book, we may never have discovered who you really were... Nurse Dalglish.'

'Book?' Alice frowned.

'The copy of *Pride and Prejudice*,' Hannah supplied.

'The one she filched from your room at Percy Circus,' Aunt Violet added.

'Yes, thank you, Aunt Violet.' Hannah nudged her, hard.

Alice laughed. 'I wondered where that had got to. I had meant to bring it with me, but I was in such a rush, I forgot it.'

'I brought it with me, so I shall be more than happy to return it to you,' Hannah said. 'I also have some letters you left behind in your room.'

'From Rafe?' Her eyes lit up. 'Thank you. I remembered them in Georgina's motor car, but it was too late to go back. I'll be so pleased to have them again.'

'I also hope you'll forgive me for suspecting you, Mr Allardyce,'

Hannah began, nervous about possibly offending him in his own home. 'I thought she might have a reason to avoid your, er... attentions.'

'I was never afraid of him, Miss Merrill.' Alice exchanged a lingering look with Gabriel. 'I had just lost my brother, my only relative apart from my aunt. An aunt – and forgive me Gabriel, I know you care for her – but who was always terribly cold towards Rafe and me.'

'And I was precipitous.' Gabriel's smile was useful. 'I should have known Alice was in no emotional state to handle a proposal on top of Rafe's death. I saw it as a solution to her pain, but I was wrong.'

Alice kept her steady gaze on Gabriel. 'Knowing he was prepared to face the consequences of interfering with a police investigation, it made me realise I was wrong to have refused him. I've changed since my brother died, and Gabriel helped me with my grief. I know what we mean to each other now and so we plan to announce our engagement when we return to London.'

A murmur of congratulations circled the table as the couple continued to stare into each other's eyes, while Georgina brushed away a tear.

'No dessert for me.' Aunt Violet waved off the maid who offered her a fruit and custard confection loaded with whipped cream. 'I've had enough syrup this evening.'

'You don't put syrup in a trifle,' Hannah responded in a stage whisper.

* * *

The evening progressed on a lighter note once all questions had been answered. Darkness had fallen outside and the candles on the table reflected in the glass, making the room feel smaller, more intimate.

'Perhaps we could withdraw to the sitting room for coffee?' Georgina rose regally and led them all into a sitting room, which was only slightly smaller than the dining room, but more intimate.

Coffee and brandy were distributed amid laughter and light chatter as the hands of the clock ticked the minutes away. The conversation reduced to an indistinct murmur in the background as Hannah's eyelids felt heavy, and began to droop, only to snap open at the entry of the butler.

'Pardon the intrusion, Mr Allardyce.' He paused beside Gabriel's chair. 'There's a Commander Ballantyne in the hall asking to talk to Mr Clifford. He says it's urgent.'

'It's almost midnight.' Georgina frowned at the intruder. 'What can the chap have to discuss at this hour?'

'Pardon my presumption, Mr Allardyce, Mrs Ure-Reid.' Darius placed his brandy glass on the mantel. 'It's important I speak to this man.' He inclined his head politely before heading for the door.

Hannah watched him go, aware she was so focused on her conversation with Alice he had barely spoken during the meal.

'Are you acquainted with this Commander Ballantyne?' Aunt Violet asked Gabriel.

'Only by reputation. He's something to do with the command of the Harwich Force which offers protection for the minelayers and air carriers operating the bight. Other than that, I have no idea why he would wish to speak to Mr Clifford. Is he a naval man?'

'Not really,' Hannah replied, unsure if Darius even had a rank. She nodded to the maid to replenish their miniscule cups of fragrant coffee and tried not to worry.

'I apologise for breaking up the party,' Darius said, rejoining them mere moments later. 'The commander has informed me that

Zeppelins bombed Norwich and Ipswich earlier this evening and were fired on by British ships.' A shocked hush ran through the company but tailed off when he continued. 'All nearby naval officers have been summoned to the Customs House as they expect a retaliatory attack in the next few hours.'

Georgina gasped and Alice paled, while Aunt Violet impulsively grabbed Aidan's hand. 'What sort of attack?' Gabriel's horrified expression showed the secret had been well kept.

'I might as well tell you, as you'll learn soon enough.' Darius paused and scanned their faces. 'A German scouting troop of eight battlecruisers and two destroyers has been spotted heading this way. The Harwich Force of three light cruisers and eighteen destroyers were ordered to move north to intercept. Warnings are being issued, but there's every chance any actual fighting will happen at sea, though it's uncertain.'

'Aren't there plenty of our mines in these waters to keep the enemy ships away?' Aidan asked.

'There are.' Darius measured his words carefully. 'But I fear German intelligence will have discovered those and will avoid them by hugging the Belgian and Dutch coasts.'

Gabriel rose and turned the handle beside the fireplace to summon the butler. 'As a precaution, I suggest you send for your luggage from the hotel and stay here at Swan's Nest.'

'We don't wish to be a bother,' Hannah began. 'If this attack is to take place at sea, we're unlikely to be in any danger at the hotel.'

'I beg to differ—' Gabriel began.

'Of course, you must stay here.' Georgina interrupted him, patting Hannah's shoulder on her way to the bell pull beside the fireplace. 'You're all our guests. I'll instruct the servants to prepare three extra guest rooms while your luggage is sent for.'

'We will be safe here, won't we, Gabriel?' Alice rushed to his side, her luminous eyes wide with fear.

'As safe as anywhere, my love.' He stroked her cheek and guided her towards Georgina. 'It's late, and there's nothing happening yet, so I suggest everyone go up to bed and try to get some sleep.'

'It's obvious why Alice ultimately couldn't resist him,' Hannah whispered, when she parted company with Aunt Violet on the landing. 'If a man like Gabriel Allardyce wanted to protect me from the world, I don't know if I would be strong enough to resist.'

'Darius ought to marry you before you go off the rails, young lady,' Aunt Violet said. 'Now take that silly grin off your face, or you'll get a reputation for being a flapper.'

'Appreciating masculine beauty and a pair of compelling green eyes doesn't make me a flapper. Besides, we have more to worry about right now than my reputation.'

19

Woken from a fitful sleep created by a combination of nerves and unfamiliar surroundings, Hannah bolted upright as a resounding boom shook the building. She stared around, disoriented, then remembered she was in a canopied bed at Swan's Nest and not her bedroom in Chiswick.

Gunfire! The thought struck at the same second another blast shook the entire house. A vase on a bureau toppled and smashed onto the floor.

Blinking her eyes into focus, she peered at her travel clock on the nightstand. It was 4.11 a.m.

The boom came again, closer this time, followed by another. Throwing off the covers, her feet hit the floor and she hauled the curtains open, flooding the room with hazy, early morning daylight.

At first, she thought a sea mist obscured the view, but as the grey cloud bloomed and swirled, she realised it was smoke. Another boom came and more smoke billowed over the edge of the cliff.

Ignoring the gown hanging on the wardrobe door, she flung

open her suitcase and dragged out the first item her fingers found
– a blue skirt she followed with a slightly wrinkled white blouse
she'd worn on the train. Finally, she pushed her feet into a pair of
slippers and hurried downstairs.

Aidan stood at the window in his shirtsleeves on the next
landing down, his braces hanging loose. He had thrown up the
sash and leant so far out she feared he might tip over the sill and
topple into the shrubbery below.

'Is it the Germans?' Hannah asked, her voice high and tinged
with panic.

'I bloody well hope so, or we're in more trouble than I thought,' he
muttered, bringing his head back inside. 'A couple of battlecruisers
are bombarding the town. There are destroyers as well, but from this
distance it's difficult to make out how many of them there are.'

Hannah joined him at the window, but all she could see was
more smoke with patches of blue sea in between.

A door banged further along the hall on that level and Aunt
Violet hurried towards them, rapidly fastening the buttons on her
burgundy skirt.

'How close are they?' she asked, frantically tucking her eau-de-
nil silk blouse into the waistband.

'About four or five miles.' Aidan continued to stare out at the
far distance, his eyes narrowed. 'I can't see any Zeppelins. Maybe
it's just the battlecruisers.'

'Fetch Darius.' Aunt Violet tapped him lightly on the shoulder.

He turned to move down the hallway, but Darius was already
striding towards them. 'Go downstairs and stay there,' he
instructed, taking the stairs two at a time.

'I don't know much about heavy artillery, but we must be out
of range up here.' Though Hannah was more hopeful than knowl-
edgeable.

'We certainly are, but the town is getting a battering,' Darius said. 'Aidan, see if you can find Gabriel and we'll take a car and see if there's anything we can do.'

'You read my mind.' Aidan turned and ran back the way he had come.

Doors opened and the slow-moving figures of Georgina and Alice joined them, both rumpled from sleep.

Hannah clattered down the last flight of stairs behind Aunt Violet and into the hall. The scream of shells and explosions continued, growing faster and more intense, so they had to shout above the noise.

In the hall, partly dressed servants drifted from the basement and attics. They stood huddled together, scared and quiet, waiting for orders.

Withers unlocked the front doors, allowing weak dawn light into the hall. The servants and guests went into the drive, their eyes shielded with their hands to see what was happening.

Gabriel appeared and stepped out onto the drive, a pair of binoculars held up to his eyes trained on the sea.

'Can you see anything?' Georgina cowered as another shell screamed towards them but fell short of the cliff.

'Looks like the *HMS Conquest*, but I cannot see clearly,' Gabriel replied. 'There are six torpedo boats. No, eight!' he yelled with growing excitement. 'Our destroyers are firing a broadside at the Germans.'

Every few seconds, another missile sailed over the water in a horrific bombardment, culminating in sickening crashes as they impacted on shops and houses in the town below them.

After about twenty minutes the shooting halted abruptly, leaving the small crowd on the drive confused by the sudden heavy silence.

Hannah's ears rang, and she swallowed repeatedly to clear the pressure.

'May I?' Darius took the binoculars from Gabriel and held them up to his eyes. 'The German ships appear to be leaving now ours have drawn their fire away from the town.'

'Did we win?' a gardener's boy shouted.

'God only knows,' Darius muttered, lowering the binoculars. 'I suspect this was a show of strength rather than a serious invasion attempt. But we won't know until the extent of damage and casualties are known.'

'A distraction to keep us occupied while the Irish nationalists disrupt Dublin?' Aidan nodded sagely. 'Just as you thought, Darius.'

'Not that the town got away unscathed.' He drew attention to the plumes of smoke rising above the cliff, a pungent smell of burning filling the air. 'I suggest we go into town and see if we can help the injured. There might be people trapped in fallen buildings. What do you say, Mr Allardyce?'

'Excellent suggestion.' Gabriel reclaimed his binoculars and handed them to Georgina.

'What can we do to help?' Aunt Violet asked.

'I appreciate the offer, Miss Edwards,' Gabriel said. 'But we don't yet know how bad the damage is. It's bound to be chaos down there. Once we have a better idea of what is needed, perhaps—'

'Go, darling.' Georgina gave her brother a light shove. 'The ladies and I will gather some supplies together. Blankets, and whatever food we can find. We'll load my motor car and bring it to the Customs House later.'

'Good idea.' Relieved, Gabriel planted a kiss on his sister's cheek, before he headed for the motor car they had travelled up in the evening before, a journey that seemed so long ago now.

'Well, at least we can make ourselves useful while we're here.' Aunt Violet wrapped an arm around Hannah's waist and drew her back inside.

'Wait.' Hannah resisted, her gaze on the edge of the drive where Gabriel's motor car had been seconds before. A flash of something white had appeared in her peripheral vision, but was gone again.

'What are you looking at?' Her aunt smiled. 'Can't you bear to see Darius going off into dangers unknown?'

'Don't tease, Aunt Violet.' Hannah winced as the shaft hit home. 'I thought I saw something in the bushes.'

'What sort of something?' Aunt Violet followed her gaze. 'Those rhododendrons are so thick I'm surprised you could see anything through them.'

'I... I don't know. I'm probably imagining it. My head is still fuzzy after being woken after so little sleep.'

'We have work to do. Georgina said to meet her in the pantry.' Her aunt wrapped both arms around her midriff. 'Dawn might be pretty here but it's still cold.'

* * *

'I haven't yet congratulated you, Alice.' Hannah broke the silence as they stood at the kitchen table arranging foodstuffs in wooden packing cases. The shelling had tailed off to distant whistles and the odd crash, then stopped altogether. 'You and Gabriel are so well suited, which came as a surprise when I was informed there was nothing between you.'

'I've always admired him.' Alice's cheeks flushed prettily. 'Even when I was still at school. When he proposed the first time, I was only sixteen, and overwhelmed at the idea of being a wife and making him happy, which is why I refused.'

'Gabriel isn't as complicated as you imagine,' Georgina said as she emerged from the pantry, apparently having heard this last remark. 'He resembles an Adonis, but he's a simple soul at heart.'

'And the second time,' Hannah said. 'After your brother died?'

'Oh, I was a mess and didn't know what I wanted. Once I felt normal again, I realised I'd been too impulsive. Fortunately, Gabriel never gave up on me. He says he's always loved me. His loyalty has proved that.' She frowned, and her hands stilled on a pack of sugar. 'Who told you he had no interest in me?'

'Josie Bellamy. I'm afraid my inherent nosiness unearthed the fact she was a friend of yours.'

'That's odd she should say that. What was—' Alice broke off as the butler sidled towards them, his face grave.

'What is it, Withers?' Georgina asked.

'It's the servants, madam.' He crept closer, his voice a reverent whisper. 'They're becoming concerned for the safety of their families after the shelling.'

'I see.' Georgina nodded. 'Of course, I should have thought of that. Send them home, Withers, but warn them to take care. We don't want to add to however many casualties are down there.'

The staff thanked their mistress and filed out of the kitchen, leaving their items behind. They could be heard on the other side of the kitchen door, discussing where they would go first and who had a spare bicycle they could borrow.

'What else might be needed?' Hannah asked, surveying the various boxes laid out on the kitchen table. 'We don't even know how many people are affected and need to make provision for.'

'Pack anything we can spare. I'm sure it will be put to good use.' Georgina darted around the kitchen, pulling things from cupboards and loading them into boxes.

Aunt Violet emerged from the scullery, her skirt sporting a layer of flour. 'I've found some carbolic and disinfectant.' She held up a box that once held Lifebuoy soap. 'Can you spare these jars of preserved fruit, Georgina?'

'I'll be glad to get rid of them. Cook has been stockpiling them for months, and Gabriel hates rhubarb.' Georgina laughed as she hefted a wooden crate into her arms. 'I'll take these out to the motor car and be back in a minute for more.'

'Where's Alice gone?' Hannah asked.

Georgina halted at the door and turned back. 'She's upstairs searching for old sheets to be used for bandages.' She tucked the full box under one arm. 'I didn't have the heart to tell her that since the shelling only lasted for twenty minutes, the hospital will probably be able to cope.' The side door slammed behind her, leaving Hannah with Aunt Violet.

'This is blackberry jam.' Aunt Violet held up one of the preserving jars she was loading into an empty wooden crate. 'My favourite.'

'Perhaps they could spare you a couple?' Hannah said, sealing the box ready to carry outside. 'I'll load this into the boot and come back for more.'

She took the path around the side of the house onto the drive where Georgina's motor car was parked. Boxes were piled onto the jump seat, and one lay on its side near the rear wheel, the contents spilled onto the gravel.

Hannah frowned as she scanned the drive, but it was empty. She circled the vehicle and halted, almost dropping the box. Behind the rear offside wheel, Georgina lay prone on the gravel, her arms flung above her head.

Dropping the box on the ground where it landed with a thud, Hannah crouched beside her.

'Georgina?' She shook her shoulder, trying to work out what might have happened. Had she fainted? Had she tripped on something and fallen?

Georgina did not stir. Her eyes were closed, and she lay motionless. Hannah placed her fingers against her neck and exhaled in relief as a steady pulse throbbed beneath her fingers.

There was still no one in sight, so she scrambled to her feet and ran back into the kitchens. 'Aunt Violet! Come outside quickly. It's Georgina.'

To her credit, her aunt asked no questions – she simply dropped the bar of carbolic soap she was holding and headed out to the drive at a run.

Hannah followed, arriving to see her aunt bent over the woman who had not moved.

'What happened?' Aunt Violet bent and grasped Georgina's wrist, her lips moving as she counted.

'I don't know. I found her like this. The servants left a while ago and there was no one about when I arrived.'

'She's alive, but out cold.' Aunt Violet probed Georgina's skull gently with her fingers. 'She has a small gash on her head, but there isn't much blood. Perhaps she fell and hit her head?'

'On what?' Hannah shrugged and cast about her for a possible cause. 'There's nothing here that could cause an injury like that.'

'Well, we can't leave her here.' Aunt Violet lifted Georgina's arm, tucked her shoulder into her armpit and hauled her to her feet. 'Take her other side, Hannah.'

Between them they carried the unconscious woman into the sitting room and laid her on the couch.

'Alice might be able to help as she's had some medical training,' Hannah suggested. 'We need to call a doctor, though.'

'I agree, but most of the medics in town will be tending to the wounded.'

Georgina moaned, moving her head from side to side on the cushion Hannah had placed behind her head, her eyes still closed.

'I hope that cushion wasn't a favourite?' Hannah chewed her

bottom lip. 'It's got blood on it now.' She paused at the door and looked back. 'I'll get the coverlet from my bed to put over her and tell Alice while I'm up there.'

Hannah bounded up two flights, her feet slowing on the second landing where the doors of the armoire stood open. A trail of sheets crossed the landing carpet to Alice's room, but there was no sign of her.

'Alice!' Hannah called, halting at the open door of Alice's room. 'Georgina is hurt and I need—' Her eyes widened and a chill ran through her.

The doors to the balcony were thrown wide and Alice sat balanced on the rail over a fifty-foot cliff drop to the sea below. Her vivid blue eyes widened as she saw Hannah and filled with a silent plea for help, but no words escaped her.

Behind her stood Josie Bellamy, a long kitchen knife with an inch-wide blade held to Alice's throat, her free arm locked tightly around the girl's shoulders.

* * *

'Josie?' Hannah crept forward, her steps slow and measured so as not to startle her. 'What are you doing?' It was a ridiculous thing to say, but seeing her there made no sense.

'What do you think?' Josie raised the knife higher, forcing Alice's chin upwards an inch as the blade touched her throat. 'Stay where you are. I'm about to finish what I started, and you won't stop me.'

'Finish what, Josie?' Hannah halted, gauging the distance to the balcony. Making a dash for it appealed, but wasn't an option. She would never reach Josie in time to stop her carrying out whatever she had planned. The house was old, and the rail set low. It would only take a light push for Josie to send Alice over the edge. The presence of the knife certainly complicated things as well.

'Why do you want to hurt Alice? She's your friend.' Hannah's hands suddenly felt clammy, and she wiped them against her skirt.

'Friend!' Josie screeched. 'She's no friend to me.' She tightened her arm around Alice's shoulders, pulling her backwards against the rail.

Alice squeezed her eyes shut and whimpered.

'How did you get here?' Hannah kept her voice conversational. Unthreatening. 'We thought you were in London.' If she could only keep her talking until help came... But from where? The men were in the town and the servants had left. There was only an unconscious Georgina and Aunt Violet. Aunt Violet! She had no idea what was happening.

Josie looked confused at the question, as if she couldn't remember why she was there. A thin line of blood trickled down Josie's forehead from a gash at her hairline to which she appeared oblivious.

'Train.' Josie said after a tense moment. 'No one questions a nurse in uniform. I booked into the Royal Hotel last night, but when the bombardment started, the window caved in. I ran outside and made my way up the hill and saw the servants leave.' Her eyes lost focus as her thoughts drifted and she gazed out over the sea. 'I came here two summers ago for a holiday. That's when we met.'

'Met who? Alice?' Hannah asked, her gaze fixed on the knife in Josie's hand, conscious that if Alice moved more than an inch, the blade would slice into her throat.

'Gabriel, of course!' Josie snarled, dismissive.

'Of course, sorry.' Gabriel? Why did that not occur to her before? She took a tentative step closer. 'We could talk about – Gabriel – but not when you're holding that knife to Alice's throat.

Put it down, Josie and I'll bathe that gash on your head. It looks painful.'

'No!' Josie tightened her hold on Alice, hauling her up on her toes. 'Don't come any closer!'

Alice gave a tiny shake of her head, her eyes fixed on Hannah in a silent plea.

Hannah froze, her hands raised in supplication. 'All right, I'll stay where I am. You might be relieved to know Georgina will be all right, although that was a nasty bump you gave her. I'm sure you didn't mean to do that.'

'Don't humour me,' Josie's upper lip curled. 'I don't care about her. Only Gabriel. He's mine. He always was. Until *she* took him away.' She aimed a contemptuous glare at Alice, whose blonde head came up to her chin, accentuating the difference in their height. 'She was never interested in Gabriel. Not until he took notice of me.'

Hannah searched for something to say which would not aggravate Josie more, when she heard footsteps ascend the stairs.

'Hannah?' Aunt Violet called out, her voice growing closer. 'Where are you?'

'I'm fine, Aunt Violet,' Hannah shouted back, then raised her voice. 'Don't come up here. I'm busy.'

'What are you talking about, busy? I need your help with Georgina, she's still—' Her aunt's footfalls halted abruptly in the doorway. 'What the hell—?'

Hannah groaned inwardly, not daring to look at her, muttering, 'She has a knife.'

'I can see that,' her aunt replied in a whisper, then louder, 'Hand the knife to me, Josie, before you cut yourself!' She made a reckoning motion with her fingers. 'Come along. I'm waiting.'

'That tone didn't work when I was in the nursery, Aunt Violet, and it won't now,' Hannah kept her voice low. 'She's not open to persuasion. Trust me.'

'It was worth a try,' her aunt whispered, her forward steps halted by Josie's harsh command to, 'Stay right there!'

'Now what?' Aunt Violet whispered but obeyed.

'I really don't know,' Hannah answered. 'Why don't you come away from the railing, Josie?' She tried to sound cheerful, but her voice shook. 'It's a long way down and you don't want to slip.'

'No?' Josie laughed, a harsh, unnerving sound. 'People fall from heights all the time and no one could survive one onto those rocks below.' She leaned a hip against the low railing, making it creak.

Hannah gasped and instinctively took a step forward, aware of her aunt Violet's low groan warning her to stay where she was.

'Why are you doing this, Josie?' Alice whimpered, her chest rising and falling in time with her panicked breaths. 'We've always been friends.'

'With you gone, Gabriel and I could be together.' Josie's voice became calm, almost reasonable. 'It's how things are supposed to be. You refused him, twice, so why should you have another chance?'

'I was only sixteen,' Alice squeaked. 'I—'

'Shut up!' Josie hauled Alice up onto her toes and pressed the knife against her throat, drawing a thin line of blood below her ear. The cut was long but shallow; not life-threatening. Although it would be sore later.

Alice released a horrified squeal but fell silent again.

Josie relaxed her arm, the knife dipping as she focused her attention on Hannah. 'Don't you see? It was me he really wanted.'

'Did Gabriel tell you that, Josie?' Hannah asked gently.

Had he led Josie on only to reject her for a wealthier subject, or was it all in Josie's imagination? The fury on the nurse's face told her it was the latter. Which made their situation even more deadly.

'He didn't need to tell me,' Josie smirked. 'You always know when it's the right person.'

'I cannot argue with that. Maybe he just doesn't know how you feel about him, Josie. You could talk to him.' Hannah smiled encouragingly at Alice, whose teeth worried her lower lip showing she fought to stay calm. But for how long?

'He came to see me at Cheyne Walk after you two busybodies left.' Josie's angry expression softened. Her arm slid from Alice's shoulders, and she took a step towards Hannah.

Hannah felt rather than saw Aunt Violet tense beside her, hoping she would not do something reckless. Her aunt never was one to submit to bullies.

Josie smirked. 'I told him Alice wasn't coming back. That she'd run off with one of her suitors and he should forget her.' She lifted the knife towards Hannah and twisted it from side to side. 'But he said I was wrong. That Alice was here at Swan's Nest with Georgina. That he was going to join them for the Easter holiday and stay to plan the wedding. *Their* wedding!'

'Josie, I promise you, I didn't know you felt that way.' Alice had not moved from the balcony, one hand against the cut on her neck.

'Listen to her, Josie,' Hannah pleaded. 'She didn't mean to hurt you.'

'Hurt?' Josie snarled, taking two steps towards Hannah so now there was barely six feet between them. 'She should already be dead! If that stupid fool had done what I paid him for, I—'

'Paid who, Josie? To do what?' Hannah asked carefully. Did she mean Duffy?

'Some boy I found in King's Cross. I paid him to follow her and arrange an accident.'

'What sort of accident?' Hannah swallowed.

Beside her, Aunt Violet gasped, but Hannah kept her gaze fixed on Josie.

Josie curled her lip. 'I left that to him. He said it would be easy, that people get run over by carriages all the time. But then she went missing. I went to the Coal Hole to tell him he was no longer needed, but that red-headed detective was following him. I knew then that if he was questioned, they might find out about me, so I —' She clamped her mouth shut as if she couldn't bear to say it. 'Nice touch with the beer though, wasn't it?'

'You pushed him down the steps?' Hannah murmured.

A movement on her right brought her attention to the window where Gabriel's motor car approached on the drive three stories below. They were too high for the engine noise to penetrate the wind from the sea, but the sight of it sent hope through her.

Confident help was on the way, but also that Josie was becoming more agitated the longer the standoff lasted, Hannah doubted they would get there before Josie did something rash.

Gathering her courage, she lunged forward, grabbed Alice's arm above the elbow and pulled her into the room.

Josie howled in protest and leapt between them. Hannah's hand was ripped from Alice's arm as Josie crashed into her, sending her into a large mahogany bureau. Her shin collided painfully with the corner, and she hit the floor, hard, bringing Alice down with her.

Aunt Violet moved towards them just as Josie brought the knife down in an overhead arc straight at Hannah, a glint of light dancing off the blade inches from her face. Panicked, she scrambled sideways, her back pressed against the wall away from the lethal blade.

'No!' Aunt Violet leapt at Josie; her arm raised to block the swing of the woman's arm.

Hannah's breath hitched and the room stilled.

Josie still gripped the handle of the knife that now embedded in Aunt Violet's forearm, the pointed blade protruding from the other side.

Alice screamed and Hannah froze, transfixed by the dark red bloom spreading slowly into Aunt Violet's sleeve.

20

Josie released the knife as if it was hot, and backed away, her eyes wide in shock.

Hannah rushed towards Aunt Violet but was intercepted by a strangely composed Alice. 'Don't touch it! We must immobilise it until we can get her to a hospital.' She climbed to her feet and ran onto the landing, returning almost immediately with a handful of cotton strips torn from a sheet.

'No hospital!' Aunt Violet insisted, her gaze fixed in disbelief on the blood oozing between her fingers and dripping onto her skirt.

'Don't be ridiculous, Aunt Violet,' Hannah snapped, aware her shin throbbed painfully. 'You'll need stitches, or even surgery to remove that knife.'

'We'll discuss that later,' Alice interrupted, tying a strip of cotton above Aunt Violet's elbow in a makeshift tourniquet. 'Now I know this is uncomfortably tight, but it will help stem the bleeding.'

'It hurts like hell!' Aunt Violet said through gritted teeth, as if surprised.

'Keep your arm raised,' Alice instructed. Grabbing a towel from a pile on the bed, she folded it into a thick wad and held it beneath her arm to stop the blood dripping onto the floor. 'Hannah, I want you to press it tight against her arm.'

Hannah obeyed, staring in stunned silence at the knife, surprised at how the shy, meek Alice had transformed into an efficient, compassionate nurse.

The slam of the front door sent Alice running out onto the landing, where she leaned over the railing and shouted. 'Up here! Quickly!'

There was the sound of rapid footsteps ascending the stairs and Aidan appeared at the door with Darius close behind him.

'What the—' Aidan's gaze went straight to Aunt Violet, transforming instantly into horror, replaced immediately by fury.

'Get Josie!' Hannah shouted to Darius, her hand still pressed against the bloody cloth. Unable to move, she thought Josie might make a dash for the balcony again, but she had not moved. Her face was expressionless, a streak of dried blood on her forehead.

Aidan stomped forward, wrapped an arm around Aunt Violet's waist and with the other took charge of the bloodied towel. 'Let go, Hannah, I'll keep hold of that. Now, sit down, Vi, before you fall down.' Gently, he eased her onto the edge of the mattress of the brass bed.

Darius eased Josie into a chair as far away from Aunt Violet, uttering soft, cajoling words and an unthreatening outstretched hand. She offered no resistance, her eyes dull and unfocussed as if at the horror of what she had done.

'I thought you were in town,' Aunt Violet said, shakily, her gaze fixed on her damaged arm.

'I was. But I'm here now.' He eased onto the bed beside her. 'I've quite a few wounds like this South of the River, but I never took you for a street fighter!' He gave an odd, stilted laugh, but if it was meant to smother his nerves, it failed.

'Not funny,' Aunt Violet snarled between gritted teeth. 'She was aiming for Hannah, but I got in the way.'

'Are you all right?' Darius asked Hannah over Josie's head, his eyes dark with concern.

'I almost wasn't, but Aunt Violet saved me.' Hannah climbed to her feet, wincing at the ache in her leg but ignored it. Avoiding his eyes, she blinked away tears as reaction set in, aware she was shaking but refusing to draw attention to it.

'We would have got here sooner, but I was held up at the Customs House and Aidan had to wait for me.' Darius nodded at the pair on the edge of the bed, both of whom seemed too absorbed in each other to pay them much attention.

'I can't believe Aunt Violet jumped in front of me.' Hannah swallowed, queasy at the sight of so much blood seeping into the cloth tied around her aunt's arm. 'Not that I'm not grateful.' She summoned a shaky smile.

'I don't know what came over me.' Aunt Violet's face was pale now and she swayed a little. 'But when I saw that knife coming towards Hannah, I just—' She shuddered.

'Where's Gabriel?' Alice clambered to her feet and smoothed down her skirt. Her fearful gaze went to the door, just as the man himself appeared in the door frame.

'I found Georgina in the sitting room, she's—' Gabriel froze splitting a horrified look between the occupants. 'What the hell been going on here?'

'It was Josie.' Alice's voice rose in fury rather than distress as she threw herself into his arms. 'She appeared from nowhere and dragged me onto the balcony. She said she was going to kill me so you and she could be together.'

'What?' Gabriel's jaw went slack, and his arms closed around her, but his gaze still roamed the room as if trying to make sense of the scene. 'What was Josie even doing here?'

Hannah composed herself enough to fill in the details of finding Georgina and how Aunt Violet had been injured.

'I must see to Georgina. She was coming round but couldn't tell me what happened.' He disentangled himself from Alice's arms. 'Will you take care of Alice for me?' This he directed at Hannah. 'I'll also telephone the doctor.'

'And the police!' Hannah called after him, but doubted he heard her.

'I don't need to be looked after,' Alice said gently when he had gone. 'I'm not as delicate as everyone believes. I'm a nurse, remember.' She smoothed down her dress, though the hitch in her voice betrayed she was badly shaken. 'Well sort of one. I obtained my First Aid Certificate.'

She brushed a stray blonde hair away from her forehead and handed more of the makeshift bandages to Aidan, who used one to mop up most of the blood that had flowed from Aunt Violet's arm.

'This will do temporarily until we get you to the hospital, Vi.' Aidan tossed a bloodied cloth aside and replaced it with a clean one.

'We tried that,' Hannah said. 'She refuses to go. I mean she volunteers at a military hospital so it can't be nerves.'

'I organise fundraising and concert parties,' Aunt Violet scoffed. 'I hate the smell of disinfectant. And I only need a few stitches. Besides, the hospital has enough to handle right now.'

'Don't be a martyr, Aunt Violet. Let us take care of you.' Hannah crouched on the floor beside her and avoided looking at her aunt's arm.

Gabriel reappeared as they were arguing. 'Our family doctor will be here in about ten minutes. He wasn't needed at the hospital as there have been fewer casualties than anticipated.'

'Which has to be good news.' Aunt Violet replied with a smile. 'A country GP, I can handle, but I meant what I said. No hospital.'

'All right, Vi. You win.' Aidan nodded, winking at Hannah over her bent head.

'How is Georgina?' Hannah addressed Gabriel. 'She was sleeping when we left her.' Was it only half an hour ago?

'She's got a headache, but nothing serious, I hope,' Gabriel replied. 'She's currently refusing to see the doctor, but I'm not giving her the choice.'

'Mr Allardyce,' Aidan began. 'Might I use your telephone to call the local constabulary to send someone to fetch our homicidal nurse?'

'No, please.' Alice paused from collecting the bloodstained scarf from the floor. 'Josie isn't dangerous. She's not herself. She simply had a – an odd turn.'

'This isn't simply someone having a bad day,' Aidan snorted, plainly furious. 'A crime has been committed here.'

'I appreciate you have a job to do, but could I prevail upon you to let us handle this? As a family.' Gabriel added his plea to Alice's.

'While conscious that I'm a guest in your house, Mr Allardyce, I'm also a police officer,' Aidan said, with barely restrained anger. 'What we have here is a case of attempted murder and a serious attack on Miss Edwards. I cannot ignore that.'

'Inspector, please.' Alice pleaded. 'We've known Josie for a long time. She's not homicidal, she's... unwell. Couldn't you let us handle this?'

'What should I do, Vi?' Aidan asked, clearly unhappy.

'To be honest, I want my arm sorted and then my breakfast. After that I simply don't care.'

Aidan huffed a noisy breath, slung one arm around Aunt

Violet's waist, and helped her to her feet. 'It seems people prefer to harbour a potential killer than involve the police,' he muttered to himself, as he supported Aunt Violet towards the stairs.

Hannah drew Alice out into the hallway, leaving Darius to keep watch by the door in case Josie's co-operation was short-lived.

'Are you all right?'

'What?' Alice frowned vaguely.

Hannah indicated the cut on her neck.

'Oh, that.' She brought a hand absently to the fine line of dried blood, as if she had forgotten it. 'This is nothing. I'm more worried about your poor aunt.'

'She'll be fine,' Hannah said. 'Aidan will make sure of that.'

'He won't arrest Josie, will he?' Alice pleaded. 'She didn't mean it.'

'Why are you so keen to protect Josie?' Hannah fought down her irritation. 'We all saw her holding a knife to your throat!'

'Because it's partly my fault. She can be volatile. She isn't a violent person by nature and she's an excellent nurse. She's always been... fond... of Gabriel, but I had no idea it was serious.'

'Didn't you realise she was trying to get him away from you?' Had Alice missed the signs, or simply not known what they were?

'She always said Gabriel only wanted me for my money. That's why I didn't tell her where I was. I guessed she wouldn't take it well, but... not this badly.'

'And Gabriel? What did he feel about that?'

'He's a gentleman, so he kept silent for a long time, but was always kind to her. He thought if he treated her politely, and with distance, she would get the message.'

'Women in love do not always take subtle hints, Alice. Though they aren't all murderous.'

'I've been very naïve, haven't I?' Alice's eyes clouded briefly, showing she was annoyed with herself. 'It was Josie who suggested I become a VAD and work at the same hospital she did.'

'To keep an eye on you, obviously.' Hannah snorted.

'It appears that way. I didn't like the idea at first, but it seemed a good way to honour Rafe, so I agreed. Josie also suggested I leave Aunt Daphne's house and move into Sister Kerr's because she and Gabriel wouldn't approve.'

'Quite the manipulator, wasn't she?' Darius raised a cynical eyebrow. 'Though she was subtle, I'll give her that.'

The ring of the front doorbell interrupted them. 'That's probably the doctor.' Alice brushed the hair out of her eyes and straightened her skirt. 'Withers hasn't returned yet, so I had better go down and let him in.'

Hannah followed her down the stairs more slowly, arriving in time to see her admit a tall, well-built man of about forty with a serious expression into the hall.

The front door stood open onto the drive, where the doctor's two-seater motor car dwarfed Gabriel's badly parked tourer.

Georgina's green vehicle half-blocked the entrance, the boot wide open and still displaying the contents of the pantry.

Hannah followed Aidan and the doctor into the sitting room where Aunt Violet occupied an overstuffed armchair, her elbow on a rolled-up blanket with the knife pointing down. Georgina dozed on a sofa beneath a coverlet pulled up to her chin, her blonde hair spread over her shoulders.

The medic removed his coat, placed his bag on the floor, and approached Aunt Violet, making no comment other than a low, and slightly bemused, 'Dear me.'

He took a small, ribbed brown bottle and a tiny glass from the depths of his bag, poured some syrupy looking liquid into it and handed it to Aunt Violet. She poured it onto her tongue, swallowed and grimaced.

'Ugh. My mother used to put it in brandy to make it palatable.' She wiped her mouth with her free hand. 'Perhaps you could do that next time.'

'It will help with the pain and make you drowsy. I'll give it a moment to take effect and, in the meantime, I'll examine your arm.'

'Is it bad?' Hannah whispered, relieved Aunt Violet gave no sign that she heard.

'It looks to be a clean cut, but I advise the lady to go to the hospital to have it thoroughly checked.'

'Could you just get it over with,' Aunt Violet said, enunciating each word.

Hannah watched through her fingers as he deftly removed it in one precise movement, eliciting a single, somewhat impolite word from her aunt.

'Will there be any permanent damage?' Aidan asked.

'It's difficult to tell.' The doctor chose a wicked-looking needle from his bag. 'You did well not to remove the implement. Penetrating injuries between the radius and the ulna often cause nerve damage. However, if it doesn't get infected and movement is not restricted, she might be lucky.'

'Do you know what's happening in the town?' Hannah asked, as Aunt Violet stoically submitted to the medic's sewing skills.

'Around two hundred houses have been destroyed.' He applied the needle expertly as he talked. 'Most people got out in time, and the last I heard, the injured numbered about a dozen.' He snipped the trailing end of the catgut and returned his instruments to the bag. Using a more conventional bandage, he rebound the wound before he leaned back on his haunches. 'Now, where's the other casualty?'

'Miss Bellamy is in the tower bedroom. I'll show you, Doctor.' Hannah rose, but he waved her back down again. 'I know where it is. You stay here with the patients. If either of them start to run fevers or are sick at any point, please let me know.'

'I'd rather go to my room.' Georgina threw off the blanket and swung her feet onto the floor, rubbing her temples with her fingertips of both hands. 'That sofa is full of lumps. I should have thrown it out years ago.'

'Allow me.' The doctor, whose name Hannah did not catch escorted her from the room.

Hannah closed the door gently, then crept back to where Aidan plumped up the pillow behind Aunt Violet's head. Her features were slack, her eyes closed, and her long lashes spread like tiny fans on her pale cheeks. She had left her hair unbound and it lay in dark ringlets on one shoulder making her look almost young.

'I hope Mr Allardyce knows what he's doing by not having Miss Bellamy arrested.' Aidan kept his voice low so as not to wake her, her aunt's uninjured hand gently in his.

'That's what I came to talk to you about.' Hannah perched on the arm of the sofa next to him. 'Josie said something up in the tower room I thought you should hear.'

'Go on.'

'Detective Pendleton mentioned someone in an overcoat with a green velvet collar push Duffy down the Savoy Steps?'

'He did. And a witness came forward to say he was on the step too when Duffy fell. We haven't located him yet, I'm afraid but we're still hopeful. Why do you ask?'

'I suggest you search Josie's flat in Cheyne Walk. I'll wage you'll find that coat in her room.'

'Miss Bellamy killed Duffy?' He looked away from her aunt briefly, his tone disbelieving.

'She let it slip when she threatened Alice. I noticed something odd about Josie when Aunt Violet and I visited her at her flat. Sh had a rash on her upper lip and above her eyes. And don't sigh, it's relevant, I promise. I think she disguised herself as a man to hire Duffy, with false eyebrows, a moustache and probably wore a man's overcoat too. He wasn't only supposed to follow Alice, but kill her, only she left London before he was able. Josie was determined to clear the way for her and Gabriel.'

'And you didn't think to mention this?' He shook his head, resigned. 'But why kill the boy? Why not send him down here to finish the job?'

'Maybe that's why she met him at The Coal Hole, to give him instructions. Only she recognised Detective Pendleton from Endell Street. Knowing you had connected Duffy to Alice, she dared not risk it leading them to her, so she disposed of Duffy instead.'

'But Duffy thought she was a man. We would never have suspected her.'

'It's possible that she panicked. If Detective Pendleton arrested Duffy, he would have coughed about his being employed to kill Alice.'

'Coughed?' He chuckled. 'Listen to you talking like a Whitechapel doxy.'

'You can blame my association with you for that.' Hannah flapped a hand at him. 'She couldn't risk Gabriel finding out she wanted Alice dead.'

'Huh, well he knows now.' Aidan stroked his chin thoughtfully. 'This is an outcome I didn't expect. Albert Kerr might be innocent of murder, but the desertion charge will stick. He's a dead man either way.'

'Perhaps you could handle the Josie situation quietly? Gabriel and Alice don't need to know about it yet.'

He nodded. 'I agree. Anyway, I wouldn't want to reveal your

suspicions until I have compiled the relevant evidence. Thank you for telling me.'

'In the meantime,' Hannah added, 'it might be wise to separate Josie from the Allardyces and Alice. For safety's sake?'

'How, if I'm not going to be allowed to arrest her?'

'The doctor is upstairs with Josie now. You could ask him to admit her to the hospital overnight? Maybe he could suggest her head wound is more serious than we first thought?'

'Good idea. I'll go up and speak to him.' Aidan tucked a stray strand of hair behind Aunt's Violet's ear and rose. 'Are you staying with her?'

'For a little while, yes.'

'Um... then perhaps you should know I... um... Look, when I walked in on that scene upstairs and saw that knife, then the expression on her face and – well...'

'Well, what?'

'I realised in that moment, I couldn't bear to lose her. Not for anything.'

'She was stabbed in the arm, Aidan. Hardly lethal.' Hannah suppressed a laugh.

'I know that, but it could have been worse. Much worse.'

'What do you intend to do about it?'

'Should I ask her to marry me?'

'Is that what *you* want?' It occurred to her then she had no clear idea of how Aunt Violet would react to a proposal. She kept her feelings for Aidan very close, as she did most things.

'I do. I've even attempted it a few times, but never quite come to the point. You must admit your aunt can be... forbidding.'

'I can't answer for her. Nor can I offer you advice. My aunt is an enigma. I rarely know what goes on in her head. I don't envy you.'

'Don't I know it Well, thank you for listening. I'd better see this medic chap.'

'Aidan?' she called him back. 'Whatever it takes to win her round, it will be worth it.'

'I know that.' He smiled knowingly at her over his shoulder as the door closed behind him.

'Hannah?' Aunt Violet murmured. Her eyes fluttered open but were unfocussed. 'Has he gone?'

'Er, yes, he has. You were awake all the time?' Hannah perched on the wide arm of her chair, careful to avoid Aunt Violet's bandage. 'Why didn't you say something?'

'He was talking about me, not to me.' She slurred her words like a drunkard.

'So you faked sleep instead? I assume you aren't amenable to his plans?'

'It's the first I've heard of it.' She caught Hannah's sceptical look and sighed. 'Oh, all right, he's hinted, but to be honest, I don't know how amenable I am.'

'Do you love him?' If the answer was in the affirmative, the question seemed moot.

'Of course I do, but that isn't what marriage is about. It's far more complicated than that. Dr Murray says marriage makes women domestic drudges who cannot function by themselves.'

'Never mind Dr Flora Murray's opinion, how do you feel?'

'Confused. If I say no, he might refuse to see me again. Gentlemen don't enjoy being rejected. And I want to see him. We've been discreet to prevent gossip. Then there's the age difference.'

'What's a few years in the grand scheme of things?'

'Perhaps, but keeping our secret adds a certain fillip to our... whatever it is we're doing.' She spoke slower than normal, her words harder to form as the laudanum took full effect. 'Being a married woman is too tradisshhnal.' She fumbled the word into gibberish.

'We are a pair, aren't we?' Hannah tucked the coverlet up under Aunt Violet's chin who shivered, though the room was not cold. 'You have a beau ready to make a lifetime commitment, and I have one who would rather leave home every two weeks and keep state secrets.'

'I cannot believe how wrong I was about Josie,' Aunt Violet enunciated each word carefully. 'I was so busy convincing you she was protecting her friend I missed all the signs. Leave her to Aidan to deal with, Hannah. She's dangerous.' Her eyelids drooped, her hand flopping to the coverlet with a slap.

Tears threatened as Hannah stared down at her sleeping aunt. If Josie had been slightly faster or closer, she could have been the one in the chair with stitches in her arm, or somewhere more lethal. She clenched her fists to stop them from shaking, bent and kissed her aunt's forehead.

'Thank you, Aunt Violet.' Her whisper rewarded with a loud, open-mouthed snore.

* * *

The smell of smoke and cordite hung in the air, and sounds of bells, whistles and shouts drifted to them from the town below the cliff a mile away as Hannah stood with Darius on the top step, his arm wrapped around her shoulders.

The tail end of the doctor's motor car disappeared through the gates, a heavily sedated Josie strapped into the seat beside him.

'She won't wake up and attack him, will she?' Hannah asked.

'I doubt it. She's got enough sedative in her to fell a horse. The hospital isn't far away. She'll be well taken care of there.'

'I know it isn't what Gabriel and Alice wanted, but I couldn't allow a killer to go free.'

'You did the right thing, Han.' He used her childhood nickname, that sent a wave of warmth into her cheeks. 'The courts will decide if she's fit to stand trial. Not you, the police, or anyone else.'

'You haven't called me that for so long. I thought you had forgotten it.'

'How could I?' He looked down at her from his impressive height, his lips turned up in a warm, genuine smile that crinkled the corners of his eyes. 'You're an important part of my life. Perhaps the most important part.'

To ask him if he meant that would sound too much like fishing for compliments. Instead, she nudged him playfully.

'This wasn't quite how we expected this holiday to go, was it?'

'Indeed, not. I feel so guilty about your aunt. Had Aidan, Gabriel and I not gone rushing into town, none of this might have happened.'

'The German attack would have.'

'You know what I mean.' He hugged her to him. 'There wasn't much need for us as there weren't nearly as many casualties as we thought, thankfully, and everything was well organised.'

'I doubt you could have changed anything. Josie was determined.'

'I couldn't have borne it if anything had happened to you.'

'Well, it didn't.' Warmth flooded her cheeks and she looked at her feet to hide it.

'I dropped in to see how your Aunt Violet was just now,' he said. 'She said you suspected Miss Bellamy early on.'

'Not early enough. I'll be more alert to liars in the future. Poor Aunt Violet. I hope it doesn't spoil this lovely house for them.' She turned to look at the pale stone facade lit by the morning sun behind them. 'Gabriel and Alice intend to spend their summers here when they are married. Although, if it were mine, I think I'd prefer one without balconies poised on the edge of a fifty-foot cliff.'

'I'll bear that in mind.' Darius chuckled.

'By the way, how is Georgina?'

'She has a sore head and is a little nauseous, but she's almost as indestructible as your Aunt Violet. The inspector suspects Josie hit her with a stone urn from the garden.'

'Poor Georgina.'

'I have to go back to London later today.' He spoke with his lips against her hair, sending shivers down her back. 'But Gabriel said you can all stay until Violet feels rested enough to travel.'

'Rested! Aunt Violet?' Hannah snorted, relishing the feel of his chin against the top of her head. 'No doubt we'll all be on the evening train exactly as scheduled.'

'Hannah.' He spoke with his lips pressed to her hair, so softly she almost didn't hear him. 'I need to discuss something with you.'

She lifted her chin and met his gaze, which was so intense, she imagined it could burn through her. Only his use of the word 'discuss' and not 'ask' made her heart sink a little. 'What is it?'

'Do you remember what I said to you when the bookshop was destroyed?'

How could she forget? Those words had kept her going for months. 'Remind me.'

'That when the woman I always wanted was marrying my best friend, I stopped caring. You know that was you?'

'I hoped that's what you meant.'

'It wasn't much of a marriage proposal, was it?' he said drawing her closer.

'Is that what it was?' Hannah ducked her head, suddenly self conscious.

Surely, he wasn't about to try again. Not while she wore the first thing she had thrown on, with her hair tangled and falling down her back. She was wearing slippers, for goodness' sake!

'I've thought about this – that is, us – constantly since the night. I've simply never found the courage or the right moment to mention it.'

'Oh, for goodness' sake, Darius, we don't have to discuss it, just ask me!'

'I will, of course I will. But—'

'What do you mean, "but"?' Had he changed his mind? The thought made her slightly nauseous.

'The Service Bureau keeps me from living a normal life, but when this dreadful war is over, I hope you'll still be here.' He shrugged, waving his free arm in a wide arc. 'Well, not here, exactly, but you know what I mean.'

'Darius, we've known each other most of our lives. I always know what you mean.' She closed her eyes and relaxed against him, keenly aware of the length of his body pressed against her side. 'We seem to have been fighting for so long, I can't remember what a normal life was like.'

'It's not over yet. But I'm determined to do all I can to help bring it to an end.'

'Then I'll wait. However long it takes.'

They stood in thoughtful silence, staring out over the cliff at plumes of smoke arising from fires in the town below them. 'And when the time comes, I expect you ask me properly.'

'Do I have to do the knee thing? Because I damaged a hamstring playing cricket at university. If I get down, I might embarrass myself getting up again.'

Hannah punched his shoulder lightly. 'Simple words are enough.'

He eased aside a lock of her hair and kissed the tender spot beneath her ear, his lips sliding across her jaw until he found her mouth.

Coiling her arms around his neck, she returned his kiss, so demanding yet unexpected. The blood surged through her veins as his arms tightened around her. Finally, he eased her back a pace, his hands on her shoulders.

'Breakfast?' He laced the fingers of his left hand through her right, his eyes filled with mischief, and something else.

'I thought you would never ask. I'm starving.'

His sideways look as they strolled back towards the house told her he knew she wasn't only referring to food.

ACKNOWLEDGEMENTS

I would like to thank the brilliant team at Boldwood for bringing this series to life: Caroline Ridding for showing me the difference between a saga and a cosy mystery, Isobel Akenhead for her enthusiasm for my characters, and editors Gary Jukes and Debra Newhouse for smoothing out my clumsy phrasing. Special mentions go to Amanda Ridout, Nia Beynon, Ben Wilson, Megan Townsend, Emily Ruston, Marcela Torres and Emily Yau. Also, my thanks to Boldwood's creative department for the stunningly beautiful covers.

My eternal appreciation also goes to my agent, Kate Nash, who has been with me from the beginning. Not forgetting the Historical Fiction Critique Group: Colleen Donnelly, Diane Scott Lewis, Jennie Pittam, Maggi Andersen, Mirella Patzer, Rosemary Morris, Susan Cook and Ursula Thompson, who read every word of this novel and shared their skills, encouragement and advice throughout.

ABOUT THE AUTHOR

Anita Davison is the author of the successful Flora Maguire historical mystery series.

Sign up to Anita Davison's mailing list for news, competitions and updates on future books.

Visit Anita's website: www.anitadavison.co.uk

Follow Anita on social media here:

𝕏 x.com/anitasdavison

f facebook.com/anita.davison

g goodreads.com/anitadavison

ALSO BY ANITA DAVISON

Miss Merrill and Aunt Violet Mysteries

Murder in the Bookshop

Murder in the Library

The Flora Maguire Mysteries

Death On Board

Death at the Abbey

Poison
& Pens

POISON & PENS IS THE HOME OF
COZY MYSTERIES SO POUR YOURSELF
A CUP OF TEA & GET SLEUTHING!

DISCOVER PAGE-TURNING NOVELS FROM
YOUR FAVOURITE AUTHORS &
MEET NEW FRIENDS

JOIN OUR
FACEBOOK GROUP

BIT.LYPOISONANDPENSFB

SIGN UP TO OUR
NEWSLETTER

BIT.LY/POISONANDPENSNEWS

Boldwood

Boldwood Books is an award-winning fiction publishing company seeking out the best stories from around the world.

Find out more at www.boldwoodbooks.com

Join our reader community for brilliant books, competitions and offers!

Follow us
@BoldwoodBooks
@TheBoldBookClub

Sign up to our weekly deals newsletter

https://bit.ly/BoldwoodBNewsletter

Printed in Great Britain
by Amazon